Phantom Express

OTHER McABEE ADVENTURES

Cassies Ruler

Confessional Matters

Scholarly Executions

The Pony Circus Wagon

Phantom Express

Joseph A. McCaffrey

1663 LIBERTY DRIVE, SUITE 200
BLOOMINGTON, INDIANA 47403
(800) 839-8640
WWW.AUTHORHOUSE.COM

First published by AuthorHouse 07/25/05

ISBN: 1-4208-5485-2 (sc)
ISBN: 1-4208-5486-0 (dj)

Library of Congress Control Number: 2005904013

Printed in the United States of America
Bloomington, Indiana

This book is printed on acid-free paper.

For Judy, Kristina, and Monica ~

Observant Presences on the Path

CHAPTER I

—◆—

"Load that sucker in real careful and watch out. He's a kicker!" Walt Scott yelled.

"I know, I know all about him," the groom said impatiently. "I can use a hand here," he said a minute later. One of the grooms helped him.

The truth of the matter was this. Scott wanted nothing to do with that particular yearling who was being boarded onto the trailer with the greatest of care. There was something about him; he'd seen it before, a devious mind – something in the eyes – calculating, mean, and just maybe murderous.

"Got him in. Lock it, lock it damnit. Good. Good riddance to him," the groom shouted.

He was the last of six horses loaded into this trailer that was heading up to Harrisburg, Pennsylvania for the three-day sale that was one of the determinative auctions in the harness horse industry. Scott went over to the trailer and checked the latches and took one last look at all of his 'kids' as he called them. When he came to the end of the trailer, his eye was caught by the yearling, Phantom Express. Scott could swear that the horse was glaring at him as one would look at a prison guard, with hatred and malice. It had a way of raising and tilting its head while looking down its long nose; its ears were pinned back, set aggressively as if searching for an adversary.

Scott had been in the business of horse reproduction for as long as his memory could reach back into his childhood, a 61-year span over which he could recover the first memory of his father who also had spent a lifetime in this arcane and secretive part of the horse business.

It wasn't that Phantom Express was the only mean horse with whom he had ever dealt. They seemed to come in small batches, an unusual year, perhaps two or three. Then there would be a relative calm. A cycle of sorts. He hadn't had a serious problem-horse for five years. And then this one, the meanest horse he had ever encountered.

His sire was Phantom of the Valley, one of three of the most gifted pacers who had ever raced. He was also a prolific stud. Phantom of the Valley was not owned by Scott, who had his own two studs who were of a lesser quality, although they had produced their share of winners and champions.

He remembered the day well when Roger Theroux had called him.

"Walt, I have a favor to ask of you."

"I'm listening, Roger."

"You know I have the filly – Cleopatra's Asp."

"Yeah?"

"I want to breed her."

"She still sound?"

"She's four. Won me a bucket of dough. Last time I looked over 300 thou. I figure her foal would be worth a fortune. I don't need her breaking down on me."

"Well, OK. I have two really fine sires, as you know. Which were you thinking?"

There was a long pause. Theroux continued, "Well, there's the rub. I don't want your sires, but I do want your administration."

"You lost me, Roger."

"It's pretty simple. I want her bred elsewhere, but I want you to be in charge."

"That's not my game, really."

"There you are; that's the favor. I intend to use Cleopatra's Asp in a few big races after she's bred, then I'll give her over to you. I want you to be at the birthing all the way through to the yearling sale at Harrisburg. I don't think anyone is better than you at that end of the business. I'll pay you top rate and give you 10 percent of the sale price."

"Who's the sire?"

"Phantom of the Valley."

"What's that gonna set you back?"

"50 thou."

Scott knew that for Theroux that amount was chicken feed. It meant nothing, in effect, even though it was a huge fee for the service.

"Now let me see if I have this right. You've arranged for a mating, and as soon as we see a conception I'm to take her over, but only after you race her in a selective, few races. Then you ship her here, we foal her and eventually get the kid ready for the yearling sale. Is that the deal?"

"Couldn't of said it better myself, Walt."

"My fee is $2000 a month besides any ancillary fees – vets, shipping, and the rest. The 10 percent of sale price is the key here. God knows what kind of money that breeding will bring."

"We're shipping her down to Hasbright Farms in a few days. I'd like it if you were there. It's all on me and five thousand on top if you're satisfied. That all is above board."

"OK, I'll head down there and keep them honest."

The van driver, a sour man named Jack Mahon, interrupted his reminiscence of the contract.

"Hey, Mister Scott. Who's going to be in Harrisburg to download this six-pack? Because I'll tell you right here and now I'm not dealing with that mean bastard at the end of this hitch."

Scott responded sharply, "Don't you worry. I'll have a man there when you arrive. And quite frankly, I don't need you talking nonsense."

"Nonsense, my neck. I saw them trying to load him. If I get there and no one's there, he can just stand there for a month."

"What did I just say to you?"

"Well, OK then. I have a permanent limp because of a wild-assed horse, and I don't intend to have it happen again."

"You made your point, now get going."

Walt Scott had arranged for the care of Phantom Express at Harrisburg with Jimmy Mason, a black man from the Mississippi Delta region, who had the skill to pretty much calm down any animal on the earth. Jimmy drove over from the Meadowlands RaceTrack in New Jersey just for this purpose. Scott had lured him with a $1,000 offer for basically a two-and-one-half day piece of labor. He was standing at the gate of the Harrisburg farm complex, waiting for the Virginia-licensed trailer to arrive. Scott had called him at the Super 8 when the trailer was about one hour from arrival. Jimmy had been briefed about this particular yearling. When Mason read the breeding and information page on the yearling, he let out a low whistle and shook his head. He then realized why he was given such a nice fee. The yearling was worth a fortune, but he was a lunatic.

The Harrisburg sale was scheduled for the second week of November and extended for six days. The yearling part of the sale went for three days. Phantom Express would be auctioned on the second day of the yearling sales, number 166 of 193 for that day. Mason, whose father had been a minister, shook his head when he noticed the sixes in the hip number 166. Not unlike most horsemen, he was highly superstitious, given to looking for signs and omens that could affect the future. He mentally filed away the number 166 – just another thing out there.

Essentially, Mason's job was to take over the yearling at the trailer and stay with him until his auction was completed. Once the yearling was returned to his stall after the bidding, Mason could drive back to the Meadowlands where he was an assistant trainer in a large racing stable, 45 miles away from that racing facility.

Mason was with two others, one of whom held a sign that read 'Scott Farms.' They stood about 150 yards from the guard's gate to the complex.

"So you the guy who's taking charge of Phantom Express?" asked the heavyset, white-haired man.

"That's me."

"Hope you know what you're getting into," the sign-bearer said as he looked toward the gate. He didn't look that different from the other white guy except he had an old, red Philadelphia Phillies hat with a white 'P'.

"How so?" Mason pretended ignorance.

Neither one of them spoke for about a minute. He figured one or the other would break the silence. The Phillie did. "Listen, we don't want any trouble with Scott."

"Won't be any. You have something I need to know?"

The two white men looked at each other for a few seconds until the Phillie raised his eyebrows and shrugged his shoulders. Non-Phillie took that as some kind of permission to talk. "He's already hurt three people. He's a kicker, and there ain't no warning. I saw him miss that little teenage girl. What's her name?" He looked at Phillie who didn't answer. "Anyway, missed her head by two inches, and she was standing about six feet behind him. He's broke a wrist, crushed a foot, and damaged some fingers. You gonna be takin' him away?"

"Nah. Just tending him till someone buys him. I heard he's a piece of trouble."

"Well, alls I can say," the Phillie said, "if they can get him to pace he's got all the equipment. He is p-u-u-ure majesty to look at, and his breeding is something else."

"Yeah, I saw."

"OK. This looks like the truck now. There second at the gate."

The Harrisburg sale catalog reached Martin Blum in early October. Blum was an avid harness racing fan whose love for the game was ignited in childhood when he and his father and grandfather would venture to Yonkers Raceway just north of the Bronx on the Major Deegan Expressway in New York and on rarer occasions to Roosevelt Raceway on western Long Island. The loss of Roosevelt as a harness track still grated on him because of the chicanery and outright lying that took place to eventually turn it into a huge shopping mall. Blum had gotten some of the story, but he knew that pieces of the dishonesty would never be discovered.

Blum's father was an investment banker and partner with Goldman Sachs. When he dropped dead of an aneurysm, Martin at 25 years of age, was worth 12 million dollars as the only heir to the fortune, his mother having died of cancer two years earlier. Now, at the age of 43, Martin was worth in the neighborhood of 100 million dollars, having made his fortune in wise investments. But if the truth be told, his true love was to be found in pacers and trotters, the two kinds of standardbred horses, different from each other because of their style of running.

Blum had 20 pacers and two trotters at the Meadowlands, and an almost equal number in Chicago at Maywood and Balmoral racetracks, and about 10 pacers at Woodbine in Toronto. He rarely made money at the game; few did. Because of this he spent more and more time learning the business. He saw it as a chess game where the board was set against him. Still, he intended to beat the odds and beat the game.

The yearling aspect was the chanciest and most difficult part of the harness game. Although not as pricey as thoroughbred auctions, for which Blum had no regard, large sums were committed to purchase standardbred yearlings many of whom would never make it to a racetrack. However, if a champion was acquired, huge chunks of money could be made. In fact, a great horse, besides winning several million dollars racing, could earn even more in stud fees. As Blum went on in the game, he was drawn more and more to this end of the business. He would tell his good friend, Herman Fischer, "Herman, one great horse, one colossal inning. Game's over!"

Blum had studied with his customary thoroughness the elements of breeding in the making of a harness horse. He knew the great pacers and trotters; he knew the great sires, the great mares, and he knew the bitterness and disappointment that under-rode the business. The auction books were a constant reminder of all of these things. Even horses with the best breeding that money could buy could very easily end up in a can of Alpo, having leeched extraordinary amounts of money to no end.

Later on in that same October week Blum called Horace Bardens, an agent whom he had used on occasion. Bardens was a gruff old southerner from Georgia whose drawl could cut through a block of titanium. He specialized in the buying and selling of horses.

"Horace. Martin Blum."

"Mornin', sir. How are things in New Yawk?"

"OK, OK. What's new down in Pompano?"

"Nothin' much. Waitin' for anotha hurricane. It's the season ya know. What can I do for ya?"

"Have you scoped out Harrisburg?"

"I surely have. Ya lookin' too?"

"Yes. I'd like you to take on five yearlings."

"Hold on, let me git ovah to my desk." There was a small pause, a sigh, and a comment. "OK, Mistah Mahtin, I'm here."

Blum started out with the four for whom he had interest. Their discussion was long and thorough. After it, Blum still had high regards for two of them. He would make a play for them.

"Now one more."

"Yeah, well let me guess."

"Go ahead."

"Ya wouldn't be interested in hip number 166 by any chance? On the second day I'm talkin'."

Blum was at once gratified and disappointed. "Is it that obvious?"

Horace's laugh was a bit like a sand grinder. "Well, Mistah Mahtin, he's the talk of everyone down here in Florida. Word is he's a dream horse. But I heard he's a bit aggressive."

"That a big deal?"

"Ah. No or yes. Hard to say. Ya know when they say this stuff early in a career ya gotta wondah."

"I can't go to the sale. You going?"

"Yeah, I'm representin' on a few. None of the ones ya mentioned."

"I'd like you to place some bids for me. Right now I'd appreciate it if you could dig into hips 71, 89, and especially 166."

"Be happy to."

"Horace, let me be clear. I'm very interested in 166, Phantom Express. Whatever you can find out, let me know." He gave him his private cell number.

"I'll start diggin', Mistah Mahtin, I promise."

Martin Blum placed one other phone call to a private detective in Richmond, Virginia. He had been given the name by a resource that he had used on occasion when he was conducting business. The message was clear and distinct – discover what was discoverable about the yearling Phantom Express.

Nothing surprised Jimmy Mason when it came to horses. When the driver took out the crossbar from the trailer and removed the gate, Phantom Express looked down at the ramp nonchalantly. Mason took hold of a grip and brought himself up next to the yearling. He spoke to the horse very gently. "OK big boy, we're going to get along real well. I don't like any of these dudes who are looking at you either. So why don't we just ignore them and get outta here." He gently reached across, took the halter, and led him down the ramp. He went without a glitch; Phantom Express was a gentleman. Mason nodded at the other grooms and led the yearling to his stall in Barn C.

The beautiful horse followed along willingly. Mason reflected that this was too easy, and because it was so he was doubly alert. It was no mystery that it was when you let your guard down that you were going to be clobbered. Mason also took note that a number of strangers – too white, too dressed – were looking over the horse. If the horse was truly crazy, he had them all fooled. Of course, that was exactly why Scott hired him. Jimmy Mason knew that he was damn good at doing exactly what he was doing, keeping the horse calm and steady.

Nor was Jimmy surprised at the number of lookers who came through the barn asking to see the horse. When that occurred, it was up to Jimmy to open up the stall door, put a lead shank on him, and take him out to the aisle. Jimmy continued to whisper in the big yearling's ear, and he continued to get a marvelous response from the horse. On two occasions out of the 19 times that he was obligated to take the yearling out into the aisle Jimmy felt a rush of adrenaline. One bidder came up right behind the horse and grabbed his back, right leg. It was a classic case for a kick into oblivion. He saw the horse tighten his leg and resist. The damn fool had the nerve to disrespect the horse with a comment, "Stubborn mother, ain't he?"

Jimmy quickly stepped over and advised the man to be careful around the horse while adding, "He's been in and out of that stall ever since he got here today. I think it's wearing him down."

As Jimmy whispered into the horse's ear, Phantom Express eventually gave his leg to the curious man who, in Jimmy's estimation, was trying to impress the young blonde who stood in awe of the yearling. As in most of these showings, Jimmy had no idea who the man was.

Nor did he have any explanation for the other incident. A 'that guy looks kinda familiar' put his fist under the horse's throat. That was common enough; it was a down and dirty test of the air passage capacity of the horse. But the man also stared at the yearling in a menacing way. The horse's head tilted, his ears went back, and he cast a sole eye on the man. At that point Jimmy came between the two of them and said, "I'm bringing him back to his stall now; he's had a long day." The man walked away without saying a word. Jimmy wasn't sure, but he continued to think that he might have seen him before. There was a mean or evil quality to him. Whatever it was, something bad had gone down between the yearling and that man.

Scott came to the barn on the first day of the yearling sale. "Jimmy, how's he behaving?"

"Oh, he's fine, Mister Scott. Hasn't done anything bad around me. Had a bunch of lookers in yesterday, and I suspect today will be real busy."

"I think so too. The yearling sale starts in another hour or so; they'll be a lot of characters milling around all day. Tomorrow, he'll be in the ring around eleven, and you'll be on your way around noon. Really want you to keep him nice and calm. Jimmy, don't ever take your eye off of him at any time when he could hurt you."

"I know, I know. Seems like he's got some deep-seated thing in him. Believe me though, he's been a peach for me so far. Oh, one thing. Guy came by late yesterday afternoon. Slicked-back, black hair – white, but dark complexion – thick, about 230 or 240 pounds – flat-nosed, maybe 40. Had a way about him. He was laying the spook on the yearling, trying to get into his head."

Scott thought a minute. Only one man came to his mind, Roman Garzo. He was not a racing track trainer, rather he was in the employ of a multi-millionaire owner named Jeremy Burgess, who had made his fortune in the dot com game – getting in at the best of times and getting out at the best of times. What Scott knew of Garzo is that he would show up at sales, purchase yearlings and train them down to within 15 or 20 seconds of qualifying, then they would be sent to different tracks where they would come under the care of track racing stables. Of Burgess he knew little except that he was probably the largest owner of harness horses in America. If he was interested in Phantom Express and there were others of similar mind, the bidding could go through the roof.

Garzo, however, was an altogether different story. If Garzo was given the care of Phantom Express, then the battle of wills between the two could only be lethal. The stare-down that Jimmy reported had Scott shaking his head in sadness. Garzo had visited Scott's barn in Virginia in August and October in order to see the yearling. Scott attended him on both occasions, and Garzo didn't have the nerve to try to lay the evil eye on Phantom Express. His visit was acceptable and proper. He looked at Jimmy and saw him staring at him. He remembered that he had been asked a question, "Jimmy, I'm sorry. I was just thinking about something. Ah, yeah, I think I know who you mean. I don't know much about him except that he works with yearlings. Works for Jeremy Burgess if memory serves me. Sorry." Scott was innately evasive.

CHAPTER II

Wes Taylor drove over from Richmond, Virginia, to Scott's farm. He surveyed the area and went into the nearest town, Great Falls, which had a population of 9000 if you could believe the small metal rectangle at the east entrance of the town that stood next to the 30 m.p.h. sign. He went to the post office and asked for the address of a man named Jack Mahon.

"I'm sorry. I'm not allowed to give that out, sir," said the 50ish postmistress.

"I understand that. But I'm here to tell him about the death of his brother. We've been trying to turn him up for about a week. I know it's irregular, but I'd really appreciate it," Taylor held up his P.I. license.

"Well, I shouldn't, but ... oh OK, you look honest."

He thanked her and headed over to Fourth and Main where Mahon lived in a duplex. He had been given Mahon's name by a contact in the horse industry. He found out that Mahon had done three years in a West Virginia prison for aggravated assault. Among other things, he had also found out that he tended horses for Walt Scott.

Mahon was about as hung over as you could get. His eyes bespoke wretchedness when he opened up the door to his place at 11 a.m. "Yeah?"

"I'm Wes Taylor, over here from Richmond. I'm doing some backgrounding for a client," he took out his license.

"A P.I.? Listen why are you bothering me?" The man's eyes narrowed.

"Because you work for Walter Scott and I need to know something. If you let me into your house and you have knowledge of a horse named Phantom Express, I'll give you 50 bucks for your time – 25 now and 25 after."

"OK. Come in." The man came awake quickly.

The living room was a disaster area. Fortunately he didn't have to see any more of the house as he left five minutes later and 50 dollars lighter. He didn't get much direct information from Mahon about the horse except that everyone was scared of him, Mahon included. Mahon also gave him the name of Vern Blood who had worked for Scott until he was fired about two months previous.

From Vern Blood, he had learned enough to realize that Martin Blum would be pleased that he had taken the trouble to hire Taylor. He called from Great Falls, "Mister Blum? Wes Taylor from Richmond."

"Oh, yes. What did you learn?"

"Well, here's what I know. This horse is mean and dangerous. No one at Scott's barn wanted to work with him. He kicks, bites, and butts – in so many words. For a horse he also has a high IQ, whatever that means. One guy who I spoke with was fired because he wouldn't go into his stall. I guess this is the kind of info that you want?"

"Yes, exactly. What else did you find out?"

"No health problems. Sound of body. Not of mind, I guess. I'll send my report."

"OK, good," Blum said.

"Well, I'm about to head back to Richmond. It seems to me that we should close the case on this right now."

Blum agreed, and Taylor went back to Richmond. He felt that he had done a good service; Blum was the kind of man to remember that. Not that Taylor would ever buy a horse, but if he were going to, it certainly wouldn't be Phantom Express.

Blum was even more enchanted with the yearling. He reasoned that if the meanness could be translated into competitiveness then this particular yearling could be the big inning that he needed.

He immediately called Harold Bardens who, by his calculation, should be at Harrisburg.

Bardens, in full drawl, said, "Moh-ning."

"Horace, this is Martin Blum."

"Mistah Mahtin. I'm pleased that ya called. I was goin' to call ya in a bit, but this will do. Here, let me step out of this buildin' so we can be private." There was a long pause that went on for about twenty seconds. "OK Mistah Mahtin, this is better."

"I take it the sale has begun."

"Yes, indeed. I already bought one for a trainer in Michigan."

"How are the prices?"

"Bout normal to a little high. No unusual occurrences at this point. What I wanted to tell ya is this, the horse that you're interested in is the talk of the sale. There are rumors

and whispers gah-lore about him. You'd think he already had
stepped a 1:50 mile."

"What have you heard about his temperament?"

"Interestin' that you ask. A spotty matter. One of
the old boys says he heard from a good source who heard
from a good source that the animal is high strung and is
more than a bit prepared to kill ya. But ya know these
good sources are ten cents to the dozen. I already looked
over the horse. Very well-mannered, at least durin' my ten
minutes with him. I've studied the x-rays and did all the
things a good buyer does; he looks to be the real McCoy.
I didn't see a pimple on him; his configuration is a grand
thing to see. Mistah Mahtin, I'm goin' to be honest with
ya. I think this bid is goin' to break records. I don't know
what you're prepared to top at, but I wouldn't be surprised
to see this goin' into the mid-hundreds, especially if the
biddin' gets spirited."

Blum feared this but continued the discussion. He told
Bardens about the report from the Richmond P.I.

Bardens responded, "Well, if that's true, I'd back off
Mistah Mahtin. If the horse is a head case, it rarely works
out. What you said sorta confirms what I heard. I can tell
you this too. The guy handlin' this animal is a major-league
groom. Most of these grooms are on the younger side and a
bit innocent. This man was whisperin' to the yearling like he
was on a honeymoon. Maybe there's a reason for him bein'
there. I'll look into that and get back to ya."

"Anything else?"

"Yeah, one other thing. Talks out there that Burgess has
an interest. I suppose ya know what that means."

"I do, I do indeed. Stay in touch. When it's time to
declare, I'll want to stay in phone touch with you."

Blum sat at his desk and thought hard.

Jeremy Burgess graduated from Harvard University with a MBA in 1979. An acolyte in Apple Computers in its heyday he made a traitorous move over to Microsoft, and in the early nineties he burst onto the national stage with an immensely supported dot com venture in the death business – funerals, burials, wills, and related services. He cashed out in 1995 with a personal worth of 250 million dollars. Stories about him abounded. On the one hand, he was seen to be a champion of liberal causes, the northwest type, forward-looking and informal. But another pattern was also culled from his life, vindictiveness and pettiness. One former associate stated that Burgess, ultimately, trusted no one and that his words never matched his behaviors.

He purchased a small harness racetrack in Indiana at the behest of his brother who had unsuccessfully been attempting to purchase it for three years. For whatever reason Burgess took a keen interest in the business and soon began investing heavily in horseflesh. His level of sophistication and depth of interest continued at an astronomical level. Yet, to this date he had never turned a profit in the business.

It was his Vice President for Track Operations who had come on to the existence of Phantom Express while he was still in utero. Burgess told him to put a marker on the matter and inform him if and when the animal was up for sale. And so it was that an alert had reached that Vice President that Phantom Express would be auctioned at the Harrisburg sale in November.

Burgess had four men reporting to him relative to his track divisions. One was the Vice President for Track Operations at the Indiana Track. The second was the Racing Trainer who oversaw all of those responsible for the care of horses currently racing at the various harness tracks around the country. The third oversaw the still small breeding end of the business. Burgess knew that he needed a prime time stud who could take him to the next level in this end of the business, thus his initial and continued interest in Phantom Express.

Roman Garzo was in charge of the fourth prong of the business. This was the purchase and training of yearlings up to, but not including, their actual racing at the track. Garzo operated at the Burgess training complex in Valdosta, Georgia, just north of the Florida line.

Burgess would be the first to admit that he was uneasy due to some of the stories he had heard about Garzo and his training methods that had been described to him as brutal, medieval, and vicious. But Garzo had a very solid record when it came to bringing pacers and trotters up to racing standards.

He recalled talking with this unusually blunt man about Phantom Express, some while ago.

"You know, Roman, this could be the horse that brings us into the top tier in this industry. I want you to study him, get a sense of him and let me know what you think. I'll go as far as I have to if you give the nod."

Garzo was expressionless. Burgess waited him out and finally Garzo said, "It could be a small fortune. If it's right, I will tell you so; and I will give it every effort I have to make him a winner." Garzo's accent was ever so subtle. He had come to the States from Sardinia as a boy. Growing up in Cleveland, Ohio, he had learned enough about the harness industry at Northfield Racetrack to launch his own stable. Eventually he migrated over to the breaking and training of yearlings, and his name became known in racing circles for this skill. When Burgess expanded into the harness business, the Garzo name was prominent on a list of potential employees. Burgess was never totally at ease with the man who had a lingering aura of intransigence and stubbornness. But, for the moment, Garzo was his man and he would follow his lead.

Roman Garzo sat in his darkened room at the Marriott Courtyard in Harrisburg. It was 9:30 p.m. and he had lit a small candle enclosed in a tin container. He was midway through a bottle of Chianti while thinking intensely about the bidding battle that would erupt tomorrow morning over Phantom Express. Burgess had made it fairly clear that his future could be made or broken with the yearling. For if he chose not to bid and the yearling succeeded, he would be held accountable, and if he bid and the yearling flopped he would be held accountable. The only real way to win would be for the yearling to fail with another barn or succeed in his barn.

Garzo determined that in these matters it was best to fail on your own than to wait for the failure of others. This thinking led him to the further conclusion that he should place the bid. However, he was not unmindful that the yearling showed scorn and projected a hostile streak.

He stared at the candle for a while before getting up and going to his sink where a teacup sat. The leaves were almost totally dry at the base and bottom sides of the cup. He held the cup under the faucet and very carefully added a small amount of water, and swilled both as he went back to the side table near the window of his room. His final swill brought the tealeaves along the upper side of the cup where they fell into a cluster that he held close to the candle.

It took him over a minute before he recognized a pattern, which once recognized, made him wonder why he needed more than a minute. It was so apparent. It showed him a figure on a mountain with a long spear facing outwards.

This was all clear to Garzo. The figure with the spear was to undertake a challenge, he being Garzo while the mountain was the horse. He continued to drink, the candle burned deep and eventually he went to bed setting his alarm for seven a.m. His fate would be in for a big bounce at about 11 a.m. on the next day, he reflected. As to his reading of tealeaves and the other many superstitious customs and beliefs that pervaded his life, no one knew and no one would ever know.

The second day of the auction began promptly at nine a.m. Jimmy could hear the rhythmically harsh call of the auctioneer from a distance. He had made himself a straw bed just outside of the stall gate and had an on and off sleep through the night. While the security around the barns was better than at most sales, no chances could be taken. The racing industry was awash with stories of sabotage and malfeasance, most of which could be easily avoided by keeping alert and vigilant. Jimmy was very proud of his workmanship and his reputation.

He had just changed the water for the yearling when Scott showed up. "Hello Mister Scott."

"Jimmy. So how's it going with the big guy?"

"So far, so good."

"I need to be alone with him for a few minutes. Then, let's clean him down, put some Show-Sheen on, and see what happens." He handed the bottle over to Jimmy. It was a product used by many sellers to make a horse's coat shine.

"Sure, sure."

"Night pretty quiet?"

"Oh yes. I slept right outside the gate, nice and quiet. Unless he's cooking something up in that head of his."

Scott looked at Jimmy shrewdly. "Jimmy, between you and me, that's the thing that has me worried. Like one of those quiet volcanoes, just sitting there and suddenly – boom!"

Scott opened the gate and disappeared into the stall. Jimmy stepped to the left of the gate. Whatever Scott was going to do was not his business. However, he figured that the Phantom was going to be exposed to a depressant of some sort, just in case he did the unthinkable and went berserk in the ring. Tens of thousands of dollars have been lost in just such a way. The trick for a good needle man was to avoid sending a horse into the auction ring who looked like he was in a coma. He was confident that Scott had experimented with dosages back in Virginia on the farm.

When he came out of the stall he caught Jimmy's eye and said, "OK, Jimmy, this is it. The game has officially started. He's up around 11:00 and they're pretty good at keeping their word. I'm going to check on my others. I'll be back around 10:15, 10:30. You have my cell if there's a problem."

"Yes sir. I'll get him looking real good for the ring."

Scott left the barn gingerly touching the deep pockets of his coat. Jimmy turned his attention to Phantom Express as he began the process of soaping down and washing the horse. He would then walk him dry before giving the yearling a gloss with Show-Sheen.

All through the process never once did the yearling manifest anything other than good manners. Jimmy was diligent in his observation of the horse's ears that stood straight up as they turned and twitched in the erect position. They were like an attentive radar at an airport. To Jimmy, they were a sign of alertness and intelligence, especially when Jimmy cross-matched them with his eyes. Most horses had rather flat and expressionless eyes. They were hard to read, many horsemen remarking that was because there wasn't anything to read. Jimmy knew otherwise, of course. And no matter what the truth of the observation was, there was no doubt in his mind that this horse was thinking. Every time Jimmy would glance at Phantom Express, his eyes would be caught and held by the yearling. There was an almost otherworldly shrewdness about him, a hidden agenda concealing a potentially lethal kick or movement that could cost him a limb or worse, if Jimmy did something that was not acceptable to the horse.

Scott came back into the barn just as the caller yelled out, "Hip numbers 160 through 170 start to move your horses out of the stalls if you haven't already. They just did 154, and we're on time."

"Jimmy, you have him looking great."

"Mister Scott, he's been real good for me. You know he likes down-home chatter. I think he's got some black blood in him," he said nonchalantly as he and Scott laughed at the jest.

"I probably won't get back here right after the auction, and I know you'll want out of here." He took out his wallet and peeled off 10 one-hundred dollar bills. "This settles our score and here's another 200 for your expenses."

Jimmy gave him a half salute and said, "It's been a pleasure. Anytime you need help just let me know."

The caller yelled, "OK, 166. Let's go."

Scott patted Phantom on the back and proceeded quickly into the auction seating area. Jimmy and Phantom Express went down the barn aisle and then out into the daylight as they crossed over a pebbled road and then into a circular corral with a diameter of about 75 yards. In it were hip numbers 164 and 165. As Jimmy looked around he felt the eyes of many observers, and as he looked he saw most all of them fastened on 166, Phantom Express.

He continued to talk with the yearling who strode around the corral with authority. He lengthened the rope in order to give the horse some play, but not too much.

164 was led out into a small area just behind the auction stand as 163 was bid upon. When that ended the process advanced. Finally, 166 was led out of the corral and into the dirt area behind the auction pit. The chatter of the auctioneer was loud, hurried, and rhythmic as each new bid brought an intense bark from him. Jimmy looked at Phantom Express and for the first time since the two incidents in the barn two days previous he noticed the ears descending back, losing their upward state. Jimmy whispered to himself, 'Ah Jesus, don't you go crazy on me now big boy?' He hurriedly went up to the horse's ear and whispered into it, "It's OK boy. It's OK. Papa going to take care of you. It's OK. Remember the meadows and the fields; you'll be there soon."

There was a pound of a gavel and the auctioneer yelled, "Sold to number 31, $24,000."

"OK, man, bring him into the ring," a voice said behind Jimmy.

CHAPTER III

———◆———

Retired marine officer Jack Scholz waited at the visitors'
parking lot at Lock and Dam 14 in LeClaire, Iowa. It was one
of the superior sites in the upper Mississippi River Valley area
from which to view bald eagles. It must have been no more
than five degrees Fahrenheit on this late January Sunday, as
the sun worked in a cloudless sky; there was only a whisper
of a wind. As he sat in his Ford F-250 pickup, the large birds
circled the dam that stretched from Iowa and Illinois across
the Mississippi River, largely frozen except for an area near
the dam itself where there was open water. It was in that
gap that the bald eagles had their way with fish who swam in
stunned confusion as they came through the dam system.

He watched as one snatched a fish in his huge claws
and flew to the tree line on the Illinois side of the river
where he joined a cluster of birds on various branches of a
leafless oak tree. The killing and eating was done quietly

and professionally. The way it ought to be. He saw the bald eagle as an apt symbol for American determination and excellence. He shook his head in disgust as he reflected on Benjamin Franklin's effort to have the wild turkey become the symbol of America. Behind the closed doors of the American establishment during the Revolutionary War – did his peers sock it to him for such a stupid idea?

His cell rang. "Yeah?"

"Jack, this is Pat. Bertrand is on his way. Should be there in 10 or 15 minutes. He got held up."

"I'll be here."

She hung up. Pat was Bertrand McAbee's chain-smoking, razor thin, red-haired secretary, probably around 45, although she might be 50 or 55. She had started with McAbee when he had gotten into the private investigation business, he having left academia and the teaching of the classics. It was probably the biggest mismatch in McAbee's life because, if truth be told, he didn't belong in the PI game. Nonetheless he was there, he paid his sub-contractors well, and Jack was a sub-contractor.

He recalled his first job with McAbee, who had taken work for a litigator who was suing a large Rock Island, Illinois, company for the wife of a man who had died at a company Christmas party. The question was this – was it required for employees to attend the event? The company had said no while the wife said yes. Her husband had been asked by his boss to stand up on a four-foot high table and fall back into the waiting arms of his colleagues. This being an example of the new trust-building spirit being advocated by the company suits. He did his part – falling backwards. His head hit the marble floor with authority, his colleagues in a drunken giggle. He was declared dead two hours later. The company brass was infuriated because the party spirit had been dampened. With vindictiveness – they held out on the widow.

McAbee needed some internal documentation relative to attending the event. He wasn't getting anywhere. No surprise. McAbee, at least back then, was about as far from a street-savvy PI as Mother Teresa was from dancing at Radio City Music Hall. To the man's credit – he was no idiot – he knew that he was a flawed PI. He came upon Jack from a third party. And while McAbee had his obvious flaws and would never make the grade, he did have some huge assets – Pat, his secretary and even more so, the resources of his brother's mega-international investigation and intelligence organization in New York City. The William McAbee firm was scarily connected. For that consideration alone, Scholz accepted the offer from Bertrand relative to the trust-building death. After all, it was no stretch to leap from Bertrand to his brother if reports about Scholz came up positive.

Within three days he had taped conversations of executives, memos, files, and a host of other data that Bertrand passed on to the litigator who subsequently scored a vacation-castle in Boca Raton as his part of the settlement. From then on Jack was a part of Bertrand's cadre of irregulars. McAbee became a good source of income for Scholz. However, to his chagrin, he had not heard a word from the big fish in New York – Bill.

Personally – Jack had ditched any and all rules in his pursuit of a case except the one pertaining to not getting caught. He himself had a stable of operatives around the country largely composed of ex-seals, green-berets, and other specially trained operatives who formed a loose confederation moving in the limbo between lawfulness and lawlessness. Nothing was off the table when the going got tough.

While McAbee knew about some of Jack's shady practices such as intimidation, beatings, and torture, he didn't have knowledge of other things that Jack had either sponsored or that he had done himself. McAbee was in that ambivalent zone when he would accept a rough practice, but then stew over it. His problem was that he still believed in some kind of ethics. Jack was no longer held by those considerations. In his judgment, this was the reason why he was a great PI, and McAbee would never fit. McAbee should have stayed in his world of books, his love of Latin and Greek, and the fairy-tale world of higher education.

Augusta Satin came to mind. She was an ex-Rock Island detective – tall, black, beautiful, smart, and a no-nonsense babe. She also was part of McAbee's world as she floated in and out of his office on special assignments. Between the two of them, Scholz sensed some chemistry. He wondered about them. So different – yet so synchronized – too bonded. But McAbee was also that way with Pat, his secretary. Just what was going on between them? If anything. McAbee wasn't as easy as he presented himself. Just when Scholz thought that he had him figured out, he'd be surprised. Like the proverbial onion – layers upon layers.

Scholz could see the Great River Road, Highway 67, for about a mile west. He thought he saw McAbee's red Explorer Sport in the distance.

He reflected back again to McAbee's office. A thought surfaced that was repulsive. McAbee made heavy use of a virtual midget, a fellow ex-academic who, Jack had learned from his own investigations on him, had been tossed out of academia as an incomparable boor and martinet. This took a lot of work in a field that grew incomparable boors like blades of grass. His name was Barry Fisk. He was a computer geek of the first order and in McAbee's words, 'a world-class researcher'. He was also an obnoxious smart-ass whom Jack seriously contemplated offing on more than one occasion.

So maybe that was it, as he saw McAbee's SUV turn into the partially-iced parking lot, McAbee became understandable when all of his operatives were put together. He could be figured out by figuring out the people who worked for him. Perhaps each of them was some kind of statement of what he was.

McAbee pulled along side his truck and got out. He was wearing a beaten-up leather coat, a pair of gloves, a scarf, and black corduroys. He raised his right hand toward Scholz and came over to the passenger door and got into the truck.

McAbee was in his late fifties. He wore tinted glasses that adjusted to the sun. He was balding, had a somewhat square face, and thin lips. He stood about 5 feet 11 inches, and his weight was nicely controlled. It was unusual not to see his gray eyes for they were the most unique characteristic about him – they had a fixing quality – unnerving sometimes.

"Jack. Sorry."

"No problem, Bertrand. I was watching the eagles, Pat called."

"What do you have for me?"

"Enough to break him."

"He has it coming."

"Well, I don't take a position on these things. You put a target on someone's back, I get him." He noticed that McAbee's glasses were untinting. His eyes were becoming visible. They gave him a hard look. He kept on, "He was pretty sloppy. His precautions were paper-thin, once I blew them aside the whole thing opened up."

"Did you have to do anything questionable?"

Scholz wanted to yell out at him words like, 'What do you think, you idiot?' but he said in response, "Do you really want to know?"

"At this point, I guess not. I hope it doesn't go any further than exposing him, that it forces him to shut down the attitude and surrender to his wife all that's due to her and the kids."

"I can't see it going any other way. Just for your information, there are four files in this bag. The first, green, is a public information folder. They would have all of it at the *Quad City Times*. The yellow file has things that cost money, informant stuff. The orange file could not appear in a trial because of what had to be done to get it. And the red file, well, pictures. Acquired in ways and with methods that it's best are not ever disclosed." He stopped and looked at McAbee whose thin lips got thinner. "I will, of course, if you ask."

There was a long pause. Bertrand eventually opened the bag and withdrew the red folder. He gazed at the 12 pictures for a few minutes before placing them back in the folder that was placed back in the bag. Finally, he said, "These are knock-out shots. He's done. You're right. I don't want to know how you got them."

"The bill is in there too."

"OK. Have a good day, Jack."

As he walked back to the Explorer he ran his hand through his sparse hair. Scholz figured that the academic PI was pretty tight about the whole thing. He shrugged and resumed his observation of the eagles. McAbee, on the other hand, drove away seemingly not noticing the Darwinian splendor at Lock and Dam Number 14.

It was two p.m. Judy Pappas had just arrived at George Washington Boulevard in Davenport, Iowa, one of the cities comprising the Quad City area which themselves straddled the Mississippi River in Iowa and Illinois. As she was fond of reminding out-of-town visitors, the river went east and west. This fact was known to destroy some drivers proud of their ability to navigate strange roads. In Illinois, the cities of Rock Island and Moline were joined by the Iowa entities Davenport and Bettendorf. The greater Quad City area had a population of over 300,000. Some thought that the area's greatest asset was the very diversity of the cities, for others that was perceived as the greatest liability. In no instance had she ever run into someone who thought that the Quad Cities could become the "Uni-city". The loyalties and rivalries were deeply etched into the citizenry.

She not only did not get out of her Jeep, she kept it running at full heat. The temperature had just eked into the double-digit column, 11 degrees Fahrenheit. She was parked within 100 feet of the bike path which coursed over Davenport and Bettendorf, extending approximately 14 miles. She saw it as one of the jewels of the community. The surface was virtually clear of any snow except for occasional packed pieces. She was waiting to run her normal 10 miles with her running partner, Bertrand McAbee. They had been running together for almost four years, and they had successfully completed two marathons.

She was a skier and had always enjoyed cold weather – within reason. McAbee called her a polar bear since their systems were at sixes and nines. She appropriately referred to him as a lizard. And just as she faltered and struggled in severe heat, McAbee would do likewise in the cold. In fact, she felt that she had pulled off a major feat in convincing him to run outside in the cold rather than running in one of the local gyms. She had taught him about gators, two shirts, two pants, gloves, ear muffs, and the like. Once in awhile she even suspected that he liked the challenge of the whole thing. On the other hand – sometimes he didn't, and he let her know about it.

Finally, his red Explorer came into sight as he turned sharply onto the Boulevard. He was late but not by much. Their coming together was due to his being hired to undo an identity theft that had caused her incredible pain. They had by inadvertence run into each other on the bike path where they would run together – both pacing at about the same times.

She found it curious that while she was pursuing a doctorate in statistics at the University of Iowa located in Iowa City, about 60 miles west of the Quad Cities, he had left the teaching profession to become a private investigator.

He gave her a long face as he left his Explorer and went to his back window which he opened. While removing his backpack, his gator, gloves, and Walkman, she came up along side of him. He had a pre-occupied look, his usual smile missing.

"Hey Bertrand – cheer up. It could be windy."

"Hah! Have you been waiting long?"

"No, no, just got here," she lied. Sometimes she would tease him and tell him that she had already run, but he didn't seem to be in the mood for it.

"Judy, I think we're crazy sometimes." He reached back into his truck and took out a skull hat. "I keep thinking of warm gyms."

"Yeah. I'm sure you do. That's the lizardly thing to do," she said lightly.

He laughed and said, "If we keep talking out here we deserve bad things to happen to us."

They walked to the bike path itself and stood in front of a line which was really a crack that had developed from one side of the cement bike path to the other, about four feet. This was pure McAbee in action now. Religiously, he stood behind the line and looked at his Polar watch which gave him a read on his heartbeat and his running time. He would not move until his watch came to the top of the minute when he would press a button twice and thus start his running. Judy tolerated this aberration and would occasionally taunt him by putting a foot over the line so as to draw a look of astonishment from McAbee, as if she had committed some crime against running-justice.

It was their custom to run about four and a half miles to the Middle Park pond in Bettendorf, all the while catching up on each other's lives. The remainder of the run took place with each listening to their Walkman. Judy listened to novels and sometimes FM music, while McAbee was usually listening to some obscure lecture series dealing with arcane historical matters. She long thought their minds drifted into very different channels.

"So Judy, how's everything going at Iowa?"

"OK. I'll be taking two courses this semester and that should be the end of my course work. How about yourself? You OK?"

"Yeah. I'm very busy. Lots of muck coming through the office these days. You can imagine."

"Oh yeah. I'll bet it's pretty dicey. You must meet some really curious people with some really tricky problems." She looked sideways at him as she wasn't inclined to bring up those kinds of considerations to him. He was close-lipped.

Finally, he said, "Sometimes I can't help feeling dirty. Now your own case was pretty clean-cut in a way. But some of these things get pretty bad. I keep turning over new rocks, and under each one there's new rot. My mother had a place down near Fort Lauderdale many years back. Soon after she died a pipe broke above her apartment and water went all over the place. It was wrecked. We had it fixed up again. There was a TV on a wooden stand that didn't appear damaged, and we kept it. I stayed at the refurbished place for a week once. But I kept noticing these huge ants. I couldn't find the source. I had a friend come in and still nothing except she noticed that they seemed to cluster near the TV. So – I picked it up to look under it at the stand. I couldn't believe what I saw. There must have been 5,000 of them living in some gray detritus. It was a horrible scene. I think I emptied a can of germicide on the area." He looked at her, his gray eyes catching her fully. "That's what it's like sometimes in this game. You can't believe what comes up at you." He shook his head and kept running.

When they got to the Walkman facet of the run she didn't turn hers on right away. She thought about what he had said. It made sense since he frequently came to the runs looking harassed. Not for the first time she wondered about his fit to the PI profession. Did he regret leaving academia? He wasn't an easy man. She could feel the demons of doubt in him, calculating that his spirit flagged in the touching of so much grief, duplicity, and rottenness.

Later, as they sat at the local Panera Bread Company, they talked more extensively about her progress at Iowa and his white German Shepherd, Scorpio, who seemed to bring great joy to McAbee as his features and voice became animated. He endowed Scorpio with human characteristics and would go on about how the dog would regularly best him by gaming McAbee through manipulation, sympathy, and any other device he could employ. McAbee claimed to be a victim of dog intelligence, powerless in the face of a superior species.

Toward the end of the conversation and the bottom of a second cup of coffee, McAbee came back to the PI business. "You know, Judy, for all the problems that I run into in my profession I will say this. Every time I think things are getting boring – I seem to get a case that really jolts me alive. Now that I finally have put my college case behind me and things have settled down, I wonder where my next enterprise will pop up?"

His college case was an illusive one that had taken McAbee back to a campus as a classics professor but also a sleuth. The campus had been haunted by a string of disappearance-murders. It was one of those cases that had brought McAbee close to death. From things that he had said in the past she knew his philosophy, those cases that came out of nowhere were the ones that had tentacles on them, the ones that could easily pop up and destroy him. She said, "Perhaps you should welcome boredom, Bertrand. You don't really need another one like that one."

He laughed, paused, and then said, "I'll tell you something, Judy, that I wouldn't admit openly to anyone else. I feel most alive when the cases have the highest danger."

"Well, I hope that your dreams don't come through," she said flatly and abruptly.

He laughed as they got up and left for their residences.

CHAPTER IV

"Well ladies and gentlemen, this is the colt who has drawn inquiries from around the world. The breeding is beyond guesswork, as you can see in your books. He is staked to every major race across the States and Canada. Let me review his breeding and the success of the blood lines."

The auctioneer droned on as Jimmy led him into the ring, the colt now in a closed area congested with over 500 people. He kept his hand tightly wound around the shank, even if he did notice that the pull and feel of the horse had abated ever since Scott spent time in his stall. But this was showtime. People watched the colt closely to see if he could handle the stress of the ring. To this point, he was on his best behavior.

Garzo made one last call to Jeremy Burgess. "Mister Burgess, he's in the ring. I'm going for broke on him. Just want to make sure you don't have any second thoughts."

"Roman, go for it. I'm behind you 100% on this. Call me when it's over. Throw in a knockout shot if you want."

A knockout shot came in the following way. The auctioneer would frequently bark out a super-high bid figure and ask someone to bid to that suggested price. Most bidders would just look at him as though he was crazy and then wait him out until he tumbled down the number scale to where someone was comfortable with a figure, or sometimes someone would just yell out a bid, forcing the auctioneer to start at that level. A knockout shot attempted to abort the whole process by the bidder accepting the first number yelled out by the auctioneer. The effect of such a move is that it tended to paralyze the audience and intimidate all bidders.

Garzo had done it before to good effect. The problem was that if you had overbid and thus paid more for the horse than it was worth, you could look the fool to your fellow horsemen. Never once did Garzo feel that this had happened to him. He would use the knockout here if the auctioneer wasn't completely out of range at the outset.

Harold Bardens had watched the colt closely, ever since he left the barn in the hands of the black groom. He noticed that the horse had lost a bit of an edge, just something in the way he walked. He put it down to Scott whipping some kind of downer into him. When #165 went into the ring he called Martin Blum.

"Martin here."

"Mistah Mahtin, I'm about to go into the arena for the Phantom. I'll be needin' some specific instructions."

"Still look good, Harold?"

"A thing to behold. Beautiful colt – no doubt about that."

"Harold – I'm giving you a $250,000 clearance. Don't go to more than that unless I tell you, keep the cell on."

Harold shook his head just slightly. He, personally if he had the money, would never have gone that far. The colt was simply too problematical.

"Mistah Mahtin, you might get him for that. I think that's a big clearance given what we're learnin' about him."

"I've thought it over, Harold, and this is where I stand on it," he said edgily.

Harold said, "OK. I'm inside – #165 just sold, and our colt is comin' on the floor. I'll do my best, sir."

Auctioneer Sammy Carney had been doing horse auctions since he was 17 years old. He was one of them who had been hired to do Harrisburg. By lot, he had drawn numbers 150 through 175. He had carefully read the credentials of sires and dams. The standardbred industry was as meticulous with breeding data as was the thoroughbred side of the business. It was rare to see a colt like Phantom Express; as he watched him come into the ring, he was majestic. As he read off the reasons why this was the star of the sale, he was still undecided about where to begin the asking price. He was concerned about someone taking out the competition with a knockout bid. He'd rather squeeze it out and hope that the price forced itself into the stratosphere as 1% of every final bid was his take of the auction.

When he had reviewed the auction segments with his associate, Paul Garden, he was told that there was a pool on the colt. The estimated ranges went from $100,000 up to $350,000. Both Garden and Carney knew that many factors influenced bidding: ego, hunches, advice, X-rays, conformity, weather, and the economy to name a few. But more than anything, they felt it was when two high rollers convinced themselves that they absolutely had to have the horse. When that happened, there was no way to predict how the bids would turn out.

"OK. Let's be modest on this. I'm asking for 75 thousand, do I hear 75 thousand?" He shouted enthusiastically into his microphone.

"AH!" shouted number one of the three spotters, whose job was to keep their eyes pinned for the bidders.

"I have 75, do I hear a hundred?"

"AH," came quickly from spotter number three.

"I have a 100, do I hear 125?"

"AH," again from spotter one.

"Ladies and gentlemen, we have a colt the likes of which I haven't seen in years. We have 125, do I hear 150?"

"AH," yelled out spotter number two.

Carney knew Garzo and wasn't surprised at his hand. Harold Bardens agented for many people, not a surprise. But the third bidder was unknown. All bidders were vetted pretty thoroughly before they were given a bidding number. So, there was very little chance of fakery, which used to haunt auctions in the old days. There was a possibility that he was a shill planted there by Scott or Theroux. But he doubted it. If it came to be known that either one of them was gaming the process, they would be ruined among the heavy hitters in the business.

"We're at 150, do I hear 175?"

"AH!" Spotter one was now glued on Garzo.

"175 – and worth every penny. Do I hear 200 thousand?"

"AH!" Spotter three, now tracking Bardens, barked his recognition of Bardens' hand.

Carney quickly gazed at spotter two who was staring at the third man. After two seconds, the man shook his head and walked toward the side of the tent. He was done. Spotter two looked at Carney and shook his right hand outward, gesturing that his man had bowed out.

At this point, Carney had two heavy hitters still pushing each other at 25 thousand clips. The attention in the arena was now riveted on the two spotters whose eyes were glued on the bidders. Carney picked up his rhythm, "I'm at 200, do I hear 225?"

Carney now gazed at Garzo, a man who wouldn't know how to manifest one emotion if he tried. Almost imperceptibly he raised his hand halfway upwards, catching the spotter's eye.

"AH!" came the bark of the number one spotter.

Now the attention turned to Bardens once again as Carney pushed his voice to a new intensity, "225 thousand – there's a reason for that – all we have to do now is watch that colt, study him – the look and stature of a champion. Do I hear 250?"

Bardens had kept Blum fully abreast of the bidding. He was disinclined to go to the last $25,000 authorized by Blum. He thought the horse already overbid. "It's our turn," he said quietly into his cell. "We're up against Burgess and his man Garzo. When they're committed at this level, it's a matter of pride."

"Go to 250, Harold!"

"Yes, sir." Harold looking directly at spotter three nodded his head.

"AH," cried the spotter.

Carney took up the beat and said, "We're now at a quarter of a million dollars. We're up in the stratosphere, folks, and for good reason. Do I hear $275,000?"

Garzo had been watching Bardens talking on his cell phone. For the first time he saw a hesitancy in Bardens for sure, if not his principal. He had waited for this. He looked at spotter one and said just loudly enough, "260."

The spotter yelled to Carney, "ΛH, 260!"

Carney was wondering when his $25,000 jumps would be challenged. Fair enough, the tens could give him a good ride too. "Well, gentlemen, we have 260, do I hear 270?"

He looked over at Bardens who seemed to have picked up a new life. His nod was firm.

It came back to Carney who now asked for $280,000.

Garzo was quick and Carney pressed for $290,000. Bardens went there and barely before Carney could throw the figure Garzo moved to $300,000. Now there was a prolonged pause as Bardens went into a cell conversation, finally coming out of it with a decided and firm "310,000".

"Well here we are – unusual waters in the standardbred industry. This beautiful colt – Phantom Express – with breeding to die for – at $310,000. Do I hear any amount over $310,000?" He looked around the quiet arena with a studied and dramatic look.

"325,000," Garzo growled out loud. His knockout punch.

There was not a whisper in the place. "In that case," now pointing to Phantom Express, "it is my duty to declare the bid at $325,000, going once, going twice ..."

"$350,000," Bardens yelled. A huge murmur fell across the audience.

"$375,000," Garzo said.

Bardens went to $385,000.

Garzo yelled "400."

Bardens shook his head; he was done. Carney said, "I have a bid from number 23 for $400,000. I am closing unless I hear otherwise, once, twice, sold!"

The audience, a majority being hard-crusted and close-to-the-vest horsemen, broke into a prolonged applause. Carney's last look at the horse saw, in those few brief seconds, the black groom's mouth almost attached to the colt's ear. He was talking to him, seemed to be a mile a minute. The colt seemed to be listening. The two of them disappeared almost as though they were joined at the hip.

Roman Garzo had purchased eight horses at the Harrisburg sale. They were placed in two horse vans and shipped to Valdosta, Georgia, where it was intended that each of the six pacers would be broken to pull a harness bike or sulkey while two would do the same as trotters. Gaiting was the cause of the difference between a pacer and a trotter. Much of the gaiting preference was due to genetics. The fundamental difference was in the motion of the legs. Pacers were gaited to move the two legs on the same part of the body in unison. Thus when the two left legs were going forward, the two right legs were going backwards. Pacers were typically hobbled; they made up the vast majority of harness-racing horses. On an average, they raced about three seconds faster than trotters over a one-mile race.

Trotters, two of the eight purchased by Garzo, were gaited differently. They raced with a diagonal style, e.g., right front leg and back left leg in unison with the opposite effect on the other legs. The use of hobbles or leather rigging placed near the legs was not necessary as was the case with almost all pacers. Phantom Express was clear and simple a pure pacer. No bloodline back at least five generations had shown a trotting proclivity.

Garzo called his assistant, Fidel Diaz, as the horses were being loaded into the van.

"Fidel, Phantom by himself is almost worth the full value of the other seven. He is to be given every piece of attention that you have. Stall him, then paddock him. Take your time. I'll be down in a week. I'll take over with him when I get there. Oh, the word up here is that he's pretty feisty."

Diaz said OK and hung up.

But Diaz would never know that Garzo's career with Burgess Stables was on the line with the success or failure of the colt. That was something that was between Garzo and Burgess.

Garzo went into the kitchen area of the sales complex. Because there were still a number of unshipped horses, there was breakfast for the horsemen. He poured himself a large black coffee and took a bagel with rocklike qualities to the cashier. While he was paying, Walter Scott came up to him, "You have a minute, Garzo?"

"Yeah, sure."

He followed Scott over to a table by a back window and sat. "So, you got the big guy," Scott said.

"Yeah, do I need to know something?"

"I'm thinking you already do."

"How so?"

"My groom tells me you were trying to get into his head."

"Is that right?"

"Well, if it is or it isn't, I think I owe you a few pieces of advice." Garzo just stared at him, not replying. Scott started to push his chair back. "Listen Garzo, I'm not going to talk to a wall or to someone who doesn't give a damn about what I'm saying. Sorry to have bothered you." He stood up.

Garzo reflected that he was being too hard. "OK, OK, sit down, Scott. I'd be appreciative for whatever you can tell me."

Scott stood still for a few seconds before sitting. "You're getting a structurally sound animal. His conformity, size, stride, lungs, heart, and all the rest are absolutely A plus."

"I know."

Scott, who had been looking at something on the table, reacted as though he had been slapped as he stared at Garzo for a few seconds. "But as you know, there's more to it. Maybe you can get into his head and change him, but if you don't, I can promise you you've got a vicious animal on your hands . . . I can see that you're unimpressed by what I'm saying to you. Fair enough. You think that because you're a Burgess man that you can't do anything wrong. Is it that his money will cure the colt?"

"Listen Scott, back off. There's no such thing as a vicious animal. He's just another dumb horse – who probably just needs the crap belted out of him. I've never met a horse I couldn't tame and make obey – and this one is no exception. You saw how your groom handled him. It's just a matter of getting the right people around him, and I'm the man. I'll break that colt, he'll obey me, he'll be a champion. So just back off. Burgess got nothing to do with this. It's between me and the colt, and I'll win. You got anything else you want to tell me?"

Scott leaned forward to within six inches of Garzo's face and said with quiet intensity, "Garzo – you're a fool. I've studied Phantom Express and he's mean and very smart. You, on the other hand, are mean and very, very stupid." Scott got up and walked away.

Garzo was going to say something nasty to the old trainer, but instead he bit into the hard bagel and took a big gulp of his coffee. It was now going to be a battle of wits between him and the colt. Given his knowledge of tracks and backstretches, he was quite sure that the course of this conversation with Scott would be passed around across the tracks of North America. It wasn't just a question of Garzo's relation with Burgess that was at issue, but rather Garzo's entire stature and reputation in the industry. So, he now looked at the training of this colt as a personal crusade. He couldn't choose a worthier adversary; he liked to think that the colt couldn't himself have a worthier adversary.

He left the bagel half finished and started to look around the kitchen and then went into the backstretch looking for that black groom who had attended Phantom Express. He was without luck. Perhaps someday he'd have to look him up because whatever he was doing and saying was working on the colt. He felt the slightest shiver of doubt work its way into his soul. But he was not the type of man to allow it to take hold. Roman Garzo was Roman Garzo, and no damn horse or loose talk from an old breeder and trainer would get the best of him. If it had to be, thinking back to a high school assignment in Ohio, Phantom Express would be Moby Dick and he'd be Ahab.

CHAPTER V

———◆———

Fidel Diaz was waiting at the unloading area of the Burgess Farms Complex in Valdosta. The lead van driver coming from Harrisburg had called ahead when he was about 60 miles north on U.S. 75. Diaz wasn't sure but he felt just a nip of tension in Garzo's voice when he referred to Phantom Express. Already, he had looked up the priced paid for the horse – $400,000. High by thoroughbred prices, but not in the record category by any means. But by standardbred prices, it was a gigantic amount. If the colt failed, Garzo might take the fall with him. Maybe this was how Diaz could get control of the Valdosta organization. After all, Fidel Diaz knew how to conduct himself among the people – something the sour and taciturn Garzo would never accomplish.

It was about a 950-mile trip from Harrisburg to Valdosta. The rule of thumb was to unload the horses and let them mostly stand in their stalls for about one to two days – with only a small bit of walking. Otherwise, they were prone to tying up and that would be a problem for the rest of their careers. Phantom Express was the second horse off of the van. Diaz studied him. He was a magnificent animal, built like a pure athlete. Just on looks alone he was in a class by himself among the 73 horses residing in Valdosta. Of course, whether he had heart and courage was a different story. It was the difference between a Muhammad Ali and a fag like Rock Hudson. He went up to the colt and saw that his ears were pinned back – he grabbed the halter and jerked it hard toward him. The colt tried to raise his front legs, but Diaz held him tight and close to his body. The horse wanted to get some distance as he stared wildly at Diaz. It was as if he sensed an enemy. At first, Diaz laughed scornfully at the colt's efforts. Then he grimaced as he had to use both hands to keep the animal under control. "Get over here and take this one into Barn A Stall One. This S.O.B.'s our star!" He let the halter go to one of the grooms and feigned curiosity about the next horse coming off the van.

Stealthily, his eye caught the hostile colt from behind. He had felt a surge of power in the animal and had just barely held on as the damn colt almost caught him by surprise and got away. If that had happened it would be Diaz who would be the first sacked over him and not Garzo as he hoped.

"Hey, Fidel!"

He looked around and saw the toothless van driver smiling at him. "Yeah?"

"You just came into touch with the devil, man. Don't turn your back on that one. Suit him up with armor. He's ready to meet death head on."

Diaz went over to him and said with a smile, "He try to kick you or something?"

"Nah. Just some talk about him. Heard enough to know that I didn't want anything to do with him. Happy when they loaded him and happy when they unloaded him. He's carrying a lot of baggage already."

"Yeah. Well, we'll see how schizo he is after a few weeks here."

"The last horse is out. You have those two you want me to bring to the Meadowlands?"

"I'll get the boys to bring 'em over."

After two days, Phantom, as he was now referred to, was put out into a paddock, a fenced area, about 100 feet by 100 feet. They let him have his way in that confined space where he would typically stand, occasionally run, eat, drink, and explore his new environment. Interestingly, Garzo's calls were daily and had an insistence to them that Diaz had never heard before.

When Garzo arrived on that Tuesday he immediately went to the paddock area to see Phantom. The colt looked down at him as he raised his head, turned it slightly and seemed to appraise Garzo with an arrogant look. His ears were pinned severely – a warning to Garzo, just as humans would warn by a clenched fist, or a dog with a growl. Garzo didn't open the paddock gate; it wasn't the time to take on this colt who was openly challenging him by all appearances. He was of mixed feelings about the matter. On the one hand he didn't need some crazy beast that could be a constant headache and problem. But on the other hand he liked the spirit of the horse if it could be controlled and harnessed into a champion's ways. If he had heart and directed it to winning races and not combatting his handlers, there would be great results, not just as a racehorse but also as a sire.

The first step in moving a colt toward the track was to accustom him to harnessing, steering, and pulling a cart. Garzo had seen horses get the hang of it in two hours, others took days and some never could get into a comfort zone with it. The process was called breaking. Phantom was led out of the paddock by Fidel Diaz as Garzo followed at a distance. Two grooms had also been ordered to the half-mile training track at the complex. One of the grooms was a heavy drinking stable-bum named Henry, whose origins were from somewhere in Maine or Vermont; the other was a thin Mexican named Manuel who had been hired by Diaz. They were both highly familiar with the process, usually done in a horse's stall, but at this point Garzo opted to do it on the track itself.

When Phantom arrived at the track, he stood there quietly, but alertly. Garzo barked at Henry – "Go get the extra lines for God's sake, Henry. Manuel – we have to harness him. Are you ready? Diaz – what's going on here?"

"What's the hurry, Roman? Is he entered in a race tomorrow?" Diaz said.

Garzo didn't say anything, but he felt his tan skin redden. He wanted to slap the bastard right there. Henry came back with the extra lines and Manuel with the harness. Garzo looked quickly at Phantom. It was as though he had an uncanny understanding of what was taking place around him.

"Manuel, put the harness on him." This involved putting a strap under the horse's tail and under his stomach to hold the harness in place, sometimes dangerous steps that could cause some yearlings to lurch, run, jump, kick, or put another way – explode. Garzo breathed uneasily as Manuel tightened all the fastenings, like buckling a belt. He was quick and nimble. Phantom barely flinched. Garzo was overjoyed. So much for the horse being dangerous.

"That wasn't hard. Fidel, put the bridle on him." Diaz gave Garzo a sideways glance and went directly in front of the horse. He held up the bridle as if to show it to the colt and let him smell it, seeking his approval. His ears went straight back, lying flat on the top of his head. Garzo saw it, came around, and stood next to Diaz. "Don't let this sucker get away with this. That bridle is going on him – if it takes us all day. I'll distract him; you put it on. Henry, Manuel, stay alert." Garzo stepped to the left of the colt and drew his attention as he always seemed to. Diaz made the move to put on the bridle, but the colt went up on his hind legs, lurching out with his feet, making an effort to stab Diaz with a hoof. "Back away! Back away!" Garzo yelled. Three more efforts were made, each ending in frustration. Finally, Garzo barked, "Manuel, put him in crossties in the barn. This is going to end right now."

Crossties were two chains that were fastened to two wooden beams. The chains could be placed on either end of the halter so as to keep the colt in one place. Manuel, with great alacrity, had him fully connected within seconds. Garzo was impressed. "Now, Diaz, let's try again." He again went up to him, and the horse lurched forward, refusing the bridle.

In the barn, they tried three more times, but to no avail. Garzo finally tried, and the colt went wild. Manuel volunteered to try to bridle him and was told to mind his business by Garzo who was embarrassed and angry. He went into his office and came out with a two by four. Diaz stared at him in disbelief but didn't dare say anything. "I'm going to show him something now that I hate to do – but this bastard is going to learn. When he's dazed – then put it on him. You'll have no trouble."

Garzo walked to within four feet of the colt and slammed the two by four over Phantom's head. He almost went down as his legs buckled. "Now, dammit!"

Diaz placed the bridle around the staggered animal. "Good, now let's get him out. Maybe I won't have to do this again to him." He looked around menacingly at the three of them. Each was upset, he could tell. He went up to the most dispensable one – old Henry. "You want to say something?"

"No. No sir. I got the lines. I'm ready to go."

Manuel led the horse out to the track. The colt strode wobblingly and haltingly.

Garzo said, "Henry, I want four lines. You, Manuel, on either side, I'll be behind. Fidel – just be around."

Henry attached one line, a long leather strap, to the left side of the bridle. Manuel grabbed it and stood about three feet to the side of the colt. He placed another line to the right, which he let fall to the dirt. Two lines came across the colt's back, they were grabbed by Garzo. Then Henry picked up the line to the right. This line process was essential to teaching the colt to steer via the lines, giving the horse a steering wheel of sorts. "OK. Let's go," Garzo yelled.

Henry and Manuel walked alongside of Phantom, keeping him walking and in a straight line. Behind him Garzo held the two lines so as to give the horse the sensation of pulling something from behind. They gingerly walked the colt around the entire half-mile track. Although his ears were pinned, he did not act up. Garzo was happy that he had bludgeoned him.

When they reached the point from where they began, the cart and rigging gear were attached. Henry and Manuel would continue to hold the lines on the side of the colt, but now he would be pulling a two-wheeled cart. They hooked the cart to the horse's gear, and he was urged to jog slowly. Phantom did as asked for the half mile. "OK – that's it. Same process tomorrow. Henry – see to it."

Henry took Phantom into the barn, took the equipment off, and began the process of washing the horse down. He soaped him and rinsed him off with a hose. He noticed that the colt had a terrible gash on the top of his head. Phantom winced when the soap had worked its way into the skin.

He walked him to his stall. There was no doubt that he was not himself. The two by four had had an effect. When he went back to the barn he saw Fidel Diaz. "You know, you better put some salve on his head. He's pretty damaged."

Diaz looked at him scornfully, "Hey, that's Garzo's problem, not mine."

Manuel was a distant relative of Fidel Diaz. They both came from the same village – 35 miles south of Laredo, Texas. When he had slipped across the border over the Rio Grande he had made his way across to Valdosta. Diaz hired him because of an agreement made between him and his mother's second cousin. The requirements were few: that he had familiarity with horses, that he had reasonably good false papers, and that he took orders without sass. In return he would have a free room with a community bath, cable TV, and $250 a week. Food and drink were his responsibility. Manuel took the deal and had worked at Burgess Stables for almost six months.

With the exception of some name-calling and threats from Garzo, he found the job of groom to be satisfactory. He had, in his judgment, one great strength and one great

vulnerability – he loved horses. Although Fidel Diaz looked
at horses as stepping stones to greater things, he rarely saw it
necessary to beat or torment them. Garzo, on the other hand,
was mean-spirited and cruel. Manuel hated the feeling he got
when he was near the man. But he was a master at hiding his
feelings and tried to stay out of Garzo's way.

The most irritating of all the events that he saw around
him was Garzo's effort at breaking the colt they called
Phantom. Over the months from the day they tried to first
hook him up to the day they began to train him – it was one
sin committed on top of another sin. Garzo used electrical
prods, two by fours, mood-altering drugs, and his fists to
bring the colt to heel.

Two weeks ago Garzo had damaged his right fist when he
punched the colt on his mouth. Too proud to seek medical
treatment, he pretended that he was fine. But watching him
try to do even simple tasks with his right hand proved him
the fake.

He had tried to bring his concerns up with Diaz but
was told in very terse and vulgar Spanish to mind his own
business, especially when it came to Phantom. Garzo, he
reminded him, had made it very clear that this colt was his
crusade and that he knew best how to make it a champion
pacer. "You feed him, water him, wash him, clean his stall
– but don't dare try to challenge Garzo. Otherwise, I will not
be able to save you from being fired. If that happens, I'm
afraid that you're on your own. He's the boss here, not me.
At least not yet."

So Manuel did as he was told. He would position the
harness and attach the training cart to the colt. Then Garzo
would come and start the horse jogging around the track,
sometimes twice but sometimes up to six times. Manuel
would watch as the slightest mis-step, the slightest falter, or

the slightest sign of something amiss was met by the slash of a whip across the ass of the colt. More often than not the colt would come in with bleeding lash marks that had been opened by Garzo's whip. On the tougher days, he would hear a comment from Garzo, "Clean this S.O.B. up," or "He'll never win over me – I'll beat the bastard to death if I have to."

Manuel would treat him with salve and antibiotic creams. But with the flesh so torn it was a losing battle. It was as though Garzo was constantly picking off the scab.

Manuel, who had studied some English in his grammar school, made steady efforts to learn the language. He would practice with Henry and two other grooms with whom he had found a friendship. Never once did he ever let on regarding his growing proficiency in the language. For some reason he couldn't explain he did not let on to Diaz that he was beginning to understand discussions. Garzo, of course, would never know, thinking that Manuel need only follow simple commands such as, "Clean him up", "Unhook him", or "Feed him".

It was with a secret delight that he overheard the following conversation on Monday.

"Diaz, Mister Burgess is coming down on Friday. I want this place spic and span. See what you can do to Phantom's marks – I don't want him looking like we're abusing him. Burgess would get a little nervous at that. So, tell Manuel to walk him, bathe him, and try to get the marks healed up. And tell him that if he's asked a question in Spanish – to stonewall it. The colt is fine, eats well, and looks great. He's never to offer anything else. If he tries something I'll throw his goddamn ass out of here."

"I don't think he'd ever do that," Diaz said in defense of Manuel.

"Yeah, well let's hope so for his sake. What I see is some sad-assed guy who is upset by blood, whiplashes, and anything he deems to be cruel. Don't need some animal lover out here."

"I'll tell him to mind himself, Roman."

Garzo had him on the track that Friday afternoon as Burgess watched closely. He had him down to a 2:20 mile, which for a two-year-old in late March was phenomenal.

Manuel figured that Phantom would be under a track trainer in a matter of about six weeks, going there when the colt hit two minutes and ten seconds. Phantom was Garzo's creation, pure and simple.

Never once, to Manuel's amazement, did Garzo touch him with his whip when Burgess watched. When he came off the track he handed the cart to Manuel saying, "Clean him up." He patted Manuel on the shoulder and, to Manuel's shock, even patted the colt on the neck. Manuel was torn by the hypocrisy shown by Garzo in front of Burgess, who on that particular day seemed distracted and hurried.

He heard him go over to Burgess, "When I hand him over to your trainers – they'll have a champion on their hands, Mister Burgess."

Burgess inspected other horses that day but was in his helicopter within two hours of arriving. He never got close enough to Phantom to see the damage that Garzo had inflicted on the colt.

CHAPTER VI

Augusta Satin drove over to McAbee's office in Davenport. He said that he'd be waiting outside his building for the ride that would take them along the Mississippi River on River Road and onto the Interstate 74 Bridge that connected Bettendorf, Iowa, with Moline, Illinois.

Augusta had first run into McAbee when her husband-doctor deserted her and two kids for Wisconsin and a medical student that he ran into while attending a conference in Madison, Wisconsin. Before he left he had emptied their bank accounts, sold off every asset that he could get his hands on and had successfully trashed her life.

Before she met the bum she had risen to detective-grade in the Rock Island, Illinois, Police Department. Soon after her marriage she had resigned from the PD and had two children in quick succession. Augusta had seen the sometimes-violent results of settling matters on one's own. Asking around for

a discreet P.I., she had been given the name of Bertrand
McAbee. Her only fear was that he was too hands-off, too
indirect, and that he would be unable to shake anything out
of her arrogant husband. She never got the whole story, but
whatever he did worked. Her ex-husband suddenly coughed
up a handsome settlement and paid maintenance for the kids
regularly.

In the meantime, McAbee found cause to ask her to do
some jobs for him. She was overjoyed as she needed the
money, the challenge, and – she had to admit – the fun of
being around McAbee whom she found to be interesting
and challenging. While she was degreed from Augustana
College in Rock Island, she had never really hung around an
academic. She admired the way he thought and the richness
of his knowledge.

As time went by she took on more and more assignments,
and she and McAbee had become close. But McAbee was
snake-bitten in romance and backed away from any hint by
her that they could have more. She had gone as far as she
could without causing a rift that could have some negative
effects on the distance that they had already traveled. The
next moves were up to him.

He was there, raising his right hand with thumb pointing
upwards and a big smile on his face. He came around and
opened the passenger door. "Bertrand – aren't you chilly?"

"No. I'm a he-man."

"Right, I forgot."

"How's everything?"

"Solid! I've got this all set up for us. You?"

"Yeah, OK."

"How's that dog of yours?" The dog's name was Scorpio, a
white German Shepherd whom she felt was slightly unhinged.
But McAbee loved him; she wouldn't dare tell him that the

dog had neurotic inclinations. After all, she probably had a full share of those herself.

"Scorpio." He laughed. "What a great guy. I wanted to bring him along, but I figured that we have enough heat on the job today," he paused, "he's doing fine Augusta – and he sends his best to you."

"Well, I should hope so."

"What do you expect to come out of this adventure we're going on?"

"He thinks we're a couple." She looked across at him. He gave no reaction. "He expects that we're going to give him five, full dossiers that will enable him to destroy five people. He's prepared to give us $3000 for each dossier."

"How good are the dossiers?"

"They were prepared by your man, couldn't be better." His man was Barry Fisk – the computer geek who had an awesome command of computer technology. He had created five fictional profiles for an identity thief from Rockford, Illinois. Augusta had been introduced to the Rockford thief by a local ID thief, Richie Takes, whom she squeezed for the contact. What she and McAbee were trying to do was to exonerate a long-time friend of McAbee who had been literally destroyed by the man. In his seventies and in ill health the experience had devastated Neal McDermott, as bills to his immaculate credit record were charged, his house had been re-mortgaged and his banking accounts stripped. He had been sent to an assisted-care institution, McAbee doubted that he could even get out of it again. "I know that this is personal with you, Bertrand." She patted him on the shoulder. "Just leave it up to us."

"It's not that easy, Augusta. I want to really make this guy pay."

"Listen. He will. Scholz is already over there with two of his boys. If our approach doesn't work – I know you'll let Jack take care of it." She drove up the ramp off of State Street in Bettendorf and entered the traffic proceeding south into Moline, Illinois. She saw McAbee staring down at the Mississippi River, the river was unsettled, white-capping, a bit like McAbee she thought.

She exited at Third Street in Moline and proceeded west toward the downtown area. They were to meet the perp, John Howles, at a local sports bar. She parked just south of it. Her phone rang, "Yeah?"

"Scholz. He's already seated. He has a buddy with him. He's in the blue van, one o'clock to you. Looks like he could be an armful. Ask him if he wants him neutralized."

She whispered the question to McAbee. He shook his head and said loudly, "No."

"Not yet, Jack. We're going in, anything we need to know?"

"I've got one man watching the van; the other is two booths from Howles – you won't miss him, and I'm watching you as I speak."

"OK, I'll keep my phone on. How's the wire?"

"All set," he hung up.

Augusta's relationship with Scholz was bipolar. While he was dependable, honest in his way, and competent, he was also vicious, unethical, and criminal in his tactics. Half of the time she detested him and wanted him as far from her as she could get him. The other half of the time she was ambivalent at best. When she thought of McAbee and his relationship with Scholz, she figured that Scholz represented the dark side of the McAbee enigma.

"So, Augusta – how are we playing this?"

"I'm a sweet-assed crook like him, and you're a suspicious boyfriend but also a crook. How's that?"

He laughed, "Got it."

She loved to hear him laugh; it took the chains off of his sometimes controlling personality.

They entered in the bar side. Basically a squared area, one-third was devoted to a bar, one-third to a tabled area with stools, and one-third to a booth area. There was a second floor that skirted the bottom floor; she had never seen anyone up there.

Howles had described himself to her. "You can't miss me. I'm 6 feet 5 inches, and I weigh 275 pounds – naked. I was a defensive tackle at Illinois and a second round pick for the Miami Dolphins. Screwed up my knee in training camp and was done. That's all you need to know about me." When she saw him, he reminded her of the giant in the Harry Potter movies. Only this one had no gentle quality about him. He was watchful and nasty looking. His forehead sloped upwards, his brown eyes were deep-set, a flattened nose, and big lips set him off from anyone else in the booths. She IDed Scholz' man instantly, looking as though he was AWOL from a Seals unit. She reminded herself to avoid getting in the midst of these two.

"Mister Howles – Augusta Satin and my friend – Bobby McArthur."

"Call me John," he extended his hand, which was huge, as one would expect. "Didn't know you were bringing anyone." He shook McAbee's hand.

She saw Bertrand wince; Howles had meant to hurt him. He had. Augusta kept herself smiling and super-polite. She saw him appraising her body like he was at a buffet. She could tell the lout liked what he saw. 'Enjoy it while you can, fat boy, because you're in for a rough ride', she said to herself.

"Have a seat." They sat. "So, you got my name from Richie Takes. How do you know him?"

"We've known each other for years. You know how that goes – we don't see each other for years, then suddenly we do and we have some things in common," she said keeping her eyes centered on the big man. He acted as though McAbee didn't exist.

"You pay him anything?"

"In kind." She let the comment lie there; letting him take it wherever his rotten mind wanted him to go.

He smiled, showing surprisingly even and white teeth. "How about you? How do you fit into this?" He nodded toward McAbee.

"I'm her boyfriend and colleague."

Howles gave a winced look at Augusta. But he didn't say anything. Augusta felt McAbee's hand on her knee; he gave it a squeeze. Damn McAbee, she thought, he'd get them both killed with his sense of humor.

"So – what do you have for me?"

"As I told you, five dossiers. Complete and updated to this past weekend. Credit card apps and/or change of addresses have been made, approved, and picked up. All bank account information secured. Not one of them has less than $75,000 in movable accounts. Their property is fully paid for and could easily be second mortgaged. They're all over 70 and vulnerable as hell." She smiled hard at him to show that she could be ruthless behind that smiling exterior.

"Where are they?"

"In this satchel."

"Pass 'em over."

"Sorry, nothing personal but Bobby won't let me do that. You see he's in on this."

"Well, Bobby, why not?" He asked the question with full sneer and in an almost falsetto voice.

McAbee shot back, "Why is the question, not why not. I don't know anything about you except what Takes told Augusta. So why don't we both make some good faith offer."

Howles looked back at Augusta, nodding his head upwards.

"He's my partner, it's his call too."

"I offered you $3000 per dossier. Take one out – I'll pick. Let me review it for a few minutes. If it's OK, we'll do some dealing."

She looked at McAbee. His ruddy complexion was a shade ruddier. She surmised that McAbee was seething. No more humor coming from that direction. "What do you say, Bobby?"

"OK."

She picked up the bag and opened it to the five dossiers. "You pick, big guy," she said seductively looking at Howles as she jabbed McAbee's leg with her knee.

"The middle one, yeah that one."

She handed it to him.

He spent about five minutes studying the dossier. He closed it and handed it back to her saying, "I have a problem."

"About what?" she said.

"Why aren't you pulling the cord on this?"

"Not my game."

"If boyfriend Bobby is good at this, why doesn't he?" he said sarcastically.

"You don't seem to understand, John Howles. I love my boyfriend. I don't take kindly to your dissing him."

He sat back and looked over the pair of them. "OK, OK. But the two of you are a strange number by any account. Sorry. So, Bobby, why don't you do it?"

"I get them from a friend. I don't like being on that end of the business, enough said."

Howles went into a visual mode of calculation as his eyes went down, sideways, and up before returning to connect with Augusta. "Whatever." He took out his wallet. "I said I'd give you three for each. Fifteen hundred now for each and when I draw blood – fifteen hundred for each time I take my hit. That's my policy." He started to peel 100-dollar bills from his wallet, not looking at either of them, suggesting that they had already agreed to the deal.

McAbee looked at Augusta and said, "Not going to happen."

He stopped counting and looked at Bertrand angrily. "That's it, or I'm done here."

McAbee said, "You've never gotten dossiers this full and with this quality before. This is professional and flawless work." He looked at Augusta and said, "I told you that $10,000 should have been minimum asking price. This is an insult."

"You know you two are minor leaguers, just like Takes. I'm leaving. Screw the two of you." He was about to get up and then thought of something else. "You two – you see this wallet? I have over $50,000 in it. No joking. You're quibblers. When you prove yourselves, I'll bring you along – but not now." Then he got up and headed toward the exit.

Augusta said to McAbee, "Hey, we never even had a chance to order anything." She gave her phone to Bertrand.

"Jack, take them in the van. We'll be out in a few minutes."

She turned around and noticed that the Seal was gone.

McAbee was stiff with anger. As he sat through the charade with Howles, he wondered why and how such a man could be spawned. There was no guilt, no shame, no remorse, and no sympathy. It was as though he was swatting flies. He couldn't get out of his mind the image of Neal McDermott, the mild-mannered, good-natured English professor at St. Anselm's College. He had retired two years previous, saying that he was going to write an epic poem about the conquering of the American Indian west. Neal had Blackfoot blood in him, and although he had an Irish soul it had been "mightily enriched", as he'd say, by Indian DNA.

Bertrand knew Neal well when he himself taught and administered at the college. Neal's daughter had come to him a few months ago and told Bertrand the brutal story about her father's financial destruction at the hands of identity thieves. It had so shaken Neal that, in McAbee's estimation, he had suffered a nervous breakdown. He was a ghost of himself on the occasions of McAbee's visits to him. His heart sank when he visited this simple man with such a guileless and pure heart.

From there it was a matter of running down the perpetrators. He told Neal's daughter that he would work to bring back whatever he could beyond what the FBI and local PD could do. Ever since 9/11, though, he had observed that the FBI had abandoned huge sectors of these investigations. People like Howles were not unaware of this. They appeared to see all of this inaction as an invitation to double their activity.

This brought McAbee to call in his hugely effective computer man, Barry Fisk. A Yale Ph.D. in History, he was unfortunately a misanthrope. Under five feet in height and physically twisted, he was unable to cross the bridge of charity, kindness, or trust and had unceremoniously been dumped and branded in higher education circles as a crank and ineffective professor. Fortunately for McAbee, he had decided to remain in the Quad City area. Extraordinarily comfortable with computers and research he had made a mark for himself as a guru of sorts. McAbee had caught him at the very beginning of this metamorphosis, and a relationship was sealed, as much as one could with him. Even still, it was sometimes acrimonious and patience testing.

Within a week the name of Howles was flagged. Then the elaborate setting of a trap began to occur. At the point that McAbee and Satin were leaving the bar and heading back to the van, McAbee figured that he was personally out $15,000 which, when such numbers would pop up, would cause him to say to himself, 'to hell with it'. He had decided a long time ago to never bow to money, accepting the medieval mantra that wisdom and poverty were comfortably associated. Not that he lived in poverty – but he certainly didn't actively pursue wealth.

So, with the use of all of McAbee's assets, Howles had been gamed to this point of the affair. He and Augusta walked quickly to her car where Scholz stood. When they got to him he said, "They're in the back of the van. We had to zap the driver before Howles got there, and Howles was a handful. 50,000 volts brought the bull down. They're both tied up like pigs with some new material that I secured from the CIA. It's amazing. They say that it could hold a car to heel, not a Mercedes – but maybe your Explorer. Isn't that something?"

McAbee noticed that Scholz came alive when things became operational. What he would not admit, except to himself alone, was that so did he. "Is there room in there for all of us?"

"Yeah, the boys will sit upfront, and I'll hang outside if you want," Scholz said.

"OK," he said.

"Bertrand, why don't I come in with you?" she asked.

"Sure."

After Scholz had re-arranged the van satisfactorily, McAbee and Satin went inside and closed the back doors. Both of the thieves were positioned uncomfortably on the floor with their hands hog-tied to their legs. They both had a dazed look in their eyes. McAbee was uninterested in the van driver as he sat with his legs stretched and crossed in front of Howles. Augusta crouched beside him. McAbee noticed that the tie-material seemed to be some kind of plastic. As he did often, he wondered how Scholz managed to get materials that were of such a nature that even our troops in the field couldn't get them.

"So, Howles! What you're going through now is not comparable to what you've done to your victims. Do you understand me?"

Howles said nothing, rather he glared at McAbee.

"I assume your look is one of understanding. How's that?" The glare didn't change. "Here's the deal, please tell me if it doesn't make any sense to you. Your wallet will be stripped of its contents. You and your associate will be handed over to Illinois Bureau of Investigation the minute we leave the van. I am submitting the tape of our bar conversation as part of a citizen's arrest. As a courtesy, the Bureau is holding off until I end my talk with you. I assume that by your glare you understand me. Oh, and before I leave, I want you to know that I have given over a 302-page report on all of your activities. The warrant for your arrest is already a matter of fact. There's one particular person for whom I'm doing this. You pretty much destroyed him. Augusta?"

"You've made your point, Bertrand, let's go."

It was refreshing to be outside the stuffiness of the van. Scholz came over saying, "We all set?"

"Have one of your guys take Howles' wallet and give it to me. The money is going to Neal McDermott. Then put it back in his pocket,"

"Will do."

When that had been completed McAbee said to Augusta, "So – do I get a ride home? Or are you going to desert me?"

As they drove the I-74 bridge toward Bettendorf he said, "As usual, you were terrific."

"Not bad yourself, for a classics prof. Howles surprised me."

"Oh?"

"I couldn't believe he was willing to take a pass on those dossiers."

"When business is flourishing, people get tough. Scary to say this but it's a buyer's market."

He looked over at her. Augusta had a short afro, a long, thin face with beautifully chiseled features. She was about six feet tall and athletic. She didn't seem to have an ounce of fat on her. She wore black corduroys and a long-sleeve, black woolen turtleneck with medium circled earrings and a pretty hefty silver chain. She didn't wear a ring. McAbee shook his head slightly and sighed to himself. He really liked this woman, but he was leery of the relationship slope. So, he kept a purposeful distance, even though it took great effort on his part. He was sure that she liked him, but not clear as to what was beyond that.

CHAPTER VII

Garzo had Phantom where he wanted him. The sinister looks, the stare-downs, the pinned ears – all of it – were due to fear and punishment. Not that either was good in itself. After all, from fear a horse could do a lot of damage. Garzo, ever watchful, never trusted him. When he'd take him for his exercise he'd always remember that a horse bent on damaging someone was in the best position to do it when a jog cart was being used. The driver, sitting close to the horse's back legs, was quite vulnerable to the horse stopping and smashing the cart and driver with a lethal kick. Phantom never tried it, but Garzo thought that the colt was measuring him and waiting for the moment. Meanwhile the colt was making great progress in bringing down his times. Garzo intended to have him race in the major two-year-old stake races and the beautifully filling-out colt was on schedule to break the competition in two.

When Phantom had hit two minutes 15 seconds he was introduced to a racing bike or sulkey. Sulkey technology over the years had improved by a shifting in aerodynamical concepts and the introduction of new and lighter metals. In essence, the sulkey had two protruding shafts which attached to the harness materials on the horse. At the back of the shafts was a cushioned seat attached to the crossbar that connected the shafts. Below sat two light bicycle tires. Not too long ago, wood was the standard material, but now different metals were the norm. An exercise or jog cart, on the other hand, was made of wood or metal and was not built for speed, but rather low-key exercise and was much more comfortable for the trainer/driver.

It was a landmark point in the training down of a colt to introduce him to the racing bike. A competitive colt would immediately feel the difference in the change from jog cart to sulkey. It was as if it invited him to show his speed. One of Garzo's former employees compared the change as similar to one where a runner would carry around a thirty-pound weight until the day of a contest when suddenly the weight would be ditched. Definitionally – the lift would be exhilarating as a racing sulkey/bike is more compact, shafts are close to the horse, and the seat is just a few feet from the horse's flank.

Except for Diaz and Manuel who were assisting Garzo, they were all watching, the grooms, assistant trainers, and visitors. Phantom came out of the barn led by Manuel who held him by the lines. Garzo noticed that the race bike had caught the colt's attention. For the millionth time, he could have sworn that the colt was thinking, sizing-up. Unlike most trainers who would harness a horse in the stable area, Garzo preferred the track proper.

Garzo held the whip in his hand as he directed Fidel Diaz to hold the horse still. The nimble Manuel was to attach the bike to the harness, and, in turn, to the horse. Manuel spoke to Garzo, "Sir – it would help me to have you hide the whip from his eyes, his vision. I think..."

"Goddamn it, you're not paid to think. Just do what you've been told to do, you spic bastard. Diaz, you better explain the situation around here or this guy's outta here. Now just hook him up," he yelled at the pair of them.

Manuel hooked him up as directed and stepped aside, ashen. There was no incident as Garzo had figured. The colt knew that his whip would tear his flesh to ribbons if that's the way it was to be.

Garzo sat in the sulkey and took the reins which were lying limp over Phantom's back. "OK – Diaz – step away and check him up." The colt had already trained an hour earlier in a jog cart at the time of 2:40; a warmup of sorts to this upcoming big step.

Phantom strode forward and the sulkey moved behind him. Garzo watched the horse's ears, which after a few seconds moved back and forth like antennae. Phantom probably was feeling the difference of the sulkey, and as he was intrigued by the change, it took his mind off of his hate and fear, Garzo calculated. They jogged the oval once and during that very relaxed half mile he went nicely. His stride and movements were flawless. He had a beautiful and natural grace. An athlete. They went around again. Garzo pulled him up in front of Diaz. "Looks good, doesn't he?"

"Sure does. You going with him now?"

"Yeah. I'm going back where I'll turn him and I'll use you as the starting point. He'll go in exactly 2:15; you wait and see." He backtracked about 300 feet, then he turned Phantom. He growled a little at the horse and hit the colt's back with a reasonably gentle whack.

Phantom accelerated and started to pace. Within the 300 feet he was picking up momentum as he came lumbering by Diaz. Garzo was struck by the power of the colt and his desire to pace hard. He couldn't let the colt have his way because he wasn't in condition to go faster than 2:15; if he did not use careful calibration and keep him steady over the mile it would be poor training, indeed. Phantom was at full attention and pulled on the bike as though it weighed nothing. He was feeling his potential. Garzo worked to slow him down so that he could hit even integers at each one-eighth of a mile, about a 17-second range for each eighth. It was hardest to do so at the start when Phantom was full of energy, but Garzo had him reach the eighth pole at 17 seconds exactly. The colt was taking direction pretty nicely, and Garzo kept his whip tucked in and away from the colt's peripheral vision. He hit the second eighth at another exact 17, for a quarter of 34 seconds. 'Perfect,' Garzo thought, pulling against the striding colt as he hit the three-eighth in another exact 17 seconds.

As he came into the stretch, he could see Diaz at the imaginary starting point. Manuel had stepped off the track and stood behind the fence that circumscribed the track. Phantom, pulling harder than at the beginning of the event, came in at 16 seconds at the half mile – a first half of 1:07.

"You're a little fast," he heard Diaz yell, for he was on pace for a 2:14 mile.

The colt pulled even harder as they began their second time around the half-mile oval. Garzo now sought to exercise more control and started pulling hard against the colt. Succeeding, he slowed him down to 18 seconds between the one-half and five-eighths. Whether out of pique, fatigue, confusion, or all of them, Phantom now began to slow down. Garzo ceased his efforts at slowing him and, rather, took to making a clicking sound with his voice, urging the colt to renew his effort. It wasn't working and to his chagrin he hit the six-eighth or three-quarter pole at 20 seconds, bringing him well off the target time. Garzo was angered and Phantom's ears were pinned back. He would not allow that type of defiance and cracked the whip across the back, right leg of the horse. It jolted him and he sped up; and just as Garzo thought he had won the day, the colt slowed up again. He lashed viciously at the animal, hitting him with five savage cracks in the space of five seconds. Phantom was bleeding and now slowing down even more – hitting the seven-eighths at 23 seconds.

Garzo was beside himself. Not just Diaz and Manuel – but probably about 15 other workers were watching him being made the fool by this $400,000 horse. Beating him all the way through the last eighth of the mile he went another uninterested 23 seconds. The colt had made an ass out of him, finishing at two minutes, 31 seconds instead of the aimed-at 2:15, a terrible effort. Actually, he could have done better with a jog cart than he had with a racing bike.

He jumped off of the bike and yelled at Diaz – "Get him into the barn and put him on the cross ties. The bastard is not going to do that to me."

Manuel and Diaz removed the sulkey, and Manuel led him into the barn where he placed him in cross ties and stripped the harness from him. Phantom was panting as Garzo came out of his office. He said, "You're not needed here. I'll call you when I want you." Garzo proceeded to shut the doors to the barn. He went up to the colt and stood in front of him, staring at him. The colt's ears were pinned back, and his eyes drawn wide. To Garzo there was no doubt that he was under challenge. He grabbed the colt's halter, breathed heavily into his nostrils, and kept a dead stare on him. He did this for close to three minutes when he stepped away and proceeded to whip the colt viciously all across its body. As a denouement, he took a large, thin stick and broke it over the colt's head, near his left eye.

Garzo went out and found Manuel who stood along the fence. "Clean the bastard up!" He walked a few steps and turned around, "Oh, and don't treat him like he's your girlfriend, you spic." He saw that there were still seven track people standing around the fence talking quietly to each other. "Hey! The show's over. Let's get some work done!"

Manuel went into the barn. When he saw Phantom – with his left eye closed and his skin whip-torn and bloodied, he sat down on the ground and cried quietly until Fidel Diaz came in and patted him on the shoulder. "Take care of him, amigo."

As Diaz watched, their battle of wills continued through late March and April. Garzo used his temper, determination, and severe beatings to force the colt's cooperation. The goal was for Phantom to hit 2:10 by the end of April, at which time Garzo would send him to one of the racing stables. There he would come under the care of a trainer whose job it would be to train him down to a qualifying time, which would then allow entry into a pari-mutuel race. Qualifying times were set by each track and usually staggered over a few conditions such as age, gait, and gender.

Garzo had finally worked Phantom down to 2:14 and had pronounced that today – April 29, Phantom would hit 2:10 or less, and he would then be shipped out after consulting with Burgess. For a two-year-old at the end of April, the colt was in a great place time-wise. Garzo felt that Phantom could touch 1:50 under the right conditions and with a good driver, but that was three months away. If only the damn horse would bow to the inevitable, that he was a beast of burden that must obey. Diaz had heard the whole story before, again and again, from Garzo. He doubted that Phantom would be great, feeling that Garzo had ruined him. When Burgess would catch on and realize that Roman was a vicious and irresponsible fool was an unknown.

He watched the big bastard stand to the side as Manuel hooked up the bike to the colt, noticing that Manuel would never look Garzo in the eye. He had preached to him to hold down his hate and disgust, that someday Garzo would be tossed and that there would be a place for him as it was clear that Manuel was a superb horse handler – having skills well beyond those required to be a groom.

As he had done since the first time in March, Garzo plopped into the sulkey seat. The vibrations of that move, shaking the bike and the close metal shafts, told the colt that his archenemy was behind him. His ears were pinned back and his eyes took on a look of terror. Diaz caught Manuel's eye. They understood, if ever a trainer had it coming to him it was Roman Garzo.

As customary, Garzo took the colt around the track at a leisurely pace. Nothing unusual occurred, the whip stayed tucked into his arm. He came up beside Diaz after the second lap – "I'm turning – we want to go in 2:10 and then we'll ship the bastard out!" He tapped the colt lightly with his whip and used the driving lines to turn him. He had taken him back to a distance where he felt that he could get a solid start and sent the horse into motion. As they reached Diaz they had a full start.

Diaz watched intensely as they tore into the first turn of the one-half mile track. Later he would remark to others that he had never quite seen such a performance, given the history between Phantom and Garzo. It was as if the colt knew that his performance would free him of Garzo. Two year olds are notoriously green, irregular in movements and inconsistent. Phantom paced perfectly through the first eighth, hitting it at 16.2 seconds, the time he would need for each eighth in order to hit the magic 2:10. Garzo never touched him; and his ears, which were pinned the second Garzo sat on the bike, were now pointed up, alert and responsive. There was no sulking, no anger ostensibly at least, and no rebellion. Phantom was all business. He hit the quarter at 33 seconds flat and proceeded to head around the far back of the track and toward the last turn. His rhythm, attentiveness, and sheer athleticism made Diaz think twice, maybe this colt will be great. As Phantom went across the three-eighths marker Diaz knew without looking that Garzo had him right on target. "49.2" he said out loud.

Garzo had him pacing within inches of the rail as he came into the stretch. At a slight angle it looked as though Phantom was coming directly at Diaz. The confirmation, musculature, and expressiveness in the colt's face convinced Diaz that the colt had found something within himself. That he had discovered the reason behind Garzo's cruelty. He even felt a tinge of remorse for questioning Garzo's methods which apparently were working. They passed Diaz at 1:05 for the half mile. But could the big colt keep it up? Or would Garzo find some way to destroy this monumental effort?

Showing no signs of fatigue he replicated his 16.2 from the first time around. At the exact place, but as far distance-wise from Diaz as he could be, the colt was again at 16.2 "May God bring you home," he said under his breath. He noticed that Manuel had run across the track and was now beside him. "Fidel – do you see this? What has happened?"

"I don't know – Manuel, I just don't know. Did you whisper to him?"

"What?"

"Did you tell Phantom that this is the way out of here?"

Manuel did not answer as he gazed at Phantom who was now approaching the seventh-eighths pole. "What time, Fidel?"

"Another 16-second eighth. If he can come home at this pace, he's out of here. Look at Garzo, he hasn't touched him."

"Not yet," Manuel said resignedly.

Diaz looked as they came off of the last turn and headed into the stretch. What surprised him most of all was the seeming effortlessness that Phantom manifested. It was as if he was watching the horse perform in fourth gear, the real power still there ready to be called on if needed. He quickly glanced at his watch; he had seven seconds to make it 2:10. And again Diaz was aware of the conflict in his heart and mind. His mind telling him that the horse had no idea what he was doing or any sense of what was at stake, while his heart told him that the colt knew that this was his day of liberation if he could hit the time and keep his composure.

Phantom strode across the finish line at exactly 2:10 and with constant times at each eighth pole. This was extremely difficult to do for a two year old – at this stage in his development. Garzo began to slow him down and eventually turned him around and brought him back toward Manuel and Diaz at a slow jog.

"How'd you like that, you doubting bastards?" Garzo said laughingly, but with a sarcastic edge to it.

"El perfecto! Roman, you both looked great," Diaz said.

He stopped Phantom and Manuel came along side of the colt and held him as Garzo jumped off of the bike. He barked at Manuel, "Clean him up and cool him out. He'll be leaving tomorrow if I can get him out of here."

The next morning Manuel led him to the van that was headed to Crete, Illinois where Phantom would be trained down to a qualifying time. For the colt's sake, if for no other reason, he was pleased to see him leave, pleased to see that Garzo would be without influence over Phantom ever again. Or so he hoped as he discussed the matter with Fidel Diaz.

Diaz held some private thoughts on the matter that he would not share with Manuel. Primary of these was his concern that perhaps Phantom's performance was a freak occurrence, that he would be shipped back to Garzo if he failed at the track grounds where trainers were not particularly known for their patience with miscreants.

As he saw Manuel lead the colt into the van he noticed that Phantom looked around uneasily, as if searching for a view of Garzo. Compliantly enough he followed Manuel. The gate was shut and the van driver came over to Diaz. "Isn't this the mean stud? The one you paid a fortune for?"

"He's not mean, as you just saw. And I didn't pay a fortune for him."

"Ha! Right. Anything I should know?"

"No, señor. Just get him to Crete, Illinois in one piece."

Diaz watched as the van left the parking area, leaving behind a trail of dust, and ricocheting pebbles and a low growl from the truck's engine. He had a feeling that this show was not over.

CHAPTER VIII

———◆◆———

Betty Broder was a racetrack trainer, meaning that she stabled most of her standardbreds at the harness track in Crete, Illinois, 20 miles south of Chicago. The track was called Balmoral. It had a celebrated existence dating all the way back to the days of Al Capone, who had a railroad extended to it and who had built a tunnel from the railroad station directly to the track grandstand. Although it once had thoroughbred racing in recent years it had become a major track in the midwest devoted to harness racing.

Broder stabled between 30 to 40 horses on the track grounds at any one time and typically kept still another 15 to 20 at a nearby farm with standardbred facilities. About half of her stock was owned by Jeremy Burgess who had started her off with three horses and who each year added more. He had spoken with her on several occasions about the possibility of her becoming his exclusive trainer in Chicago. She had resisted. There was some indefinable quality about him that she instinctively distrusted.

Broder had come up the hard way. She dated a high school classmate who groomed at Sportsman's Race Track in Cicero, Illinois. Although she quickly gave him up she did not give up the track. Dropping out of high school at the age of 17 she took a job as a groom at Maywood Harness Race Track in Maywood, Illinois, a nearby Chicago suburb.

By the age of 23 she had acquired a license to be a trainer from the United States Trotting Association (U.S.T.A.), which is the interstate governing and record-keeping organization of harness racing in the United States and Canada. The procedures used for such licensure by the U.S.T.A. was a record of five years handling horses, passing a written test and a successful background check, some sponsors, and paying an annual licensure fee. Each state required U.S.T.A. clearance before submitting the trainer to its own set of regulatory practices. It was possible, for example, to lose one's license in Illinois but to still have one in Florida, the necessity being U.S.T.A. licensure.

Broder started out with two horses and progressed her way up to her current level over a 15-year period of time. She wasn't particularly liked by her male-predominant colleagues, many of whom were dubious about women working in the backstretch – especially at the level of trainer. She wasn't liked either because of her out-in-the-open lesbianism and her proclivity for hiring women only for her stable. Coarse comments and whispered-to-vocalized insults came her way for several years before she finally found a peace rendered, in part, by vituperative and vicious retaliatory gestures and comments on her part toward her tormenters. In a piece done on her in *The Chicago Sun Times* she talked about her problems which tore her up emotionally until the day she launched her own offensive. She was quoted, "After months it was as though I was on an airplane – climbing up through the clouds and then suddenly into the blue sky. The only way to stop dogs is to bite them back harder. Now they leave me alone."

She knew that Burgess was aware of her history. Given that he was a Seattle liberal, her battle against female and lesbian bias she found around her probably impressed him. Her private take on Burgess was that he was a trickster, but he was her trickster. She had been given an article from *Business Week* by one of her owners. It dealt with Burgess. The article made him out as vicious, vindictive, and paranoidal. But she had not seen it to this point, at any rate.

Of course she had heard all about Phantom. The money, the quirky personality, and the potential. She looked forward to receiving him and intended to take the 2:10 that Garzo had secured down to a 2:03 by the end of May when she was looking to qualify him for racing to begin in early June. Balmoral had a huge two-year-old race series that began in September; the track also could serve as the centerpoint for some lucrative races elsewhere in the Midwest, and in the Illinois fair circuit.

Her biggest problem was not with the colt or with Burgess – it lay with Roman Garzo. Phantom wasn't the first promising colt to come by way of Garzo and Burgess' place in Valdosta. Frequently, the colts were in some way or another damaged goods. Betty didn't believe in beating or scaring horses. In fact, she thought it to be the worst of approaches, believing that horses were already pre-disposed to be scared. It wasn't, she reasoned, her lesbianism that led her to hire women almost exclusively – it was because they typically treated horses in a milder and gentler way. Garzo was the antithesis of everything that she professed.

She reflected on his call. "Hey, Betty. I finally got Phantom down to 2:10, and Mister Burgess wants him sent up there. OK to ship him tomorrow?"

"Sure. What do I need to know about him?"

He paused for too long. "Well, he's got a will of his own, but I think that I checked it. Be ready to whip him."

"Roman, please. You know that that's not my style. I don't need another colt who wastes half his energy flinching and cowering."

"Look – what do you want? A horse who wastes half his energy trying to kill you? I'm shipping him out to you. I don't need the attitude."

"Yeah – right Garzo. It'll take me a month to have him believing in himself again. And I'm going to tell you right now – if he is a headache he's going right back down to Valdosta. I just don't have the time to handle a misfit."

"He should be there in two days. Hope you don't have to find out the hard way what petting and kissing that kind of colt will get you."

"I'm not clear. What exactly should I watch for?"

"I've been trying to tell you. He has his own ways, be careful."

Garzo spoke in code language. She surmised that what he had just said was that the colt was dangerous as hell. What he didn't say and never would – was that he personally was very much part of the reason for the danger. She wondered whether the poor animal was not already ruined by this chest-beating moron.

She was called by the guard at the grounds gate. Was she expecting two horses from Valdosta? The van came through the backstretch and parked outside of Barn R where she typically stabled most of her stock. She knew the van driver.

"Howdy – you bringing me two nice head here?"

"They didn't bite me yet. That one on the end, you better keep an eye on him."

"Oh?" she said.

"Well, he had quite a reputation even before Garzo got him, that's all I'm saying."

"Lots of money on his head."

"I'll say." He lowered the plank to the ground, creating a ramp.

"Alicia – Alicia!" she yelled. The small, intense-looking woman of about 30 years of age came out of the stable. "Let's take a look at this big boy. You need help?" Alicia looked at her as if hurt by the question. She didn't respond as she and the van driver opened the gate. Alicia took the lead rope very gently and spoke inaudibly to the colt as she walked him down the ramp and onto the hardened dirt of the backstretch. Broder was instantly impressed. The colt was beautifully proportioned, his legs strong and straight, his face highly intelligent. Alicia walked him for a few minutes before she came back and stood him in front of Broder who now moved close to him for a more careful investigation.

She walked around him a few times. She knelt down and felt his legs for hot spots and conformity. The hot spots were a sign of swelling and pain, and the tight kneading of her knowing fingers would tell her of bone or muscle problems. She stood up again and studied his face. She pressed her lips together as she saw the lash marks across his head, and then as she examined more closely she could see the lacerations around his back and legs. They had almost healed, but they were still in evidence. The poor animal had been subjected to severe beatings. "Damn you, Garzo," she muttered under her breath. She then came up to his face and opened his mouth and examined the colt's teeth and gums. They checked out fine. The welts, the bruises, the lacerations would all eventually heal over. They were physical only. But what had Garzo done to the colt's psyche? His spirit?

The van driver had unloaded the second horse. He was looking at a small book, probably figuring out what and who he would take on a return journey to some other stable elsewhere in the country. Betty went up to him and said, "I notice some marks on this Phantom horse. You have anything to do with them?" She knew that he didn't.

"No, no – ma'am. I don't know anything about that. I just changed water and fed them on the way up. I saw some of them too. They're not that fresh. I'm out of this, believe me."

"Does Fidel Diaz still work for Garzo?"

"Yup. Just saw him the other day when I was loading these."

"Have a cell number for him?"

He did, and he gave it to her.

"Anything else?" he said.

"Nope, unless you have something you want to tell me."

"Nope. I gotta get to Hopeland. I have two of his going to Ocala."

"Go east two rows. It's on the end."

Betty Broder knew Diaz. They weren't close, but she figured he was a solid horseman who had little appreciation for Garzo and his tactics. She went into her office and closed the door.

"Diaz," he answered on the first ring.

"Fidel – Betty Broder. Have a minute?"

There was an uncertain pause. "Sure."

"I just got this Phantom colt."

"Yeah?" he said warily.

"Just between you and me, OK?"

"What?"

"Why does he look like he was in a Nazi concentration camp? Don't tell me that you're becoming a lasher," she said disingenuously – knowing full well that Garzo was the one who was the 'lasher'.

Diaz was upset – his voice trembling. "Don't put that on me. You know better. The colt was not under me except for stall care. He's a Garzo product."

"So what do I need to know?"

After another delay, "Between us, the colt has incredible potential. But he was dangerous when he got here from Harrisburg. Now he's doubly dangerous in my judgment. What I fear is that he's like a volcano – really active but seemingly dormant. If he's pushed too hard, I think that he'll crack."

"Thanks, Fidel. I'll remember this and stand by you if this thing blows up."

The distance of harness tracks ranges from a low of a half mile, to five-eighths, to three-fourths, to seven-eighths, to as long as a mile. Except for some rare instances, most harness races are run over a one-mile distance. The varying sizes of the ovals frequently dictate strategies in races. It is not uncommon that a successful horse on a one-mile track can be highly ineffective on a half-mile track and vice versa. On a one-mile track there are only two turns in the entire race as opposed to a half-mile track where four turns are demanded or on a five-eighths-mile track where are three turns in a race. Some horses are not handy on turns, some are. Horsemen become well aware of the foibles of their animals and try to adjust accordingly.

Because of his considerable size, Betty Broder had determined that the one-mile oval at Balmoral would be ideal for Phantom as larger horses tended to fare better with fewer turns. The colt, therefore, would not go to her farm which had a training track that was just three-eighths of a mile, even smaller than that of the training facility at Valdosta.

Alicia was assigned the care of Phantom. She was born in Oxford, Indiana, and found her way to the harness business through her father who, more by way of a hobby, would always seem to have a pacer or two on his farm. Oxford was a magic word for those steeped in the history of harness racing as it was the birthplace of a famed standardbred by the name of Dan Patch who would perform at unheard of levels in match races throughout the United States in the early twentieth century. He was regarded by many as a freak of nature who was ahead of his time by 70 to 80 years. Perhaps – he was comparable to what Babe Ruth was in baseball.

Alicia did not have a life of joyous events. She had married twice and divorced twice with a child from each marriage. Both marriages were marked by severe physical cruelty. By the time that she was 30, she had a metamorphosis which led her to seize control of her life. She left Indiana, surrendered both of her children to the husband-abusers, and left for Chicago. Six months later she was working for Betty Broder. As a groom she was assigned the care of five horses. This involved, as Betty would say, the perception that she was to see the barn as an assisted-living facility. She was to feed, bathe, exercise, water, groom, and give complete maid service to each stall. When the horses raced, she was to be with them at all times before and after the race until the horse could be re-stalled. Vet care and shoeing was to be monitored by her in conjunction with Betty. Although low paying, it was a challenging and full-time job. Like many of her peers, she lived on the backstretch in a rent-free, one-room facility – about 9 feet by 12 feet. What she put into the room was her business. She had a television, a small bed, a chest of drawers, a small desk, a rocker, a small refrigerator and microwave – the room was full. Bathrooms were community affairs split only by gender.

"Alicia, I'm giving you a huge responsibility. This horse already has $450,000 and more into him. He's expected to compete at the top level of two year olds. He is more important than anything you're working with. I printed out his training schedule. By May 25 or close, I want him at about 2:03. He's 2:10 now."

Alicia had looked at the schedule. It was a bit aggressive for a two-year-old, but it was possible. "I'll do it Betty – I'll do my best."

"He's from Garzo. He's been beaten. The colt has a reputation for meanness, or at least a reputation for being difficult. Be careful around him. When you train him, I want to watch."

The schedule earmarked training in a sulkey once a week, with four miles of light pacing in a jog cart on a daily basis. After two days of walking the horse for 20 minutes, she fitted him to a cart for the first time and took him out to the track. She figured that it was unlike the laid-back Valdosta. On the Balmoral track during training times between six a.m. and one p.m. there may be at any one time 20 to 30 horses along with a tractor or two. The one-mile size of the track was daunting. Immediately, she noticed his ears. They were pinned. He jerked forward as he was directed to move to the rail and gain a steady momentum of about four minutes per mile for three miles. She could feel his power. Athleticism exuded from him. He wanted to pace hard, but she held his reins tightly and leaned back in the cart to get control over him. She noticed that he was curious as he looked around at his new surroundings, but his ears remained pinned.

Horses are herd animals, adjusting to the principle of dominance. Was he sending some kind of message to the animals who passed him? He was the new stud on the block? She didn't know and was forever suspicious of projecting human desires and motives onto animals. But this one was special. He had a way about him – an imperviousness.

Her arms were exhausted after the exercise that had lasted a little over 12 minutes. It was her introduction to Phantom; she knew that this really was an unusual animal.

"So how did it go out there, Alicia? I just watched the last five minutes or so. It looked like he wanted to take off," Betty said as she came over toward her after the colt was placed in cross ties.

"My arms are really sore. He's a puller. His manners are pretty good, but he's got attitude. His ears are pinned something terrible. There's something going on inside his head."

"What do you mean?"

"He's thinking. I don't know. He's thinking about things other than just the business of pacing. I don't know how to explain it. Just a feeling that I get."

"Can you handle him?"

"You better believe I can."

Betty walked away. Alicia was angry with her. She didn't like being second-guessed. She'd bring him down to 2:03 by the end of May, easily.

CHAPTER IX

Pat, McAbee's secretary, through all the years that he was in the PI business, watched Barry Fisk who was sitting in the ACJ waiting room. He was reading the latest issue of *Time Magazine*, tisking his way through it – like a prohibitionist in a saloon.

She was of mixed feelings about him. On the one hand, he was a nasty, vituperative, and ungrateful man. She had overheard him described as being too mean for human companionship. She knew that he had graduated from Yale with a Ph.D. in history and that his interest was in Lewis and Clark and their relationship with Thomas Jefferson. Apparently, his thesis argued that instead of their mission being one of exploration, it was rather one of deception and malevolence. When Pat and her husband planned to travel in some of the areas that Lewis and Clark had traversed, she sought his advice, only to be rebuffed harshly by him. Later,

McAbee explained to her that Barry had never traveled into those lands and that perhaps she had embarrassed him. Whether or not that was true, the incident was entered onto a long list of complaints that she had with him and his abysmal social skills.

But on the other hand, she sympathized with him. She found him to be woefully insecure. This led him to be suspicious and untrusting in almost everything that he did. His diminutive size, 5 feet at best, his painfully slanted posture with one shoulder raised unnaturally with the other sloped almost down to his chest, and a face no mother would willingly claim, she understood some of his acidity toward people and the world. McAbee told her once that she pitied him rather than accepted him as being a flawed human being. One of those comments that would fly out of McAbee's mouth that caused unintended hurt.

But it was hard to deal with him whatever the psychology of the matter was. He regularly insulted her, and to her chagrin he regularly insulted her boss McAbee – not to his face but rather behind his back. When she would report this to McAbee he would laugh and say something like, 'Barry Fisk is a walking and talking psychiatric chart – whatever he says is in the spur of the moment, nothing more, nothing less.'

Fisk liked to play head games with her – constantly trying to shake up her composure and put her on the defensive. She wondered about how he was brought up – whether his parents or teachers were mean to him? Whatever the causes of his personality, she was tough with him and was not above launching assaults on his insecurities if such had to be done.

So, here he was, seated, feet off the ground and tisking his way through *Time*. She knew that the tisking was his attempt to draw her into a discussion, which in turn would give him an opportunity to be mean and scurrilous. She would have ignored him except that McAbee had asked her to treat Fisk as someone important to the ACJ Agency. She knew that McAbee had the highest regard for Fisk's analytical abilities, that he had helped him break some major cases, and that McAbee felt that Barry was an indispensable piece of armor in his arsenal. So she thought to herself 'if I engage him it will just enable him to act nastily to try to hurt me, but if I don't engage with him he'll complain to my boss that I was unsociable'.

Accordingly, she chose to engage. "Lots of tisking going on over there, Barry. Something I should know?" She asked this as gently and kindly as she could given that it felt like she was putting her hand into a beehive.

"Oh, so she talks."

She said nothing knowing that he was inept at maintaining a silence when he saw the possibility of a battle.

"I'm reading, at the moment, about something you could understand actually."

She put the nails of her right hand into her left palm. "What would that be?"

"Addictions."

She said nothing.

He continued, "It's about addictive behavior. It is about how so many American corporations rely on people to continue self-defeating and death-provoking behaviors that comprise addition. You do drink, don't you?"

"Yes," she said warily.

"Well – there you are."

"I drink moderately. What does that have to do with corporate America and addictions?"

"One person's moderation is another's death wish."

"You're losing me."

"My guess is that you probably drink too much."

"What?" she was getting angry.

"Such would explain why you come across so harshly sometimes and why your eyes look like red-lined maps." He stopped, looked straight at her and smirked.

Her nails dug deeper into her palms. Pity was now far removed. In an ideal world where acts went unpunished she would like nothing better than to slap him silly. She thought it best to ignore him, and she did.

"I think that your silence speaks loudly. My point is this, whiskey makers, or tequila makers or whatever your favorite poison, is a corporate product, and that corporation links to other corporations, and it is in their interest to keep you as you are. But here's the tisk. *Time* complains about this but absents itself from any condemnation even though as part of the media they are the indispensable deliverers of the message. Now do you understand why I'm tisking?"

"All too well. You're really profound," she said in full irony.

"You can't hurt me with those comments you know. I know how smart I am. And so does that regressive classics boss of yours."

"Barry, I'm going to leave my desk for a few minutes. I'll be back." She started to get up and reach for her purse which was in a drawer in her desk.

"Ha ha! Make sure you bring your cigarettes. Slave to addictions! You're just a tool of the system. A sorry victim of corporate America."

She noticed that he now swung his small legs to and fro. He was excited, looking for signs that he had stung her, forced her to submission. She had seen this often, the jittery-feet movement brings a sure sign that he had just delivered the coup de grace or was about to.

Her anger was now getting the best of her. She walked toward him noticing that his feet ceased to move. She imagined that he was fearful of violence. In fact, she knew that he was petrified of Jack Scholz during meetings with McAbee. Only because of McAbee did he feel safe, that Scholz was controllable. On several occasions Scholz had murmured to her that, "runts like Fisk will be the first to go if America goes into revolution". She stood over him, although she herself was not a large woman, and said, "That's enough from you, Barry Fisk. I know that part of my job is to make this office hospitable and friendly. And I do that. But if you think for one second that means I have to take your senseless comments you're dead wrong. You clear?"

Looking up he said, "Tisk, tisk, Pat. You started the conversation. I'm not here to see you anyway. And if your boss would learn to show up on time I wouldn't even have to speak with you."

Half-turning she said to him – "Examine your own habits Barry. You're addicted to being a bore and an ass." She left the office and went to the women's washroom where, since no other tenants were on this floor of the building, she took out a Camel cigarette and lit up furious with herself. Most of the times she finessed the bastard, but this was one of those times when he got her, good and hard. She shook her head in disgust. As she relaxed a bit she smiled to herself. He was good with his objectives – he came in wanting to get under her skin and sure enough he did it. McAbee would say that she let him do it. That she gave him power over her. It wasn't Fisk but rather she who allowed victory to be grabbed. He would also ask, and it was hard to respond, why did she allow him to do that when she knew full well what he intended? McAbee had recommended that she read Epictetus, one of his friends from classical times.

McAbee came into the office about two minutes after Pat had returned from the bathroom. Fisk had decided to come after her again for she had never been easy for him. He had to admit to himself that she did scare him a bit. She could be quite imposing with her red hair, tight lips, and digging blue eyes. When she had stood over him he thought that perhaps he had broken her, that she would physically assault him. But McAbee held all of these violent types in check, didn't he?

"Pat, how are you. Barry," he looked at his watch, as if he didn't know how late he was, "sorry to keep you waiting."

"It's perfectly OK by me; you're paying from the minute I open my front door. So if I sit here for two hours, it's on your tab. I don't get many chances to read trash like *Time* and to be pestered by secretaries, you know."

McAbee then turned toward Pat who was clearly flushed with anger. Some kind of understanding passed between them, Fisk noticed. McAbee said, "How could anyone pester you, Barry? You're so unruffable," he smiled knowingly.

This was a regular tactic employed by McAbee, divert and jest. Barry wasn't good on that field of play, typically responding that McAbee was wasting his money by being late and chitchatting. "This is all OK with me. It's on your meter."

"You're right; let's go into my office."

McAbee's office was dominated by two symbolic entities. On a main wall he had a huge print of Raphael's 'School of Athens'. A few years before he had gone over the personages represented in it from Plato, Aristotle, Socrates, Pythagoras, Averroes, Euclid, Heraclitus, and the like. He was struck by McAbee's sheer enthusiasm for this Renaissance fresco. He had never found that kind of excitement in his study of the past, except for a glint of pleasure at exposing the myth of Lewis and Clark.

Another wall in the office had a large set of book shelves which housed the entire Loeb collection of the classics – over 500 green- and red-covered books, each of which had the original text on one side of the page and its translation on the other. The green-covered books were Greek, the red Latin.

They had had their arguments about them. Barry recalled one conversation. "So does that classical crap ever run out? Are you on some kind of perpetual subscription list that Harvard Press can soak you for a hundred or two every year?"

"And what do you want me to put in its place? Should I replace Cicero or Thucydides with the speech writers for Clinton or Bush?" McAbee rejoindered with a flash of anger. "Should I replace Thucydides with CNN or Fox News? Barry – you're a futurist with no future. Find your way back to substance."

"Ha!" he replied feebly, surprised by McAbee's forthrightness and ardor.

He had other books there also, some medievalists – Aquinas, Maimonides, Avicenna, not part of the Harvard Press. He noticed another collection for the first time. He asked, "May I?"

"Of course."

Fisk removed a Tiffany-blue covered book; there were about ten of them. "Oh no," he said as he read the back cover, "A new Harvard series? The Renaissance! That will never end, will it?" he asked ruefully.

"I don't know about that, but I'm sure that I will never live to its completion," McAbee said lightly.

"So, does Harvard with its waspish bias just excise the medievalists? Anselm, Aquinas, and the rest, doomed to a literary hell?"

McAbee laughed. "They would probably say, as did many in the Renaissance, that their Latin was flawed and therefore wanting in style. They weren't worthy of entry. Of course it's bias and professionally pathetic, but it's not my battle. What they do is good even if it's flawed by bias. There are other editors and publishers out there other than Harvard."

Fisk put the blue book back – it was a mystical theology book by Ficino. He glanced at the end of the last row and once again he saw that Francis Bacon ended the collection. It was as though Bacon ended all that McAbee found interesting. "I see that you still have old Francis Bacon holding up the end of the collection."

"You know why. He's the transitional between the old and the new age."

"Since we're well into the 21st Century I thought you'd move forward a bit – like to Voltaire or Kant?"

"Forget it, Barry. Now sit down. I want to talk with you about some things."

Barry sat, knowing that once McAbee got to business it would be just that.

"We successfully took down Howles last Saturday – I sent you a brief email."

"I got it."

"This guy Howles was saying some nasty things. We're a bit concerned."

"We?"

"Augusta, myself, and to a lesser extent Jack Scholz."

"Scholz? Scared of something?"

"I didn't say scared, I said concerned. It appears that Howles is part of a network that extends into Chicago. The Illinois Bureau thinks that it may involve one of the inner city prison gangs."

"Howles was white."

"So what? Race ends where profit begins."

"I never received any indication of this. Are you sure this isn't just the Illinois police smoking hashish?" Fisk was an adamant foe of police departments and agencies. McAbee, on several occasions, had to extricate him from police tentacles by using his overly powerful, overly connected, and probably overly corrupt brother who ran an investigation agency in New York City. On several occasions Fisk had penetrated into some of the doings of that brother's firm. What he saw was scary. He secretly connected the line in his mind that went from Bill McAbee to assassin, albeit assassin for the supposed righteous.

"Could be. There's going to be a criminal trial for Howles. They're trying to sweat him to give up other names. So far – no luck. We're wondering if he is expecting some heavy work on the investigation witnesses. I think that you're out of the circuit – unlike Augusta and Jack. But you know how this goes. Witnesses have to be identified and your name might appear. Also, they might be able to backtrack through your work. I'm just giving you a warning, Barry. Look around."

This was all bad stuff to Barry. He wasn't about to defend himself physically. Violence immobilized him. And now this, a piddling case in which he was to generate a few files to reel in a crook. He hears inner city – the gangs. Creatures from the second century, like the Germans, nothing to lose. Make a living by causing havoc in his backyard. Great! "So what am I supposed to do? Hire a bodyguard? Bring a gun? Come on, Bertrand. Keep my name out of it. They won't be able to track back to me. The only way this will happen is if the cops divulge my name. Surely, you can control this?"

"I'll try, Barry, but I just want you to keep an eye. OK?"

"OK, OK. What else?"

"I need you to investigate the backgrounds and doings of three people. They're not related to Howles. This is a different matter. We think that there is some industrial spying going on toward a local company. Inside job type of thing."

He knew what this meant. When McAbee said 'backgrounds and doings' he meant a full-court press. When he was done he'd have every financial record, dental exam, medical record, and any other kind of record out there. This was his forte, his game. And he owed a lot of his wherewithal to this classics troglodyte sitting across from him – McAbee had probably over the years of their association given him over $50,000 gratuitously to develop his incredible computer capacity. He took the names and put them in his pocket. "That it?"

"Yes," McAbee rose.

"Oh. And if I see someone in my backyard, what do I do?"

"Call me right away. Or Scholz."

"Yeah. Right – I'll call Scholz. He probably armed the guy to begin with." He left. He didn't say anything to Pat.

CHAPTER X

―――――◆◆―――――

Alicia never touched him with a whip. Into mid-May it was without fail a matter of restraining him from getting too far out beyond himself and thus inadvertently coming up with an injury to his still-to-be fully developed limbs and muscles. Every time she took him out to train she came back with sore arms and a hurting back. On non-training days, when he was merely being exercised with the jog cart, he would pull some of the time. But with the sulkey or bike, streamlined and light, he would take the bit sharply and do all he could to run as fast as his legs could move, probably associating the racing bike with speed.

By May 15, she had him down to a time of 2:07; a 2:03 by the end of May was well within sight. On this day she was going to make an evenly rated 2:05, attempting ranges between 31-32 second fractions for each quarter of a mile. The calibration was extremely important. Nothing unusual occurred during the entire rigging process. She came from the barn area of Balmoral onto the track. As usual, she took him around the track oval twice – a two-mile exercise at little more than a saunter.

She turned the horse the 'race way' about half way up the long stretch distance at Balmoral. Alicia took out her stopwatch as she turned the big colt around readying him for the biggest mile of his life. She noticed to her left that across the infield of the track, behind the outer fence, that at least five Broder employees stood above the rail at a section of the outer fence that could be reached by ladder to a raised platform. Their bright yellow caps gave them away. Betty Broder had told her that she'd be there watching. There was a feeling of intense excitement in the barn.

"Well here goes Phantom, show me what you have." She tightened her gloved hands on her whip and driving lines as the colt moved forward steadily gaining speed. As they hit the starting line she set the stopwatch in motion as Phantom tore across the imaginary mark in full pace. Within five seconds she knew that by the end of this mile every muscle in her body would complain. He hit the eighth pole at 15 seconds – too fast. She gripped the lines tighter. Now she was leaning back in the bike halfway to a prone position in her effort to hold the big colt. By the quarter pole she was still too fast at a 30.5.

They had swung into the long backstretch, a straightaway for over a quarter of a mile, tempting the colt to go even faster. He did so as she was forced to be almost flat back on the bike in her effort to restrain him. He did the three-eighths in 14.5 seconds, way beyond what was desirable. The strength of the horse was beyond anything she had ever experienced. She felt fear for both her and the colt's safety as the lines were starting to be pulled away from her by the streaking horse.

In a desperate effort to gain control, to free her hands for the reins only, she threw her whip forward and out of the bike to the right of Phantom's head. Looking back later, it was at this point that what was going to go wrong went wrong.

Balmoral Park during the morning training times has a series of gates leading to the track from the backstretch and vice versa. These gates, which occur along the surrounding outer fence, are kept scrupulously closed during live racing. But during morning training it was the custom to keep the gates open to the track, thus allowing horsemen from the various barns to easily bring their horses onto the track in order to exercise and train them. A person training a horse, as Alicia was doing, would hardly notice whether or not they were open or closed.

Phantom's head jerked as he saw the whip fly from her right hand. He slowed down perceptibly for Alicia, too much so, too abruptly. And then he did it. He swung away from the inner rail and tore across the width of the track, barely missing a collision with two horses being exercised in the middle of the track and proceeded to dash toward the open gate. She pulled frantically to get him under control as he went through the gate and along the outer rim of the stable area. There was tremendous danger now to both of them as they traversed this corridor which was full of grooms, trainers, horses, veterinarians, shoers, guards, cars, vans, and the many underpinnings to a racetrack.

A groom yelled, "Loose horse, loose horse!" People scattered as Alicia managed to slow him a bit. A powerful Swedish trainer by the name of Nils Johannsen timed his move as he grabbed the lines of Phantom and hung on as he was dragged standing and slipping for about 50 feet before the sulkey and horse came to heel. Alicia's heart was beating faster than any time she could remember as she jumped off the bike and tried to help Nils manage the colt.

"Lady! Please! This horse needs a strong hand. Please be careful." He walked away rubbing his left leg.

Alicia looked back and saw a formation of six yellow-capped people running quickly toward her. Betty Broder was among them. They came along side of her and helped her calm the colt whose eyes were wide, ears pinned, and who was making an effort to jump up and send his front feet into some imaginary enemy.

"Get that horse back to the barn. Alicia, are you OK?"

"Yes, yes," she said now with tears flowing freely down her cheeks. "God, I don't know what happened. I was just trying to slow him down."

Betty patted her on the shoulder as she glared at the bystanders who had watched the events and this particular scene with feigned disinterest. One by one they shuffled or walked back to their respective barns. Three of the Broder grooms led Phantom back to his barn, now quite watchful of this colt with newly seen attitude. "Let's go to the kitchen."

"Let me go with him," Alicia said in protest.

"No, I said the kitchen."

"But ..."

"Alicia, stop it now, I don't want a scene out here. All of these cretins love to watch what has happened in the last five minutes. Now walk with me – quietly to the kitchen," Broder said with intensity.

Alicia did as she was ordered by this blunt and no-nonsense woman. She realized that besides the embarrassment of the incident with Phantom, that she had caused embarrassment for Betty Broder. Any defiance now could get her canned. She loved the work too much for that.

"Get a coffee or Coke for yourself and come back here." Broder had chosen a table on the far end of the horsemen's diner.

Alicia bought a cup of black coffee and wondered what she could say to Betty Broder. When she sat she noticed that Broder was already halfway through a Marlboro cigarette. "You didn't want anything?"

"No. And speak quietly, very quietly. What happened out there?"

"He was going too fast; I tried to slow him. He's incredibly strong, nothing like anything I ever handled before, Betty."

"I saw you. You were almost parallel to the ground. I saw that. Tell me about the whip."

"I never once hit him since we got him, never once. I just had to get him to slow down. We went a 14.5 second between the quarter and three-eighths and he was already too fast on the first quarter, 30.5. I just threw the whip to get more control. He kind of buckled, I don't know, his ears flattened, he slowed just a bit, almost like he staggered but he didn't and then he saw that open gate and went for it. I don't know what to say. I never saw such a thing. Have you?"

"Once," she said ominously, "once." There was a long pause. "I had a maniac in my stable a few years ago, his name was Forgotten Years. He ran off the track several times. I eventually got him under control with some big-time blinders and some big-time discipline. Sucker was claimed by some damn fool from Florida. I don't think that he ever won a nickel with him. But that's not the point. He was a bag of crap, an $8,000 claimer, who could care? This is a $400,000 colt that Burgess adores. He's the big hope of the two-year-old season and it seems that he's a psycho."

"Should I have let him do what he wanted?"

"Of course not. You had your orders. I wanted a 2:05, not a 2:00 or a broken-down colt – who damaged an ankle or something because he was going too fast. Alicia, you didn't do anything wrong. I think, though, I need a stronger set of hands on him. No offense meant – but you can't handle him."

"But ..."

"No, hear me out. I'm going to put a seasoned driver on him from here on in. You can have him in the barn; but when it comes to jogging or training him, I want someone else. This isn't a discussion, it's an order."

"But what happened out there, Betty?"

"Something and someone you don't know created this situation. His name is Roman Garzo. I think that he probably ruined this animal. So, Alicia, nothing personal but I can't afford another one of these events. Otherwise he's going back to Garzo and he can explain to Mister Burgess what happened. Let's get back to the barn. And by the way, if anyone asks you, tell them that there was a broken strap on his equipment. I don't want him getting tagged as some kind of nutty horse. I'll talk to Nils; he'll come on board."

Alicia was downhearted, but she also felt some relief. She never wanted to go through this kind of thing again.

Nils Johannsen was approached later in the day by Betty Broder. Nils seemed to be about 40 years old. He had come to Balmoral two years ago by way of Pompano Race Track in Florida and ultimately from Stockholm, Sweden. His specialty was the training of trotters; he was highly regarded for this skill. He and Betty had always gotten along well.

He had huge hands; his upper body was thick to the waist, below which it fell into rapid thinness. He had agreed to train Phantom in four days as well as broadcasting that a broken strap had caused the colt to go haywire. Samuel, a groom in her barn, was chosen to jog him.

"So Nils, I don't know what to tell you. He's incredibly promising, but I think that he's a bit whacko. Alicia just tossed a whip near him, but there's little doubt that caused the runoff."

"She is not strong enough for him. He's a big stud. She should not have been training him," he said in a thick, Swedish accent and without rancor.

"Well, she had trained him in 2:07 without incident," Betty felt slightly defensive.

"You want an even 2:05. I will do what I can with him. I won't even bring a whip onto the sulkey with me. No horse has ever been able to out-power me, and this one won't either," he pounded the table emphatically.

"Then we're on – four days. Why don't we wait until close to noon? Almost everyone is off the track by then."

"That is fine. I will come over."

True to his word, he appeared in Broder's barn at about 11:45 a.m. Phantom was in his pacing gear but still unattached to the racing bike. When Alicia saw Nils, she began to attach the sulkey to the rigging. Betty came over and said, "Well, here we go again, Nils – 2:05, very even in fractions."

He removed his stopwatch and checked it. "Well that will be it," he said curtly as he sat in the sulkey seat and urged the colt from the barn to the track. He took him for a warmup mile, first.

To Betty's relief Phantom did a perfect 2:05, hitting almost each quarter at identical times. After he came off the track he walked to the barn. Nils yelled to Betty, "What a colt! He's barely breathing. I've never seen a two-year-old like this. When do we go again?"

"Next week, 2:03. I want to get him to 2:03 by the end of May and then we'll qualify him. Samuel is schooling him to the gate next week." Gate practice, or schooling, is a precondition to qualifying horses. Unlike thoroughbred racing where horses race from a dead start, harness races begin by horses following a long, collapsible gate structure attached to a starter car. The long gate has numbered areas, about a foot square, to which horses, sequentially numbered, move behind. They typically follow the car and gate for about a quarter of a mile as it picks up speed heading to the starting point of the race. When that point is reached the car speeds forward and the gate ends close, forming a long column over the hood and roof of the car. The car then proceeds away from the rail toward the perimeter of the track. It then follows the race, and its inhabitants become still another way of looking for fouls in the race that could be brought to a judge's attention in evaluating the fairness of the race.

Two-year-olds don't come naturally to the gates with numbered squares. Thus, the track allows for schooling practice for young horses. The gate is extended and the young horse is brought to the designated square – to which he would be trained to follow once or twice around the entire track at a slow speed. Some two-year-olds get the hang of it very quickly; others need much more work. The underlying principle is simple enough, in races where a split second can affect the outcome of a race and thus the awarding of purses in the thousands of dollars; it is critical to have horses trained to accept the gate and thus start a race with no disadvantage. In the case of Phantom – the schooling went smoothly and without incident even though the filly next to Phantom broke stride and refused to go to the gate. Phantom was focused, well behaved, and undistracted. This bode well when it came to his first qualifying race; it was one less thing about which to worry.

On May 23, Nils trained him in 2:03 with not much difficulty. The colt wanted to go faster, but Nils' strength served him well as he was able to maintain fairly even quarters.

"So, Betty, when is Phantom going to qualify?" Burgess said.

He never identified himself when he called. He assumed that it would be known who he was. She did know. It wasn't the first time he had called and his reedy voice was quite distinct. "Well, sir, I've trained him in 2:03 two days ago. I want him to do a 2:00 in a training session, probably in about five days. Then I thought I'd qualify him."

"What time does Balmoral demand for two-year-olds?"

"2:04."

"That's great. Call me when he's entered for the qualifier. I just might come out to see it."

"I will, sir," thinking that she didn't want him around at that time. She wasn't convinced that Phantom would qualify smoothly.

"How is he?"

"Oh, oh fine."

"Any problems?"

She thought quickly. Did he get wind of the incident? She had to be quite careful in her response. "Every two-year-old has quirks. Generally, he's fine. He's high-strung, and if we didn't watch his training times carefully – I think that he could damage himself – he tries real hard." It was candid but also oblique. She hoped that he'd let it drop there.

"Good, good. Well, call me as soon as you're sure that you're going to qualify him. I have some business in Chicago, but it can wait for this."

On a now empty Balmoral track on May 30th at 11:45 a.m., Nils turned Phantom toward the starting line, which was about 350 yards ahead. He felt tension in Phantom, a nervousness and edginess discernible by watching the way he breathed, the movement of his head, and, of course, the ever twitching ears. True to his word he did not bring along a whip. He looked across the infield and noticed a small army of Broder's yellow-hatted grooms along the fence. But it wasn't just yellow hats. There were far too many others watching – curious about the colt. There was no use trying to conceal his identity, a track held few secrets. Loose talk and rumor were the fuel of almost all backstretches. All the extra lookers knew that Nils was aboard the extraordinary animal who a few weeks ago had brought the backstretch into a state of panic as he raced uncontrollably through its back regions. They also knew that he was a $400,000 colt.

Nils whistled softly as Phantom took the bit firmly and began to accelerate toward the starting line. Nils realized that his arms and legs were in a state of high tension as he kept control of the colt. It was as though Phantom wanted to break away from the bike and the driver, and shed all of the equipment that held him.

Nils kept his stopwatch curled in his left hand as they bore across the starting line and moved quickly into the first wide turn of the one-mile track. Nils aimed to stay at three 31-second quarters and then to try to bring him home for a 27-second last quarter. It was important to see if he had anything left at the end of a mile. The great champions always did.

Phantom went across the first quarter pole at 31 and one-fifth, causing Nils to give him a bit more headway. He hit the next quarter in 30 and four-fifths. Nils was right on schedule as he glanced toward the yellow caps who were now just about 60-feet across the track from him, behind the outer fence. He heard one yell from there, "Go, man, go." Then he was by them and quickly heading into the second long turn. His watch had him at 1:33 at the three-quarters. He came out of the turn and bore into the straightaway heading toward the finish line. He let out the lines slightly and growled – as if tempting the colt to show him something. Phantom did as he was asked, coming home in 27 seconds flat, completing the mile in 2:00.

He brought him down to a slow ramble as he went toward the yellow caps who were now out on the track awaiting the return of the young star.

He jumped off of the bike and went directly to Betty. "Quite a colt you got there, Betty. He's ready to qualify. But I want to tell you now, he's on a high edge. A keg of dynamite. I don't know how to say it, but I sense a characteristic in him, a recklessness or something. But he's a great colt. Pick your driver very carefully."

He walked back to his own barn. His wife came toward him. She said, "That's some colt."

"Yah, it is. But I am glad to be done with him. I wouldn't want to qualify him. I don't know how he'll act with drivers yelling, whips flying, and other horses straining beside him. I will watch him with great interest, there could be fireworks."

CHAPTER XI

Days before any race is run on a track a randomized drawing occurs, typically in the racing office of the respective track. Betty rarely attended the drawings, knowing that she'd find out soon enough which race she'd be in and, more importantly, the post position of her entries. Each race had a particular parameter or condition; for example, a claiming race for $20,000, or a race where a horse hadn't won $5,000 in its last five races, or a race where a horse had never won a race as examples of an extraordinary number of possible conditions. Besides entering a horse who fit a particular condition, it was customary to name a preferred driver for the horse. If the horse was successfully entered but the driver had been chosen by more than one trainer, the driver would usually choose the horse that he felt would be the most competitive. Bettors, of course, watched this factor closely as extremely good drivers – who, perhaps, dominated their tracks, might be chosen by three or four trainers in a particular race.

But Betty Broder didn't make her rare appearance that day to check for the drawing of a pari-mutual betting race. She came to check on the draw of the non-betting qualifying races beginning at 10 a.m. on June 6th. Qualifying races were held to determine whether a horse was fit to race to a minimum standard set by the racing secretary of the track. The racing secretary oversaw the scheduling of races and was the supervisor of the overall track schedule. He was an employee of the track ownership, but he had a position that dictated his being on good terms with all the constituents of the track.

"Have you drawn yet for the qualifiers?" Betty asked, knowing that he hadn't.

"Will in about five minutes," Bogey said.

"OK." She studied Bogey for a minute. He rarely gave eye contact; he didn't in this case. He was bald, massively overweight, and had a huge, flat nose. But to her, his lasting feature was that she had never seen him without an unlit cigar in his mouth which he tossed back and forth between his fat lips.

"How many qualifying races will there be?"

"Looks like four."

A few minutes later Bogey yelled out to the sparsely-filled room, "Gather 'round, drawing for the qualifiers first, then Wednesday and Thursday night's betting races."

Betty and one other person whom she didn't know walked to Bogey's draw process. The few others were probably concerned about the races for Wednesday and Thursday nights.

Bogey said, "This is going to be as fair as I can make it. First race is for fillies and mares – I've got six for that, second for seven two- and three-year-olds, third and fourth for the rest, seven in the third, and six in the fourth." He put six numbers into a box for the first qualifier and called his assistant over who proceeded to pick blindly from the draw box. This determined the post positions for the first qualifying race. "OK, now for the second: two- and three-year-olds got seven." He nodded toward his assistant.

Betty felt nervous, a rare feeling for her relative to the simple process of draws. Her heart sank a bit when she heard that Phantom drew the seven hole or post, as far from the rail as he could get in this particular race. She didn't stick around for the rest of the draws.

On her way back to her barn she called Burgess and left a message with his secretary that Phantom would be qualifying this coming Wednesday at about 10:10 a.m. out of the seven-post position. His secretary seemed to act as though she couldn't care less. Betty hoped against hope that Burgess wouldn't be notified and that he wouldn't even show up.

She thought hard about what driver she would ask to sit on Phantom's bike. She would have preferred Nils, but he long ago had given up on any competitive driving. It was then that she decided to ask Anton La France, an old-time driver from Montreal, known for his patience, particularly with young horses. The only problem with La France was relying on him to show up for anything at ten in the morning. She'd press hard on him and hope that he'd be there for her, reasonably sober.

Wednesday broke hot; it was already 70 degrees at 6 a.m. Betty had positioned fans all through her stables in order to keep the horses cooled off. She had ordered her grooms to get the horses onto the track as early as possible – to avoid the coming heat of the day. But it was Phantom who occupied her thoughts.

By 8 a.m., Alicia had turned her full attention to the colt that seemed to sense that something unusual was in store for him. He held his head a little higher; he cast a long look at anyone who came near him by a tilt of the head and a wide-eyed stare. His ears were racing to different positions as though he was trying to hear some faint signal in the air. When anyone, other than Alicia, passed near him his ears would press down and back, about as pinned as any horse could have.

For qualifiers, many of the standard race rules were relaxed. Drivers, for example, would drive in t-shirts, there was no betting, and the races would be run quickly in 10-minute intervals. The trick to qualifiers was to meet the prescribed time set by the track's racing secretary. As long as the horse came in at the time set or any time better than the set time, he was qualified to pace or trot in a betting race. For many trainers, it was of no import where their horse finished in the qualifying race. What was of import was beating the prescribed time.

Prescribed times varied. Trotters, for example, were usually given two more seconds than pacers since their gaits slowed their times, on an average, of about two seconds. With pacers, two- and three-year-olds were usually conceded a few seconds as well as fillies and mares. Aged horses and geldings, on the other hand, were not offered concessions. Each track had its own parameters. Tracks in larger cities with big purses usually enforced higher standards as bettors eschewed lesser horses, finding them difficult to handicap. Smaller tracks with small handles, perhaps barely staying in business, would not be in a position to set high standards. Some compared the whole thing to major and minor leagues.

At 9 a.m. sharp Alicia took Phantom to the paddock or holding area, a large barn and stable complex where racing horses were to be housed prior to races. At Balmoral this area, off the racing track itself, was in the middle of the stretch of the racing track. Samuel had already warmed him up once by having him leisurely pace three miles.

Betty came up to Alicia who was brushing down Phantom. "Mister Burgess is supposed to come to the track at about 9:45. He wants me to sit up in the grandstand with him. I don't have a choice. When Anton comes over, tell him again about the whip; I don't want him to touch Phantom. Make sure you get that message to him. I already spoke with him a few days ago. But – hell, he's drunk more often than not. How's Phantom behaving?"

"He's alert. He knows that something is up. Tense as a rabbit in the open."

Betty patted her on the back. Her phone rang.

"I'm about five minutes away Betty. I'll pull in at the clubhouse entrance. Meet me, will you?"

"Sure, Mister Burgess, I'll be there." She turned toward Alicia. "Great. Mister Burgess is early." She looked at her watch and said, "It's all in your hands, Alicia. Just make sure La France remembers."

At about 9:50 the announcement came across, "The first qualifier is going off in ten minutes." Alicia saw the fillies and mares being led from their stalls by their grooms, sometimes with the trainer present. The chosen drivers were waiting. She saw Anton La France. He was driving the five horse. He took the filly with his hand and led her for a few seconds and then he jumped onto the sulkey seat and led her onto the track.

It was hard to tell, Alicia thought, just what kind of condition La France was in. If truth be told, she reflected, he always looked drunk and hungover. He was short, very dark, and always seemed to have a three-day beard growth. Brusque of manner he spoke with a heavy French accent. On the few times that she dealt with him, he had treated her nicely enough, not that they ever had long and complex discussions.

She looked back at Phantom who was staring at her with one eye cocked as it were. She wondered just what was going on in his head.

Every once in awhile – with no rhyme or reason that she could detect – a practice announcer would call the qualifiers. He wasn't the usual caller or announcer but simply someone who knows someone and who would ask for the gig. Hardly anyone watched qualifiers except for those in the respective stables from which they came, owners and friends, and some bettors who were hoping to spot some hint of potential for a betting race. On this particular day, it was some young man who knew someone and who was going to call the four qualifiers over the track's loudspeaker system.

Alicia heard the call of the first race as she did final preparations on Phantom. It was a call that only the poor guy's girlfriend might like. Pathetic. The kid stumbled through names and was confused between the names of the number three and number four pacers.

"Get ready for race two," the announcement came across the loudspeaker. She took Phantom from stall seven in the second race section of the barn and led him out. Anton La France walked toward her. His face was ashen beneath the black stubble.

"Anton, Betty spoke with you. Be careful with him; he's very high strung and please, please don't use the whip."

"Yeah, yeah," he jumped on to the bike and headed toward the track. Under her watchful eye he just pulled onto the track and proceeded about 20 feet when he stumbled off of the bike. He motioned toward a groom to grab Phantom and keep him still. La France went to the rail and began to wretch up last night's supper, this morning's breakfast, probably a fifth of whiskey and scarily, at least Alicia thought, at least a pint of blood. By the time she had reached him the outrider who oversaw the conduct of horses before the race came over and yelled to Alicia, "You better get yourself another driver. I'll tell the starter car. Step on it, will you?"

Alicia ran back into the paddock and the first driver she saw was Brian Broad, a young and aspiring driver who seemed to be a nice guy. "Brian, quick, we need you on our horse. Anton is sick. Can you qualify our horse? He's out on the track."

"Hey, yeah. I was getting ready for the third, no problem."

"But Brian, this is a big deal colt. No whips, OK? He's very temperamental. Just go about 2:02, that's all we want."

"OK, OK," he ran toward the track with Alicia behind him.

"OK?" she asked.

"Sure, sure."

She immediately called Betty's cell. She answered on the first ring. "Betty! Anton is very sick. He's still sick along the rail here. I had to put the nearest man on him, Brian Broad. I explained it all to him."

"Brian Broad? Are you kidding me?"

"No, he was available. What was I supposed to do?"

There was a long pause; Betty said tensely, "We'll be down after the race." She hung up.

Alicia now felt sick at heart. Phantom was becoming a jinx for her.

Brian Broad sat in the bike and took the lines from the groom. Only then did he ever look at the colt in front of him. Alicia or Alice or whatever her name wasn't kidding. This colt looked good. He urged him forward and he responded nicely. The starting car came alongside of him, and the judge who sat in the car during all races yelled across to him, "Take him around once and then we're going to do the race. Get moving a bit, we're already late."

Broad was 23 and had started driving on the county fair circuit in Illinois when he was 19. He had taken to catch driving at the Indiana harness tracks. Eventually he moved to Michigan where he shed his (P) status. As a (P), he was a 'provisional' driver who would keep that designation in racing programs until he had accumulated enough satisfactory starts to be taken off of that dubious status. When the 'P' was removed, he had ostensibly equal status with other drivers.

But he knew as did everyone else in the harness game that there were drivers and there were drivers. The really successful drivers might be chosen to drive in every race on a card (usually between 10 and 14 races per night or per card) while some drivers might only be chosen once or twice per night. It was hard to break into the top ranks due to the fact that trainers typically chose the best drivers – who if they were chosen by more than one trainer for a race would choose the horse they thought had the best chance. The trainer who was chosen against would have to come up with another driver, and this was sometimes how Broad got to drive.

He knew that the best way to succeed was to keep his head down, his relationship with trainers good, and to be around at the right times, as for example with the qualifiers, and getting a break like spelling Anton La France. He noticed that the colt had drawn outside – the seven post as this was the number attached to a pad on each side of the colt. As he drove around the backstretch, he came up on Dan Murphy who was aboard the three horse in this qualifier. "Dan, are these all two-year-olds?"

"Two- and three-year-olds. How come you're driving him?"

"La France – sick."

"You know about that colt?"

"No. What do you mean?"

"He's the one who ran off the track a few weeks ago and almost killed a bunch of people in the backstretch."

"No! This is the one. I heard about it. Crap." They kept moving around the backstretch in lockstep.

"Big bucks wrapped up in him I hear," Murphy said.

"Great, watch the crazy bastard go goofy on me."

Murphy laughed and fell back letting Phantom pull at Broad as the move toward the starting line advanced. When he came toward the far turn he saw the starter car up ahead with its gates fully extended. It was the job of the driver to put the horse's nose as close to the number on the gate as possible and then to follow the gate as it picked up speed as it moved toward the starting line. As in all things, some horses were blazingly fast off of the gate and went for the lead, whereas others did not have much gate speed and those would quickly search for the rail and as best a position at the beginning of the race as they could find. Unlike betting races, strategy was usually not of high import in qualifiers – finishing at or below the qualifying time was what was important.

As the car picked up speed and crossed the starting line, the starter shouted, "Go," and the starting gates winging out from the top of the car closed abruptly, making a distinct clanging sound as the car sped up and raced away from the horses and toward the outer fence. The starter and a judge would now parallel the racing horses to make sure that the rules of a race were kept.

Broad felt a slight hesitation in Phantom as the gates swung inward, inexperience, he thought. Quickly, his thought shifted as Phantom flared forward with tremendous force. He looked across toward the rail realizing that he was already ahead of the number five and number six horses as he pulled back hard on Phantom, managing to get him away in fifth along the rail. This took great effort, his body leaning back, almost flat on the bike as he tried to restrain him. Phantom was trying to run over the fourth horse with the number two on his pads in front of him. Twenty seconds into the race he decided to pull him for fear of an accident. The fact was that he was having a brutally hard time restraining him.

The lead horse in the race had the number four on his pads. He hit the quarter pole at 29.1. Within a few seconds of that Phantom was by him, now at the front end of the race. Broad was still stretched out in the sulkey, arms sore, legs stiff as Phantom was looking down the long backstretch, hearing two particularly noisy drivers screaming at their horses, and also surprisingly, beginning to hear the thwack of a whip on the flesh of a few of those behind him. He carried the race to the half-mile clock in 58 seconds flat. Broad looked back and saw that he was a good six lengths ahead of the pack behind him. They weren't kidding, this was a special colt, but there was a problem. He was sure that they didn't want him to go this fast. 2:02 was the desired time. At this rate he'd go less than two minutes. No trainer wanted that on a young colt at this point of his development.

Unfazed by his new times and new speeds, Phantom paced on about to head into the start of the long turn between the five-eighths pole to the three-fourths pole of Balmoral. At this point, Broad started to pull him in hard – wanting to break his speed in the third quarter and bring him home gently in the stretch. Phantom fought him all the way around the turn; Broad was getting upset with the colt and with himself. Could he not handle a good colt? This was not a way to gain approval and win confidence. He looked back quickly and saw Murphy's three-year-old stalking Phantom while all of the other horses were a good 10 lengths back.

He used every muscle in his body in an effort to hold back Phantom. He had only marginal success. Murphy's horse was now parallel to them, angering Broad who did want to win the race.

Broad applied the whip to Phantom's upper leg – two quick thwacks and then a release on the lines. The colt hesitated; Murphy's horse sped by. Broad thought that the message had not been delivered successfully. He was distracted for a split second before Phantom, looking hard right, must have seen the opening leading to the pre-race paddock area. He changed direction without slowing and started to race off the track at a 70-degree angle. Brian tried frantically to slow the horse that either had not seen that a pole-gate closure had blocked the opening or who could care less as he tore toward the four-foot tall iron poled fence. He hit it going at least 25 miles per hour; the pole gave a foot and then held the horse that collapsed in pain. Broad's ultra light sulkey flipped, hurtling him into the air, over the pole and onto the ground behind the pole. He remembered feeling great pain in his back and that his arm hung without seeming direction. He gazed at the horse that was down on the ground already with a towel over its eyes, a quick-thinking groom trying to divert it from panic. He tried to move before he felt a few hands restraining him. He felt a darkness entering him, then he passed out.

CHAPTER XII

It was six a.m. sharp when Bertrand McAbee's phone startled him awake. Scorpio, his white German Shepherd, jolted himself up to a standing position on McAbee's king-size bed. He walked toward the phone as if ready to answer it before McAbee pushed him aside. "It's OK Scorp, it's OK. Down." The dog sat and then lay down. As Scorpio aged, sudden noises and unusual, unforeseen events seemed to distress him more and more.

He answered the phone after the third ring. "Hello?"

"Hey, brother, what's up out there? Aren't you at work yet?"

It was his brother, Bill, who would next pretend that it was eight a.m., stating that he could never get the difference between eastern and central times. Bertrand fell into the act. "Hey, do you realize that it's only six out here?"

There was a phony delay as this extraordinary news was absorbed. "Damn! Can you believe that? I thought it was eight."

He was already patting Scorpio's head as he said, "Gee Bill, I know that it's hard on you. And I know that you want something. What's up?"

"Have you ever heard of a conservative, Jewish synagogue in Rock Island, Illinois?"

"Sure, my lawyer goes there, or at least he did last time it came up." He didn't inquire further. The reason for the question would come.

"How about a place called Hampton, Illinois?"

"Sure. Tough little place along the Mississippi in Illinois. Floods a lot in the spring and summer, and it has the reputation of growing some bad customers, not that I ever met any of them." Again, no attempt at whys was sought.

"By now I'll bet you're asking why I'm asking."

"I asked that, Bill, when I heard the damn phone ring at six. Only you call at that time."

He laughed. One of his traits was to take joy in the grief of others, as long as the grief was just frustration. "I have a few more pieces, then we'll talk. Did you ever hear of Abraham Horowitz?"

"Bill, let's cut the twenty questions. And no, I never heard of him, I think. Although as I grow older, when you start telling me about him, I suddenly remember. But for the record, no."

"He's been a key figure in the recovery of Nazi looted art. Lots of people don't like him. He's seen as arrogant and brash, and all those things that we like in a lawyer who represents us but what we hate in those who don't represent us. Got it?"

"Even without a cup of coffee it makes sense. So, where are we headed?"

"Horowitz is coming to speak to the congregation in Rock Island next Sunday night. He's a bit of a rabble-rouser in the sense that he reaches into the gut-anger of Jews. Because of that some right-wing groups, I mean really right wing, don't care for his message. These groups think that Jews should be happy to have survived the holocaust and let bygones be bygones. They use all of the anti-Semitic cant that they can dig up and throw. Got it?"

"Sure."

"Well apparently there's a cell of these would-be Nazis in Hampton."

"And?"

"I have one name. Doesn't matter where I got it from, but it meets the gold standard. I'd like you to run it down and see what's there."

Bertrand, now fully awake sitting at the edge of his bed, said, "What's this got to do with Horowitz coming here? Are these Hamptonists peaceful?"

"That's the problem, no. We think that there might be an effort to kill him."

"What?"

"I know, I know. Some of the data says they might try to blame it on Arabs. They have elsewhere."

"How rough do you want to get?"

"The name I'm giving you can not afford exposure as you'll see. Make it rough enough that Horowitz's safety is beyond doubt. How's that?"

"Will do ... how is everyone?"

"Great. Mary sends her best."

"Same here to everyone. And how about your safety, Bill? Any more attempts?"

"No, we're keeping the hordes away for the time being. But, Bertrand, remember one of these days they'll probably succeed. I fully expect you to seek revenge."

"Guaranteed. But why don't you try to stay safe so I don't have to go down that road."

"Call back and let me know how this thing goes, here's the name; John Austin, lives in Hampton." He hung up.

Bertrand sat at the edge of the bed and reflected on Bill. He headed a massive consulting and investigation agency in New York City. It had international reach. Bill, himself, was connected to a variety of spy agencies, police departments, federal groups, and so on. His clout and connections had aided McAbee in several major cases on which he had worked. Several years ago, however, Bill had missed being assassinated in the elevator of his office building by a German skinhead whose complaint was that Bill had helped the German police break up a particularly lethal cell of them. The would-be assassin was never heard from again. Bertrand was sure that he had been tortured and murdered. Bill had a ruthless streak the width of a 10-lane highway. Even still, it was because of him that Bertrand was established in the investigatory game himself after he left academia. They were, therefore, connected in the same game but at different levels. For Bill, it was an all-consuming affair; for Bertrand, it was an interesting past-time on a road that he would travel until he became disinterested.

For a few seconds he thought about whom and why Bill was doing this job. He shrugged. It could be anyone from Horowitz himself to Israeli intelligence to the FBI to some person to whom he owed a favor. He didn't offer, and Bertrand didn't ask. But several things were clear – there was danger afoot and worry.

He put on a sweatshirt, pants, and the rest of his running gear. It was either get in a few miles now or probably kiss off all exercise for the day. Scorpio watched him impatiently as he swallowed a glass of orange juice. "OK, big boy, ready to go?"

Scorpio tore up the stairs and pawed the front door. They walked toward the park, about three blocks from his condo. After Scorpio addressed his plumbing needs they began a slow run. McAbee was only going to go about three miles, wanting to get to his office by eight a.m. He had scattered appointments on his calendar; he would try to have them changed.

He brought him back to the house at a walk. Scorpio was dealing with the beginnings of arthritis, not nearly as conditioned as in the old days when he could maintain himself handily on a 10-mile run. McAbee's heart went out to him as he peeked a look down and his eye was caught by Scorpio who was, perhaps, wondering why they were walking so fast. He poured his Purina Dog Chow into a large, red, plastic bowl and refilled his yellow water bowl. Scorpio no longer attacked the food bowl, rather sniffing at it and biting into a few pieces of the brown nuggets. McAbee patted his head while saying, "Come on now, boy, you gotta eat kid." He went up to take a shower.

He took Scorpio out to a run he had built in the back of his condo. Scorpio struggled against going into the run for a few seconds and then relented. When he was younger it was more of a battle. McAbee turned and locked the gate. He was walking toward his garage when he heard his next door neighbor, Gloria.

"Bertrand, Bertrand. Do you have a minute?"

He turned and said, "Sure, Gloria. How are you?"

Gloria had been a neighbor of his for years. She had known him when he was married, was there through his rough divorce, and she loved Scorpio, often tending to him when McAbee's erratic schedule created problems in the care of Scorpio. McAbee didn't appreciate her at awkward moments. He forced himself to focus on this good woman.

"Just wanted to let you know that I may have to leave town for a few days. A second cousin of mine in Omaha is very sick. They don't expect him to live."

He saw this as a good reminder as to just how essential she was to his life and Scorpio's well being. "I'm sorry. Were you close?"

"Not really. But as you know I'm pretty thin when it comes to family. So every cousin is important, I guess."

"Can I do anything?"

"I'll leave you a note in your mailbox. Maybe you'd be kind enough to watch my place?"

"Of course I will, Gloria."

She turned to Scorpio whose front feet were up on the wire fence. He whined, and she of course accommodated him with small talk and placed her fingers inside the cage – catching his nose with a pat. McAbee knew that other than himself and Gloria, no one could do that without probably losing a finger or two. Territorial Scorpio wasn't exactly friendly.

By 3 p.m. McAbee had quite a profile on John Austin of Hampton, Illinois – thanks to the efforts of Barry Fisk. He knew Austin's blood type, that he had acne as a teenager, that he had his appendix taken out when he was a 22-year-old senior at Northern Illinois University in DeKalb, majoring in finance. For some odd reason, he lurched rightward out of the Republican Party, became involved with the Libertarian Party and then he left that organization and drifted deep into First Church of Jesus the Supreme. He became a minister in that organization which Fisk linked to some second amendment defenders and with greater difficulty to some extreme views on race. The anti-Semitism was shrouded by a number of high-sounding front groups usually headed by the words 'Jesus' or 'Americans'.

McAbee wrote a few key words on a small sheet of paper and placed it into his sports jacket. He was to have an interview with John Austin at four p.m. that day. Austin thought that it concerned the opening of a bank account at his bank in East Moline, Austin being president of such.

At 3:15 Augusta came by with a small case in her right hand and was immediately sent through Bertrand's office door that was ajar.

"OK, my friend, clothes off!" she said dogmatically ironic.

"I was afraid that this day would come. Liberated women ordering men around like they were sex objects."

"I don't see the clothes coming off, Mistah," she said lightly.

He took off his blue sportcoat and eggshell, collarless Perry Ellis ribbed shirt. As he did that he realized that this was a first.

She walked to the door and said, "Pat, I need a witness. Your boss is an exhibitionist!" Pat came in and laughed when she saw Bertrand standing in mid-office, bare-chested. "You see, you see."

"As God is my judge," Pat went back to her desk.

"Augusta – some day you're going to need a wire," he said.

"Whoops. OK, I apologize. Well, I don't know. You're so diplomatic and sensitive; you wouldn't notice."

He laughed and said, "I prefer your touch to that of Scholz."

"I sure hope so." She opened the case and removed some wires, a tube of lubricant, and some tape. "Boy, I'm going to have to work around all that hair." She did so – adeptly and without further comment. "OK Bertrand, you know the drill. Let's check it now. I'll go into Pat's office. Just talk for about a minute." She left the office, heard him read a few lines from Plato's *Republic*, and came back. "Now we're all set."

He had already put his shirt on. He grabbed his coat and said, "We better get going. It's hot in here, isn't it?"

"No, I don't think so." Then she looked at him, seeing something in his eyes, because she added, "Well, I mean, not any longer now that your shirt's back on."

He gave her a whimsical smile. They left for East Moline, which naturally enough was a small city east of Moline, Illinois, with about 18,000 people. Part of it fronted along the Mississippi River. He had briefed Augusta on the drive, which took them from Davenport to Bettendorf, then across the I-74 Bridge to Moline and then along the Ben Butterworth Parkway into East Moline and to its very modest downtown. The bank was in a two-story, salmon-bricked building. They parked a block from it. It was 3:57 p.m. "Wish me luck."

"Be careful, Bertrand. He sounds like a nut to me."

He felt the wire as he walked the block and entered the lobby of the bank. 'Another reason to save with your friendly, locally-owned bank open until 5 p.m.,' the sign in the lobby said.

The bank had four teller windows. One of them was without a customer. He went up to a window seeing a sign that read 'Ellen Smith'. With a practiced smile she said, "Can I help you, sir?"

"Yes. I'm looking for John Austin – I have an appointment with him."

"Oh, OK. His office is back there on the far left. He has a secretary – just go up to her. Is that all?"

"Yeah, thanks."

He turned and went toward Austin's office. It was fronted by a blonde in her mid-fifties. She had a curious way about her. He sensed army about her. Perhaps she had worked on the federal government's Rock Island Arsenal, a huge employer in the Quad Cities and a regular contributor to the double-dipper syndrome which had so bothered a former colleague of his at St. Anselm's College that he ran as a third-party candidate for congress to outlaw the practice of drawing a full government pension and then proceeding to still another pension in the private sector. He got his head handed to him in the election, declaring that this particular congressional district in Iowa was controlled by double-dippers whom he was sure were double voters. He was an economist, to McAbee that explained much about him.

"Yes sir, may I help you?"

"Yes, my name is Bertrand McAbee I have an appointment with Mister Austin."

"I'll see if he's in." She had quickly glanced at her calendar. She went into his office and came back in an instant. "Just go right in sir, he's expecting you."

John Austin was corpulent. That word struck at McAbee with considerable force. He had all of the hustle down as he stood and held his hand out over his large desk. "Pleased to meet you, Mister McAbee. What can I do for you?"

Bertrand sat down and withdrew the small sheet of paper on which he had written some comments off of his analysis of Fisk's work. He reflected that John Austin did not seem the assassin, at least, until he looked back at him and saw a pair of calculating brown eyes which, when noticed, turned back in a flash to friendly ones.

"Call me Bertrand, sir."

"Of course; and me, I'm John."

"John, I'm going to get right to the point with you." His friendly eyes went hard. "I know a lot about you. More, I can tell you, than I would ever want to know." He passed across his small list to him.

Austin stood up and asked angrily, "What's this about, McAbee?"

"I'm trying to tell you, it's about you. Now if you'd sit down and hear me out I think that you'll be happy to have done so."

Austin stayed on his feet, looking hard at McAbee. Then he sat. "You have five minutes – maximum."

"That'll probably do it. Let me explain my mission. There's a man coming into Rock Island soon. His name is Horowitz." He noticed that Austin's eyes gave an ever-so-slight recognition of the name. "You're a prominent man in this community, sir – a banker, a preacher, a political connoisseur. The problem is this. As long as you're obscure and no one gives a care about you, no problem. But, you see, you're not obscure. You draw attention."

"What the hell are you talking about?" He yelled out, "Helen!" She came in – in a sort of slithering motion. She didn't walk so much as slide.

"Yes sir. What can I do for you?"

"Call the police, right now." Helen left abruptly.

"You should leave immediately, McAbee."

"Before I do, may I say one more thing?"

He hesitated. "Go ahead."

McAbee looked down, thinking. Then he said, "I've seen some of your anti-Semitic screeds, John. Be careful.

If it gets out, you'll lose every major account in your bank. All I want from you is this, Horowitz, he's not to be touched, and I wouldn't be here if there wasn't some concern. Do you understand me, Austin? Don't make me get tough on this. You won't win. The power behind me is obsessional and unrelenting. I'm easy." He smiled. Then he heard the siren near the bank entrance.

Austin glared at McAbee but didn't say anything. There was a slight commotion in the lobby.

Time was running out. McAbee was wondering how this whole episode would transpire. He sat and looked calmly at Austin.

Finally, the fat man said quietly, "Nothing will happen to Horowitz. Now get out."

Helen slithered in with a uniformed East Moline cop. Austin said with an impressively manufactured smile, "Officer, I'm sorry. No problem here. Just a misunderstanding. Mr. McAbee will be leaving now, won't you?" He looked at McAbee expectantly.

"Oh yes. My business is done," he got up and started to walk from the office.

Helen hissed out, "Are you sure, sir, he should be let go? I didn't like him from the start."

McAbee stopped, turned, and caught her eye. He said, "Miss ...," he caught himself, thinking of Epictetus, the great ancient stoic who would have counseled McAbee against wasting his time in idle chatter with useless people. He turned and left.

When he got into the car Augusta said, "That was quick. Do you believe him?"

"Yeah, I do. His eyes told me everything. He's done, at least with any thoughts about Horowitz. But he'll be back. He's a critter."

"I heard his secretary. What were you going to say to her?"

He looked at her. She stared intently at him. "Something very nasty and very unnecessary. Let's just leave it at that. But I did get the feeling that the two of them are cut from the same rock. A bad pair. I sense that we might get into it again with them."

Later that night he called Bill who hung up satisfied. But Bertrand committed one of Scholz' men to be around during the Horowitz appearance, just in case.

CHAPTER XIII

———◆◆———

Kalona, Iowa is sometimes referred to as the Kalona-nation. It is a town about 20 miles south of the University of Iowa in Iowa City. The difference between the two cities is vast. Iowa City, population about 50,000, is home of the Big Ten Hawkeyes, and probably the most liberal city in Iowa with its cosmopolitan ambience and international student body. It has a medical school, a law school, and numerous doctoral programs besides the full gamut of undergraduate programs. But in that 20 miles between Iowa City and Kalona it becomes apparent that the 21st Century has been rolled back into the 19th Century. The town of Kalona is controlled by a rigorous and defensive Amish population that eschews electricity, motorized transportation and other modern amenities. Of course, not everyone is Amish; the town has cars, banks, and restaurants alongside of hitching posts for horse and buggy transportation.

Kalona also has an auction site that draws from around the area. It is primarily home to livestock auctions that occur in a small ring surrounded by tiered seating housed in a large barn-like edifice. The entire site has a number of pens and stables where the animals are housed in anticipation of the auction. On the first Saturday in November of each year there is an auction of a variety of horses, some thoroughbreds, some westerns, some quarter horses, and some standardbreds. Although the horse industry in Iowa has been on a precipitous decline, there are still those who stay active.

Prairie Meadows, now principally a casino, just outside of Des Moines was built in the mid-80s as a racetrack. Iowa was then innocent of the creep of gambling. In a few short years, gambling riverboats were approved, lotteries were established, and this parade spread to other states – Illinois, Mississippi, Indiana, and so on. Each, in turn, was protesting the lost revenues that went to Iowa and then to each other. As in dominoes, each state took the path to gambling as another way to raise money. To this day, some hold the state of Iowa responsible for starting this chain of events throughout the mid-section of the country. Prairie Meadows complained bitterly that the riverboats were given an unfair advantage over a simple racetrack, eventually the powerful Des Moines legislators forged a bill that allowed slots and other forms of gambling onto the racetrack, but it was demanded that live thoroughbred racing must go on. This kept a dying horse industry alive on life support. Also included in this compromise was that a percentage of monies would be diverted to county fairs to support the grand old sport of harness racing. Prairie Meadows was mandated to even have a few cards devoted to harness racing, with an attendance that could be shoed into a small school bus.

It was, then, a November pastime for those few hearty souls who still did race horses to show up for what was to serious horsemen a scavenger hunt in Kalona. Many of the horses were broken down or just too lousy to compete even in races filled with losers like themselves, thus their ending up in November in Kalona-nation. Others were unproven yearlings or two-year-olds with faint hint of promise.

Some of those attending the auction were lovers of standardbred horses. They made it their hobby to compete in the fair circuit around Iowa in the summer. The purses for those races were supported, in part, by a takeout from the revenues of the gambling industry in Iowa. A solid horse could earn a nice little sum during the fair-races, and if the horse was really good it could be shipped to Chicago for some serious racing when the fair circuit ended in late summer. But fair racing was oftentimes a dangerous adventure, the tracks were frequently poorly maintained, the drivers were scary amateurs, and the horses were not well mannered. Collisions, falls, fouls, and a host of other calamities befell both horse and driver. When the fair season ended it was typically time to send the stock to Kalona and attempt to secure some new stock for next year.

Willis Clohessey had been a standardbred man all of his life. Even as a small child he remembered the farm's track that his father had created around a field of corn. By the time he was seven he would exercise the pacers that his father kept at the farm, always at least three, sometimes up to seven or eight of them. When he was 18, he had decided to become a driver and trainer and had moved to Chicago in pursuit of the dream. He was beginning to make his mark when he was called home, his father being killed in a tractor rollover. Willis was the oldest of eight kids. His duty was to take over the farm. He did.

Eventually he got married, had his own kids, and forgot about Chicago and beyond as a career. But he never let go of standardbreds, the Iowa fair circuit, and the occasional horse that would be sent to Chicago, Michigan or Ohio for advanced racing.

Willis was now 64 years old. His kids were gone, three boys and one girl, none of them having the slightest interest in farming. Eventually, he knew, he'd have to sell out and retire to town. He dreaded that day because he knew that it wouldn't just be the end of farming but also the pursuit of his avocation – the harness horse industry.

The Kalona sale had 151 horses for auction, of which 37 were standardbreds. Willis looked over the sheets again while he ate an Oreo cookie and sipped a Diet Coke in the Super Eight Motel in Kalona on that Friday evening before the sale. He had interest in five horses, but there was another one that his eye kept roving back to. He was Phantom Express, a six-year-old with breeding to kill for but with a footnote on the offering page that said, "He is not raceable due to a serious track accident. However, he has been used successfully to draw a buggy at slow speeds. Still young – must sell due to move to Oregon." He wondered what kind of accident the animal had suffered.

The auction started at 9:30 a.m. the next day. Willis was checking out the five horses that interested him. He had gotten it down to four; he would bid hard for them. At 8:45 a.m. he strolled over to hip number 66 where Phantom was located.

"Willis Clohessey," he held out his hand to a young Amish man who had a requisite beard, a long, thin face, and wore wire-rimmed glasses.

"Noah Brown," they shook hands.

"This your horse?"

"Yes. Care to see him?"

"Please."

Noah took Phantom out to the middle of the aisle and held him steady. Willis looked at Phantom. He was overweight and clearly out of condition. The horse stared at Willis – a cocked eye watched him as if appraising him. He felt his legs; there was a huge bump on the left knee. He put his hand against his chest and throat to gauge his air potential, and he looked at the horse's nostrils and teeth. He said, "Good looking horse. What's the deal? He was bred superbly to race. Do you know what happened?"

"No, can't say really. I got him from my uncle in Lancaster, Pennsylvania about two-and-a-half years ago. He told me that he was in a bad track accident, that they tried to bring him back but couldn't. He was going up for sale to a slaughterhouse in Pennsylvania, but my uncle picked him up. The horse's got a good way about him, but you can't lay a whip on him, that's what I was told."

"Where did you get all the information on him?"

"Oh, my uncle had it. He's registered with the USTA. They have all that, I guess, or someone did."

"Why don't you take him to Oregon?"

"Too much money to ship him. I'll buy out there. My uncle brought him here from Lancaster; he was bringing other stock out here in case you're wondering."

"Have you ever tried to race him?"

"No, no way. I have a child and a wife. We just want transportation."

"A lot of people looking at him?"

He laughed. "No, to be truthful, you're only the third one. There are so many broken down nags in this sale; I'm afraid he doesn't stand out."

Willis walked around again, feeling and probing the big, powerful horse. He shook his head and thought to himself, 'The accident is a pity; this horse was meant to race.'

"I'm going to put him back now, if you're done."

"Yeah, I'm done." Willis walked away. He looked back and caught Phantom's eye. It was glued on him. Then he disappeared into his stall.

The auctioneer came to hip 66 by 11:30 a.m. Willis had already made successful bids on three horses; and he had lost track of the schedule as he and several old-time acquaintances chatted about past times. It was only by sheer coincidence that he heard, during a conversation lull, the name Phantom Express. He said to the two men he had been conversing with, "Excuse me, I want to look in at this one."

He stood behind the last row of seats as the big horse stood in the ring. The only bid registered at $650, a price that renderers would pay. He assumed that that was the nature of the bid. He held back, then the bid went up to $750 as two other men joined in the action at 50-dollar increments. Willis wondered what the horse had gone for when he was a yearling. He had already lost out on one horse that he wanted, and his van held four horses. So, he thought, maybe he should take a leap and buy this one. This thought process transpired in a matter of seconds. The auctioneer was asking for $800 and was already saying, "Going once, going," when Willis raised his hand. The auctioneer yelled out, "I have $800, do I hear $850?" He looked around, paused for a few seconds and once again intoned, "Going once, going twice, sold to bidder number 17, our friend Willis Clohessey, for $800."

Willis drove out of Kalona-nation with four horses that day. He wondered to himself whether any of them would be worth a damn.

By April of the next year Willis had made several inquiries to old-time friends in Chicago and Ohio. They'd ask around about Phantom Express, they couldn't recall the name offhand.

Two weeks later he was called by a Chicago trainer named Eddie Shreve, whose name and phone number registered on Clohessey's caller ID.

"Because you're a friend of a friend I thought I'd call you about that Phantom horse. He went wild in a qualifier here at Balmoral and ran into a metal bar at about 30 miles per hour. He'd already done some crazy things. Word was that the racing secretary banned him from the track. I was told they paid a fortune for him. Personally, I thought he was long gone – in a can of Alpo or something. That's all I know. Good luck." He had hung up, never leaving a name.

Clohessey checked the qualifying records with the USTA, which keeps an official record of all harness races, including qualifiers. He ran the June data of four years past and saw that the only competitive race ever run by Phantom was a qualifier. The horse had shown incredible times for a two-year-old through the first three-quarters of the race before an ending notation on his line that read DNF. Why did he not finish? He crashed a gate, why? Was it broken equipment, did the driver have a seizure, what exactly happened? He jotted down three names that showed on the documentation: Brian Broad, Betty Broder, and Jeremy Burgess. He wasn't familiar with any of them.

Broad was no longer in the racing game, they said at the racing office. He had lost a leg in a racing accident. Betty Broder was a trainer stationed off-track in Crete, Illinois, and Jeremy Burgess was a horse owner, no further comment given.

Willis called Broder and identified himself as a part-time trainer in Iowa. By the time he got that out she said, "Sorry, Mister, I don't take horses. I have enough right where I am."

"I'm not calling about that. I'm trying to get some information about a horse I bought at an auction that you trained."

"Oh. I'm listening," she said warily.

"Phantom Express is the name."

There was a huge silence. "What do you mean? You bought him? My understanding was that he was sold to a renderer in Pennsylvania a few years ago," she commented sharply.

"Well he may have been. But he's in my barn right now."

"Well, Mister Clohessey, if that's true you're dealing with a bad luck horse. I hope to God you're not intending to race him or anything like that."

"I don't know what to say to that. I put him in a bike two months ago, and he took to it like a fish to swimming. I mean to say, he's not even close to racing form, but I sure do like what I see. That's why I'm calling."

There was another long pause. "Real quick on this. He was bought for $400,000. He was ruined by a nut-trainer named Roman Garzo. When I got him he was already ruined." She said plaintively. "I got him down to 2:02, then he was in a qualifier. The chosen driver was sick, and a kid got him. Laid a whip on him, and he crashed a gate, the kid lost his leg, I lost the horse, the owner, and every horse he had in my barn. So, you see, I'm no lover of this animal. They did some big-time surgery on the colt's chest area, look, you'll see the scars, and one of his legs. He was taken away from me and sent back to that Garzo in Valdosta, Georgia. Not long after I was told he was sold to a Pennsylvania trainer as a huge tax loss. That trainer gave up on him, and supposedly he went to a canning factory."

"Did he have potential?"

"Hell yeah. But Garzo ruined him; I've been trying to tell you this. He made a living beating the hell out of horses. This one couldn't handle it. Whatever you do, don't show him a whip. But more so, he's bad luck. I don't know if you've been in the business long, but there are bad-luck horses. This is one. My advice to you is this, get rid of the sucker."

"This Garzo? Where can I find him?"

"Don't know. But I'll tell you this, if you get that bastard of a colt racing he'll find you." She hung up loudly.

He called the USTA and asked whether Garzo was a licensee. "Nope, hasn't been for two years. Can't give you anything else."

So the trail went cold as Clohessey continued to work with Phantom. He now knew enough to conclude that the stares, the looks, and the edginess of Phantom were not due to some inherent madness in the horse, but rather a monumental fear in the animal. Willis was, above all, a patient man who understood the anxieties of horses. He would argue with other trainers that his job was to be a therapist for the animal – a doctor, a counselor, a coach, and ultimately a friend. Most would laugh at him, a few would agree.

Phantom became a reclamation project. Whatever surgery was done on him seemed to be successful; he showed no signs of disability. He glided around the track as though he owned it and week-by-week his times went downward. By the middle of July, Phantom trained a mile in 2:10 on a serviceable three-eighths of a mile track at the farm. He calculated that he could easily hit a 2:03 on a contoured, professionally-graded track.

But he wrestled with the comments of Betty Broder whom, he found on further checking, was a respected trainer in Chicago. He agreed that there was such a thing as a bad-luck horse. He had had two in his life; it was as though a dark cloud hung over them and all who dealt with them. And although Phantom was much more relaxed around him, he would occasionally catch a look from the horse that sent a flash of fear through him. Horses were not smart; but this one had something within him that would make a person think twice about that assumption.

At this point in time he received a call from Josh Swift, another part-time Iowa trainer. "Hey, Willis, what are you doing this weekend?"

"Same old, why?"

"I'm bringing up two of my colts to that new track in Madison, Wisconsin. Want to give me a hand? I'm going to qualify another, on Saturday morning. Come on, you need a break."

"I'll make a deal with you, I want to qualify one of mine up there. What kind of track is it?"

"One mile, and it's lightening fast. Qualifying time is 2:02. And it's a deal. Why don't I come by on Friday morning about 10:00 a.m? There's room in my van. How's that?"

"You have a deal, Josh."

And so it was that Josh Swift and Willis Clohessey drove out of West Branch, Iowa, the birthplace of Herbert Hoover, the first and only president from Iowa, across Interstate 80 and then north on 61 through Dubuque, Iowa and into Wisconsin where they went due east to Madison.

"This that horse you bought for $800?" Josh asked.

"Yeah."

"You going to say anymore about him?"

"Nope, not until I see him race. All I want is a very seasoned driver for the qualifier. I've concluded that that's essential."

"I know just the man."

CHAPTER XIV

———◆◆◆———

There were to be five qualifiers at Madison Downs. Phantom Express was in the last of them along with five other horses. Except for Phantom, the others were old, seasoned pacers who were coming back after a few months of inactivity. From what Willis could gather in the paddock most of them were returning from injuries that had sidelined them. One of them was a pacer who had lifetime earnings of over $270,000. A nine-year old, he was a class horse who had been in a number of races over the years. His name was Cherokee's Puzzle.

Phantom was to be driven by an old-timer who accepted that he should abandon his whip and merely try to qualify him at the exact time set for a successful qualifier, 2:02. The old-timer's name was Jim Benson, a gentle-tempered man with a powerful physique.

Just before the qualifiers started, Benson took Phantom out onto the track for a warm-up. Willis watched him with some apprehension, not too sure what exactly would happen. The warm-up seemed to go without incident.

When Benson came back to the paddock Clohessey asked, "Seem OK?"

"Yup. A bit jittery, watchful. But he's keyed. How many races he have under him?"

Willis answered, reluctantly, "One, a qualifier a bunch of years ago. He didn't finish, had an accident."

"Oh. One of those, huh?"

"Yeah, one of those."

"Age?"

"He's six."

"A lightly-raced six," Benson chuckled.

"So, you know what's expected. He's whip-shy. Just a reminder, I'd prefer that you didn't even take one out on the bike with you. That OK?"

"Oh sure. It's not the first time, you know?"

"If you can get me a 2:02, I'd be happy. He's a puller, however."

"I'll do the best I can."

Willis washed Phantom down and threw a light, cotton blanket over him. The temperature was already in the lower 80s. He sat outside the stall on a short wooden seat. About 10 minutes later, at 9:52, he heard the loudspeaker, "Qualifier One, getting ready. It goes off in eight minutes flat." He looked back over his right shoulder; Phantom was staring down at him, wild-eyed. He figured the horse knew enough about racing conditions to feel the tension in the air, reduced as it was by the informal and relaxed environment surrounding qualifiers. Willis arose and went to Phantom.

He put his hand on the long neck of the horse and stroked it while he spoke gently to him. Phantom relaxed, his ears standing up at attention, no hostility apparent.

When his race was called Jim Benson came over and helped Willis hitch him to the sulkey. He looked at Willis and said jokingly, "See," he held out his hand, palm up, "no whips, no buzzers, no pepper spray. We'll do fine."

Phantom went out onto the track without incident and Benson urged him forward. There was enough time for this pacer to take one trip around the mile oval at a relaxed pace. From what Willis could make out Benson and Phantom got along well.

He watched the starting gate's wings spread out across the Cadillac and then begin its slow climb to speed as the horses filed into line in front of their numbers. Phantom had the four post. Clohessey removed the binoculars from his chest and put them to his eyes as Josh came alongside of him.

"Good luck, Willis," he patted him on the shoulder.

Willis said nothing as the gate started its rush to the starting line. All of the horses were on it as it swung inward over the starting car that now sped up and out of the way for the six pacers.

Benson kept Phantom out for a few seconds before he moved him in toward the rail – finding the fifth spot as the number six horse went for the lead and battled successfully for it with horse number two. Behind two were one and three, and behind Phantom was five. The number five horse was none other than Cherokee's Puzzle – the real class of the qualifier.

The six horse went by the quarter pole in 28.1, his driver trying to slow him a bit, for a moderate second quarter. He wasn't having much success as the pacer, now fired up by the quick start, wanted to sustain the speed.

Phantom was being held nicely by Benson who was about a second off the leader who now hit the half at 58.4. Willis figured that the lead horse would tire soon as he had been off from racing for over six months. Then he noticed that Cherokee's Puzzle was coming off the rail, the driver was hesitating, trying to flush out Phantom so that he could get a second over trip, meaning the chance to draft off a horse in front of him. Benson, to his credit, didn't take the offer as Cherokee sped by him only to be given a second over trip by the number three horse who swung out into the second tier. Willis quickly looked at the leader who was being whacked gently but constantly by his driver. By the time he brought his binoculars back he saw that Phantom was now off the rail and glued to the back of Cherokee.

The three horse was now alongside of the tiring six horse. The one and two horses were locked on the rail behind the six while outside of them in almost perfect unison were the three, the five – Cherokee, and the four – Phantom. They went across the three-quarter marker at 1:30 as they came into the quarter mile stretch.

In an instant Cherokee fanned out three wide and almost effortlessly captured the lead from the six horse that was coming toward the finish at a crawl. Phantom pulled into the void left by Cherokee and followed the three closely as they both passed the six horse. After Phantom cleared the six both the one and two finally broke away from the rail, freeing themselves from the now pathetic effort of six. Every driver knew their mission was to get their horse qualified, winning was not essential.

Cherokee, however, was another story. Apparently that driver was under orders to bring him in at a good time, and he did, finishing the race in a 1:58.1. In fact, all but the six-horse qualified. Phantom, held tightly, finished with a

2:01.3. Willis was overjoyed, the horse showed discipline and a willingness to race without any untoward occurrence.

When Benson came back to the paddock area Willis went out and caught the lines. "Good drive, Jim. You brought him in real nicely."

Benson jumped off of the seat as Clohessey walked Phantom into the paddock. "That's a real good horse. I don't know what the past is, but I do know this, I could've given Cherokee there," he pointed across the aisle, "a run for his money. A man doesn't need a whip to deal with him. What I don't understand is this."

Willis looked at him attentively before saying, "What's that?"

"He's pretty race savvy. I held him, he obeyed. Even in the stretch I had a firm hold on him, and he relented. He didn't fight me, but I could sense his energy. Feels to me that he should have been racing instead of sitting in some barn."

Willis was excited as Benson spoke. He said, "Do you compete in pari-mutuel races?"

"Yeah," he answered defensively.

"Well, I'm going to enter him. Non-winners of one. His maiden race. I'd be privileged if you'd drive him."

"You've got a deal."

On the way back to West Branch, Willis repeated most of his conversation with Benson to Josh Swift. He finished with a query, "Can you believe this? A six-year-old horse that has never been in a betting race? With a chance?"

"It's a great story; I hope it ends well for you, Willis."

Kent Limmer had watched the qualifier that Saturday morning. He was a professional handicapper and a full-time gambler with mob connections. Forty years old, he walked with a bad limp, due to his having been beaten-up by two enforcers when he was 24 years of age. He had physically resisted the beating. That caused him to be held down by one of the attackers as his knee was hit viciously four times with an aluminum baseball bat by the other. After his reconciliation with the mob two years later, he was told that the baseball bat was used only because of his stupid effort at resistance. "Pay your debts Kent, or the other knee is next," they said.

He never borrowed again from them. He used his brains to full avail and worked with an almost religious zeal to beat a betting system where typically about 20% of every dollar bet was taken off the top to support the racing enterprise. He reasoned that 20 cents of every dollar was chump money and that that money was to be paid by the unknowing suckers who happened into the betting side of racing.

Few watched qualifiers, and of those who did, few could match his understanding of things. He scanned for equipment changes on the horses, driver tactics, how a horse warmed up before the races, and physical problems to name a few. He kept them in a computer devoted to every race and every horse on the grounds.

He had come across to Madison from his base in Michigan because of his mother whose health was in steady decline. He decided to spend the summer in her house, but he would not give up his livelihood.

He liked what he saw of Cherokee's Puzzle who put on a terrific display in the last half of that qualifying mile. He had watched Phantom and was impressed by only one thing – he had finished the race. When he had checked him out he saw that he was a DNF in the only race he had ever paced, a qualifier at that. His assessment was that he qualified, but that he didn't show much of anything in the process. He calculated that Cherokee's Puzzle had carried him through the third quarter and into the stretch. He figured that a number of the successfully qualified horses would show up soon for betting purposes.

Limmer was about 6' 2" and thin as a rail. He had blonde hair, a hawk-like nose and an elongated face. Other than gambling and handicapping he led a spare, sordid life, enmeshed in apathy. His one area of vulnerability, he felt, was that he still did some business with the mob. In fact, he was their official handicapper – in Michigan and now Madison. After all, they had a tremendous need to wash money and racetracks served that purpose admirably. With his handicapping skills he was good enough to return to himself and his sponsors about 110% of every dollar bet. Did he make mistakes? Did he squander huge sums on bad bets? His answer was always to be yes. But – did he score massive returns on the basis of his analyses? Did he hit on some trifectas and exactas where the return of investment was sometimes a $100 for every two-dollar bet? Again, his answer was yes.

So it was that Kent Limmer left the track that day to have lunch with a down-and-out trainer, Larry Roberts, whom he had known in Michigan and who had moved to Wisconsin with the advent of the new track. Limmer knew that there was a thin distinction between the word moved and forced. He suspected, in fact, that Roberts had been nudged pretty hard by the Michigan Racing Board, but he wasn't positive about it and Roberts had not been forthcoming.

They sat in Norma's Cafe situated four blocks from the track. It was a haven for truckers whose depots were close by. It was a first-class dump, but this was where Roberts wanted to meet. Limmer acceded to his request because Roberts had, on occasion – but not often, given him a useful tip about one of his horses or some other inside tidbit that he could use in making a bet.

Roberts ordered a double cheeseburger, French fries, and a Pepsi. A man of about 50, overweight, ill-proportioned, and if truth be told, uglier than sin with his red nose, spottily shaved face, and rat-like eyes. Limmer didn't like to be seen with him. He felt that it hurt his image. On the other hand, most of the truckers who were in the place were hardly a step-up from Roberts.

This meeting would cost Limmer the price of lunch and a 50-dollar stipend. He figured that half of the time he had made money from a Roberts tip – a good rate of return. He figured that Roberts gave him, in sum, about a 160% return. He was a valued correspondent, as Limmer would say.

While they waited for the food, Limmer, who had ordered a small salad, French dressing on the side, said, "So how are you doing over here, Larry?"

"Crappy. I'm down to five horses. The purses are so-so, and I'm limping along. One of these days, though, I'm going to get a great horse; you wait and see."

Limmer had been hearing that line for years. He figured that Larry's chances for a 'big one', a great horse, were about one in 500, while his chances for the 'big one' relative to a heart attack were about one in two over the next three years. "Go for it man," he said without enthusiasm. "So what do you have for me?"

"I have a horse for you. A non-winner of one. He's coming over from Minnesota, doesn't have to qualify here. He's been racing in some county fairs there. His trainer's assistant told me that they brought him here last week. Had him out on the track two days ago, and he went 1:58 and was barely breathing at the end."

"There's a good reason they're non-winners of one."

"Well, that's the whole point. His odds will be long. His fair lines aren't that good, couldn't get around on those lousy ovals; he's big. Big-big. Needs a big track with long, easy turns. They drew this morning; he's a cinch. None of those damn horses in that race will break a two-minute mile. The trainer thinks he could come home in 1:57."

"Do you have the advance sheet?"

He dug into his pants' pocket and found a dirt-smeared sheet of paper. He laid it on the table and pointed to a name in the seventh race. "That's him!"

Limmer took the list and read the name, 'Cobra, Cobra'. He had remembered seeing his name in the entry box, but he had never seen the horse in the flesh and he knew nothing about him. Limmer was leery of non-winners of one races. Two of these horses had raced over 30 times, yet had never won a race. For two others, this was their first pari-mutual race. A non-winner of one race literally meant just that. These horses did not make an all-star team. Handicapping them was hell. On the other hand – given this datum from Roberts, money could easily be made. He scanned the list downwards.

1. Downer's Look
2. Doitwell
3. Sorry About It
4. The Banker's Friend
5. Cobra, Cobra
6. Jimmy Steffen
7. Wild Bills Food
8. Phantom Express

None of the names were new to his extraordinary memory. He was already attaching odds to the list. Of the eight, he thought the best chance was for Downer's Look (1) and Doitwell (2). Not only were they the most promising, they had drawn the best posts and had solid drivers. He now recast the list in his mind, as it might be handicapped in the racing program.

(1)	Downer's Look	2 – 1
(2)	Doitwell	5 – 2
(3)	Sorry About It	4 – 1
(4)	The Banker's Friend	4 – 1
(5)	Cobra, Cobra	6 – 1
(6)	Jimmy Steffen	10 – 1
(7)	Wild Bills Food	12 – 1
(8)	Phantom Express	20 – 1

There was no doubt that if Cobra, Cobra was as he was told, lots of money could be made, not only in straight win bets but in the more lucrative combination bets, e.g., picking the top-three in order – a trifecta, or picking the top-two in order – an exacta, or picking the top-two in any sequence – a quiniella. He remembered quickly that this race also featured a superfecta, picking the top-four horses in perfect order and that it was in the pick-four sequence at the track – meaning that the winners of races four, five, six, and seven would also be a factor in the betting. Cobra, Cobra could produce a gigantic return on investment for both himself and his ill-tempered associates. He became so engrossed with his calculations that he was jolted when the waitress placed his salad on the table while saying, "Salad with French on the side."

Roberts was already chomping down on his burger when Limmer became fully aware of his surroundings. But he couldn't shake himself away from his musings. "So, Larry, how sure are you of this assistant trainer? Is he a druggie or drunk?"

"Hey, no man, he's the real item. He owes me a favor. He wouldn't screw with me. But," he finished chewing and washed down the burger with a big gulp of his Pepsi, "remember, it's racing and nothing is sure. They're horses. I don't need you coming back to me and barking about you losing money."

"Have I ever done that?" Limmer asked with a hint of a smile.

"No, no. Can't say you have. But there's a first time for everything."

When Limmer returned to his mother's house he went directly to his computer and he stayed on it for a full three hours. He pulled down the records for all eight horses and studied them with great care. He found no good reason to change the handicapping odds that he had placed on the seventh race.

He then worked on the fourth, fifth, and sixth races so as to get some combos on the pick-four which, if hit, could be astronomical.

In the end, he excluded only one horse from all of the possible betting combinations, a horse from Iowa with an unknown trainer named Willis Clohessey and with a driver, Jim Benson, who should have hung up his whip and helmet ten years ago. The horse's name was Phantom Express.

The next day he called his contact in Chicago. He was suggesting a full range of bets through all of the possible combinations of $8000. The answer was, "That's a whole night of betting on basically one race. But if you think so, do it. What are you personally putting on it?"

"$2000."

"You still think that the odds will hold?"

"They'll drop a bit. But my answer is yes, pretty much so. The track is hooked up to the national network; races four and five are solid races with good horses. I think that we'll come out of this in good shape."

"Well, you're due, you know. You've been cold since you moved to Wisconsin."

"New track, new track. You have to live with these horses to really get to know them. So you're OK on this? It will clean out a big section of your account over here."

"OK, just win!"

CHAPTER XV

———◆———

"So Pat – what's on the agenda today?"

He supposed that he had surprised her. She glared at him, as she had for all those years when he had quietly opened the door to his suite and came in front of her and spoke – just short of shouting. There was a good chance that she wasn't surprised at all, that it had become a ritual between them, complete with his exclamatory approach and her feigned surprise.

"You know, one of these days I'm going to keel over from the start that you give me."

"Yeah, right. You look real scared."

She smiled as she looked at her appointment book. "Three scheduled for now. One of the appointments came in yesterday from an old student of yours, a Peter Clohessey. Familiar?"

"Sure is. I had him in class about 15 years ago. He seemed to have a natural aptitude for studies. Came from a farm family, I don't remember, maybe around Iowa City or West Branch. I wonder what he wants."

"He's not coming in. He called from Tulsa. His father is coming in." She looked down at her note, "His name is Willis. Something about a racehorse."

McAbee rubbed his chin and looked closely at Pat. "What kind of racehorse?"

"Harness," she paused, "I know."

"I didn't think that this sport would come our way again."

She gave him the rest of the schedule. He went into his office and saw five files relating to updates on cases currently under review. Before he looked at them he reflected on the last time he had become involved in a harness horse case. It had ended with Augusta Satin barely escaping being murdered by a serial killer and the unlikely ending at his house when the killer had determined that McAbee was his nemesis. Thanks to Scorpio, his neighbor Gloria, and a handy baseball bat, the case and the killer had been successfully closed off. Like many of his most dangerous cases, it had started off innocently enough only to eventuate in a close call in a highly lethal situation. He wondered what Willis Clohessey wanted with the ACJ Agency.

Clohessey wore his sixties well. White-haired, about five feet eight inches, he had a thoughtful, almost monastic, air about him. His eyes were greenish-gray, projecting a clear and steady gaze. His lips were thin and his face deeply creased as was true of a vast majority of Iowa farmers who lived a life under the sky.

"Your son. How is he?"

"He's well. He's making lots of money in the futures market. He sends his best to you. He said for me to tell you that he still works on his Greek to this day." He smiled – was it sadly?

"He was one of my best students. He could easily have gone into the classics, but he was edgy about their future. For a 22-year-old, he had a good sense of things. The classics are very vulnerable in today's colleges and even where there's some regard for them, the next administration may take aim at them. It would not be a good thing to be in your 40s and worried about whether your department would be closed down by some short-sighted and ignorant administrator."

Willis said, "Now I know where he got his insights. For a second, I thought I was listening to him."

"I think that the real question is this – is he happy?"

"I don't know. Sometimes I wonder. Maybe he was quoting you when he said he can be very happy and very poor or so-so happy and pretty rich." He gazed at McAbee and then went on, "I think that the latter best describes him."

McAbee smiled. Willis Clohessey had hit it on the head. There was no easy answer to any of life's choices. "So, I hear you have a horse?"

Willis laughed. "Yeah, I guess that's one way to put it. Let me explain my situation to you." He recounted his lifelong interest in harness horses as he edged his way to the agenda of the meeting. "I remember the case you had worked some years back. So had Peter. My assumption is this, you know something about the racing game?"

"Yes, that's a fair comment. I learned a lot from the case. I even met a few horses on my way through the case," he said lightly.

Clohessey smiled. "Here's the situation. I bought a horse last autumn at a sale in Kalona. No big deal – I only paid $800 for him; he's six years old now. If truth be told, I had an extra stall in my van, and I bought him somewhat on a whim. There's a lot of mystery around him, and I've been successful to a degree in throwing some light on his history. But then I hit a wall. It's not satisfactory. I spoke with Peter, and he recommended using your resources. I'm willing to spend $1500 to get to a few truths about him."

McAbee listened carefully to the man but felt that it all wasn't hanging together. "I'm not a numbers man, Willis, but I do know when something doesn't add up. You spent $800 for a horse, and you're willing to spend $1500 to get some information on him. I know from Peter that you guys have a great interest in history, and from that the causes of events, but the numbers don't add up." McAbee held his hands out, palms up.

"I think you will. As I said, I've been working around pacers for years. Most of them were so-so, what can I say? I had two really good ones; they both made me some serious money on the Chicago circuit. In fact, one of them helped send Peter to St. Anselm, not a cheap place, I'll tell you." His eyes emitted a flash of humor. McAbee put his hands in the air in a gesture of surrender but said nothing. Willis continued, "This horse's ability has no end that I can see. That's what brings me here. He's six, like I said, but he has never raced in a betting race. There are mysteries to him that I have to know. They've branded him a bad-luck horse. Cursed."

"Who is 'they'?"

"One of his previous trainers; but then she hung up on me. She mentioned another trainer whom she said ruined him. The horse was in a serious accident; his driver lost his leg. He was sold for dog food, but he was saved and ended up on the front end of an Amish wagon, and then came Kalona. I have a lot of pieces, but I don't know if they're from the same puzzle. I'd appreciate your help."

"$1500 won't go too far – as long as you understand that. I'll give it a full effort, you can be sure. But help me a bit. The horse hasn't raced? How do you know he's so good?"

"He qualified last week in Madison, Wisconsin. He'll be racing this Saturday – his first betting race. You'll see how good he is." Clohessey showed just a hint of pique.

McAbee said, "I wasn't calling your judgment into question. But a qualifier is a lot different from a race if I recall things correctly."

"You're right, you're right. But I think that he's ready to break out and assert himself. Oh, and by the way, when he was a yearling?"

"Yes."

"They paid $400,000 for him." He hit the desk hard with his hand and said, "How do you like that?"

McAbee didn't respond. He changed the subject back to what it was that Clohessey wanted to accomplish from his agency. "So what do you have on that pad, Willis?"

"All the names, all the dates. Everything that I have managed to gather on my own." He handed it across to McAbee who read it closely.

"As I recall, the United States Trotting Association, USTA, is the supreme record-keeping agency for harness racing," McAbee said as a half question.

"I did do some checking there, but they weren't helpful with that Roman Garzo, for example. And I don't know who put him up for sale when he was a yearling. I really want to know all these things. I'm going to treat this horse as though he was a two- or three-year-old just coming to the track. I have to know a lot of stuff because this horse has the potential to knock people's socks off."

"I have a marvelous computer man. If there's anything to be found out in that medium, he'll do it. The rest of it will involve footwork, that's where things get pricey. But I'll do my best. By the way – is this the horse's name?" McAbee pointed to the name at the head of the page.

"Yes. Phantom Express."

"You know, Willis, I have fond memories of harness racing. I met some really good people, well maybe fascinating is a better word. Their individualism is admirable. It seems to be their greatest strength and, if I may, their greatest weakness."

Willis looked across at McAbee as though weighing this remark. After a few seconds he said, "That's a pretty savvy take," he paused and then said, "Well, I guess I'll be leaving. I'll give your regards to Peter. Any words of wisdom for him?"

"Maybe just something from Socrates, 'Know thyself'."

"I'll pass it on."

They shook hands, and Willis Clohessey left his office.

Pat came to his doorway. "Are we opening a file?"

"Yeah. We are."

"Interesting guy, isn't he?"

"Yes. But it's another horse case. Remember the last one? Cassie's Ruler!"

"Don't you even think that, Bertrand."

Two days later McAbee was in Chicago with Augusta Satin. They had been summoned by a Cook County grand jury. They were both done within the hour as some new evidence was presented by the FBI to the county attorney. At that point both McAbee and Satin had only to confirm what they knew about the particular crime, which was unexceptional and incidental.

"OK, Augusta. Tell the truth. You were prepared to spend the day up here."

"Yes, that's true. Are we going to have a holiday?"

"How about driving south of Chicago to a place called Crete, Illinois?"

"Ah ... OK," she said with hesitation. "It doesn't sound like the Shangra La that I was envisioning, but I'm sure that I have it wrong."

They got into Bertrand's red Explorer Sport and buckled up. He reached across his back seat and grabbed an Illinois map, which he handed to Augusta. "Would you be kind enough?"

"Oh, that's it. I'm a navigator. And here I thought we were going on a fling."

"It is a fling. But you won't see it as such until we get to our destination. In the meantime, let me tell you about this case that I picked up two days ago. But I'll warn you, it's about harness horses and racetracks."

She glared at him. "Not funny, Bertrand. I saw the grim reaper last time we did this. Racing and me are not commodious."

McAbee picked up the edge in her voice. He was angry at himself for not anticipating the gravity of the situation. She was right; she had suffered a close call and surely tracks were not her favorite venue, even amateurish and poorly maintained farm tracks would probably stir up some bad memories. He looked over at her quickly and said, "Augusta, I'm sorry. Pretty insensitive on my part. What if I drop you off in downtown, and I'll pick you up on my way back? You have your cell?"

There was a thoughtful delay. Then she said, "To be frank, yeah, you were insensitive. But you're a man; and it's widely known that men, even the best of them, can be dopes."

She reached across and patted his shoulder gently. "But that aside, I am a professional, and I've got to get beyond the incident. So, no more. We're going down to Crete, wherever the hell that is."

He didn't say much for a few minutes. Then he took to very slowly explaining the case that came his way via Clohessey.

She responded when he finished. "I have to say that this one sounds innocent enough. But knowing you and the things that happen around you, God only knows."

He caught the shake of her head. He considered himself fortunate to have her continue with him down to Crete. He wasn't going to press his luck with some kind of comment that would renew her ire. Augusta was extremely stable, but every once in a while, especially when an emotion had spilled out, she could be volatile for a serious piece of time.

They found the farm where Betty Broder stabled. It wasn't easy when they got off of the main road and started to wind their way around Illinois' secondary and tertiary byways. Only a small lettering on a mailbox indicated that they had found Buttery Field Farm. They drove forward.

"I take it she's waiting for you?" she said with a touch of irony.

"Not a chance. I didn't even expect to come here today." He felt that Augusta was still a bit edgy and perhaps feeling that she had been manipulated. He added, "Augusta, this was on the spur of the moment. I really did think we'd be at the mercy of that grand jury for the whole day."

"Bertrand, I'm sorry. I'm being a bit of a bitch. It's just the horse-thing."

They drove up to an infield where there was a triple-barn complex on the east and a two-story frame house on the west of the property. The parallel barns were pre-fab and extended lengthwise for about 150 feet each. Directly in front of them was a warm-up track that was probably three-eighths of a mile in circumference.

They got out of the Explorer and walked toward the barns. A 50ish black man came out of the barn closest to them. He was holding a pitchfork. "Can I help you?"

"Yeah, we're looking for Betty," Augusta said.

Bertrand appreciated her quick pick up, noting to himself that she sounded like some long-lost friend of Betty.

"Next over," he nodded his head toward the next barn and went on his way.

"Bet you didn't know that Betty and I are the best of friends," she said under her breath.

They entered the long barn that was wider than it appeared from the outside. It had stalls on either side with the main door open at the back end of the barn as it was at the front. He counted at least seven figures moving about in the center aisle. Directly to their right was an office; he could hear a fax machine churning out some copy. A woman sat at the desk talking on the telephone. She looked like the boss; he concluded that it was Betty Broder. He heard her saying, "Yeah, it's surgery; and it's iffy. Your call, but I can tell you this, he's not going to be any better without it." There was an unheard response. Then she said, "Well that's the problem. He may get worse. But if he got better, he'd go up a few notches." Another delay. "OK, just let me know." She hung up and shook her head and sighed. Then she must have sensed them, because she turned quickly. She said, "Yeah, you want something?"

They came forward. Bertrand held out his hand, "Bertrand McAbee. I'm a private investigator in Iowa; and this is Augusta Satin, same."

She didn't hold out her hand to either one of them, although he noticed that she held her gaze on Augusta. He pulled his hand back.

Broder said, "Exactly what do you want?"

Augusta took the lead; "We're working for a guy who already called you, Willis Clohessey. Quite frankly, he's in a bit of anguish after he spoke with you. We know his family and told him we'd try to find out some more about a horse you trained, Phantom Express. Could we spare us a few minutes?"

Betty, eyes pressed on Augusta, said, "Sit down. Let's make this quick."

Bertrand was well aware that his role in this discussion was to keep his mouth shut and let Augusta do the work. If he had been alone, Betty probably would have used the whip on her desk on him.

"Let me start. There are mean horses. Don't ever let anyone tell you different. Maybe it's two out of every 100, but this is one of them. The son-a-bitch had an eye – he'd cast it at you. Full of hate and malice. I know that some say it's fear and that you should treat them nice and all that crap, and for most that's true, but this one – no! What caused him to be this way? He was exposed to a guy named Roman Garzo who was the yearling trainer for Jeremy Burgess. Ever hear of Burgess?"

Augusta said, "Not the tech guy?"

"Yeah! That's it. The tech guy. He has a big complex in Valdosta, Georgia, and he let this Garzo have his way with young horses. Garzo was a psycho, but I think it's likely that the colt was already prone to be mean. Between that and the Garzo treatment, the colt became a maniac. But Burgess was blind about Garzo. So, I'm sent the crazy bastard, and we learn the hard way that if he sees this," she pointed to the whip that was on her desk and for the first time in five minutes she gave a quick glance at McAbee, "he goes nuts. Had one incident with him where he ran through the backstretch and almost killed a few bystanders. When we went to qualify him, he tore off the track and smashed into a thick, metal bar at full speed. And guess who's sitting in the grandstand watching all of this – Jeremy Jesus Christ Burgess himself. Poor driver lost his leg – sued me and Burgess and took home a solid settlement. But that was it for him driving. Burgess, one mean SOB, fired me on the spot and took every horse that I had for him, a $70,000 a month account! And, some of the best horses on the track." She stopped.

It didn't take a grief counselor to know that Betty Broder was still raw from the experience. McAbee felt that Augusta needed to offer the consolation. Broder looked at him as though he was vermin. He'd try to figure that out later.

Augusta offered a response, "Wow! This is a horror story. I'm really sorry for you."

For a second it looked as though Betty would crumble. But she came around, "Yeah. It was really unfair. Burgess, Garzo, and the damn colt."

"So what happened to the colt?"

"Everyone thought he was a goner after the accident. But, there was a vet right there in the paddock area. Within 20 seconds he was on the horse, quieted him, and later that day performed surgery. But you have to know something, I was already fired by Burgess, who went berserk."

"But, do you know what happened?"

"I know some of the story. About three months later they shipped him back to Valdosta, to Garzo. He proceeded to beat him religiously until, I was told, the horse stopped on the track one day and started to drive his back feet into the cart and barely missed killing Garzo. After that nobody wanted anything to do with him. The rest is murky. I know he ended up in Pennsylvania with some sorry-assed trainer who got the message real quick-like. I understood that he had been sold to some tanners – good riddance! And now you come along, and this Clohessey, and I'm told he's racing. Hard to explain. But you tell that Clohessey that he was warned. He's dealing with a killer. This is no run-of-the-mill horse. Anything else?"

McAbee thought it was time to say something. "Why did they spend $400,000 for him?"

She looked at McAbee like he was a rat who had crawled into the barn. "Why? He had the best breeding that money could buy, that's why. Mister, if you can catch a horse from ground zero and bring him along, win with him, and then breed him, you can make up for wads of other mistakes. One star can cancel 100 mistakes. Burgess had the dough, the interest, and, he thought, the right horse. What he didn't know, I guess, is that Garzo and that horse were like TNT together." She looked back at Augusta. It was clear that Bertrand's kind of questions were dismissed after her last answer.

Betty got up. "Not much else to say."

Augusta rose also but asked, "This guy – Roman Garzo. Have you been in touch? Have you heard from him?"

"Crap! You have to be kidding me. I don't even know if the bum is alive. I do know this; Burgess finally dumped him." She thought for a minute. "Oh, I told that Clohessey-guy. If he manages to get Phantom Express on the track and he has luck with him, he better keep his eyes open. That Garzo and Phantom Express, that's like Ahab and Moby Dick, you better believe me. Nothing personal, but I hope this is the last time I see you about this matter." Now she came within a foot of Augusta and said, "But you're always welcome if you'd like to hang here." She shot Bertrand a dismissive look, after which it morphed into a look of disgust.

As they drove away Bertrand said, "I really made it on her greatest hits list."

Augusta broke into uncontrollable laughter which was intermittently replayed without warning, all the way back to Iowa across Interstate 80.

CHAPTER XVI

———◆◆———

Scott Harris called the races at Madison Downs. Considered one of the best harness track announcers in the country, he had been lured with a profit-sharing plan to Madison Downs from the Chicago circuit. He grew up in Aurora, Illinois – a far Chicago suburb, which at one time had housed a harness track before falling victim to a fire of interesting origins. If asked, he would quickly recount his infatuation with harness tracks, feeling that at the age of five, he already knew what he wanted to be as an adult, a caller of races. His father, a racing fan, agreed with this mixture of history and mythology until he died two years ago.

It was customary for Scott to arrive at the track at about 5:30 p.m., two hours before race time, at which time he would begin the memorization of every horse in each race. He was proud of his ability to do this, and he found that when questioned by most racing fans, it was their most asked query,

'How do you remember all the horses?' or 'How do you keep them apart?' He used three variables – the driver, whose colors were a constant, the pad with a number and a specific color matched to each number, and finally the pacer's name and look. Since most pacers raced once a week, he became familiar with them even though their color was usually dark brown. Some, for example, were small, some large, some had peculiar gaits, some drew the same driver week after week. With enough practice, Scott could usually look down from his booth, about 75 feet above the track surface, and identify half of the horses just by looking at them. How did he answer the fans? "Concentration and lots of pre-study." Was it true? Sure, why not?

Only one race, as it was, demanded extra attention – the seventh. This was the non-winners of one race. Some of the horses had competed previously at Madison; after all, the designation merely referred to being a non-winner. Some of the horses he had never seen before. The eight horse in that race drew his attention. He remembered the name, but he couldn't place it.

At six p.m. he called the racing secretary of the track, Phil O'Brien, an old veteran who had worked for years at Fairmont RaceTrack in Collinsville, Illinois – just outside of St. Louis. He also had been lured to the Madison track.

"Phil, this is Scott. Anything I need to know?"

"Ah, yeah," there was rustling noise, "In race two scratch the five, Holiday Transport, lame, nothing else."

"Holiday Transport? He's the lamest SOB on the track. Lame! He's been lame all his life."

"Hey, what can I do Scott?"

"Question. I'm looking at the seventh. What's the deal with this Phantom Express? Why do I think I know him?"

"Don't know that much about him. Iowa trainer. They told me that he's been injured for a long time. He's coming back."

"Was he injured in Chicago?"

"As I recall, yeah."

"If he's the one that I'm thinking of, he's crazy. I thought I recognized that name. I don't know if you noticed his bloodlines?"

"Sure did. But here's the deal on that: Holiday Transport, who you just bashed, has great bloodlines too, and he's a lame critter. If the horse is hurt or crazy, it doesn't matter what his bloodlines are."

"As usual, you're right. Call me if there are any other changes, my friend."

He made a mental note to keep an eye on Phantom Express when he came out to warm up, probably after the first and fourth races. The horse had interesting possibilities.

After the first race, a number of horses entered the track. They were warming up for future races. Bettors could ascertain who the pacers were because they would wear side pads that were color-coded to the relevant future race and numbered to the specific horse. The warm-up color for the seventh race was orange. Scott drew his binoculars and looked for the number 8 against the orange pad. He wasn't picking it up on the track. He looked over at the paddock area, then he saw him. A big, stately-looking animal crossed the pathway in the backstretch paddock and came onto the track. His ears were pinned back, and he held his head at a slight slant. His gait was perfect as one of the worst but most patient drivers on the track, Jim Benson, took Phantom Express around the oval at a slow and measured pace.

As Harris prepped once more for the coming second race he kept an eye on Benson and Phantom until they left the track in advance of his announcing the entries for the coming second race.

After the fourth race, Phantom was brought out again. Scott noticed that Benson was more aggressive with him and, in fact, he seemed to let him loose for about a quarter of a mile on the back end of the track. The horse had a command to him – a certain style, presence, that Scott liked. In all likclihood, he reflected, he'd be a big disappointment in the race, however. Some horses had a way of looking good in warm-ups but were unable to deliver in the stress of a race. Scott took his eyes off of him as the track manager brought visitors up to the booth. By the time he was finished with them, Phantom had exited from the track.

The entrants for the seventh race came out of the paddock and went across the starting line in numbered sequence as Scott called their name, their driver, their trainer, and the owner of the horse. He looked at the odds which were changing every two minutes. His eyes trailed to the eight horse that was currently, with four minutes to go, at 18 – 1. The program, which showed a pre-calculation, had him at 15 – 1.

Harris made his final survey of the entrants, comfortable that he had mastered all of the names of the horses. His screen showed there was an unusual amount of betting for this kind of race, a difficult one to handicap, after all, their being non-winners of a single pari-mutuel race. He figured that there was some 'steam' or inside information in the backstretch about these horses. Cobra, Cobra was currently showing odds of 3 – 2, but in the program he was listed at 5 – 1. But non-winner races had such nuances. Simply put, bettors did not know much about the horses, and any hint of inside information was grabbed greedily.

He saw the starting car come onto the track and position itself at about a quarter of a mile ahead of the starting line. In the distance he heard the starter saying into his microphone, "OK, let's get these horses to the gate." This was Scott's cue to bring himself to full attention. All of the horses were turned in the direction of the outstretched gate and their attention was directed to their respective numbered square on that gate.

Scott intoned, "Less than one minute to go. Get your bets down on this seventh race." Ten seconds later, the starting car began to accelerate slowly as the eight pacers found their places. "The horses are on the gate and moving to the starting line, in post-position order, one – Downer's Look, two – Doitwell, three – Sorry About It, four – The Banker's Friend, five – Cobra, Cobra, six – Jimmy Steffen, seven – Wild Bills Food, and eight – Phantom Express. And here they go, they're off! Cobra, Cobra quick to the lead, falling in behind him is Banker's Friend, then to Doitwell, to Jimmy Steffen searching for the rail but unsuccessfully. Sorry About It settles into fifth, the one horse – Downer's Look slow off the gate sixth, and Phantom Express watches them all. Wild Bills Food off-stride and out of the race. So, we're down to seven. Jimmy Steffen is now moving up to challenge Cobra, Cobra as they hit the first-quarter pole in a speedy 28 seconds flat. Cobra, Cobra is fighting Jimmy Steffen – he will not cede the lead as Doitwell pulls to the outside from the three spot and is following Jimmy Steffen, Banker's Friend drafts in second place behind Cobra, Cobra. Sorry About It pulls out and falls in behind Doitwell, third over, Downer's Look stays on the rail and behind him last is Phantom Express. Back up front, Cobra, Cobra has put away a tiring Jimmy Steffen as he hits the half mile in a blazing 56.1. He's been used heavily; can he keep it up? Doitwell now goes three wide as

Jimmy Steffen tires badly, following Doitwell is Sorry About It three-wide. Now Phantom Express to the outside follows Sorry About It. Banker's Friend is lagging in the two hole and backing up Downer's Look. Cobra, Cobra is now being challenged by Doitwell on his outside. Sorry About It fails to keep up as three-wide Phantom Express goes around him and takes up the chase as they near the three-quarter pole. It looks like a three-horse race, Cobra, Cobra at the three-quarters in a blazing 1:25 as they hit the stretch. Cobra, Cobra puts away Doitwell who is done, the only contender now is the big Phantom Express who takes the measure of Cobra, Cobra. Step by step, they're into deep stretch, now they're eyeball to eyeball, Phantom is pulling away from Cobra. A huge upset in the making as he pulls away from the field with each stride crossing the finish in a brilliant 1:54 flat, second Cobra, Cobra, third Doitwell in an extremely spread out field. I can't tell you how huge a victory this is for this six-year-old horse that has won his first pari-mutual race in this most extraordinary manner. An incredible return!"

After he announced the official finish, the payoffs on the varying betting modalities and the participants in the winning picture, he immediately called Phil O'Brien in the racing office.

"Yeah?"

"Phil, what in God's name did I just see out there?"

"I don't know either. I've haven't seen that much in my life. A six-year-old nothing! Can't get over it."

"Maybe that Iowan is feeding him some strange grain."

"No way. Clohessey is as honest as they come. I think that it's a horse that found himself all of a sudden. It happens, you know. But it's not typical. Gotta go!"

Scott Harris wrote down the payoffs for this race. 45.20 to win, 18.60 to place, 12.00 to show. The exacta paid

82.20; the quinnella 48.80, the trifecta paid 820.60, the superfecta paid 2,024.20, and the pick-four paid 3,910.40. He shook his head; a bettor could have made a nice little fortune on this race.

Kent Limmer looked down at the 63 different tickets on which he had spent $10,000. Not one of them was worth a penny. It would take him a month of solid handicapping and good luck to make up for the shattering loss that he just endured. He looked down at the winner's circle. An edgy horse stood there, looking as though he'd try to kick everyone around him into the bleachers.

Holding Phantom's bridle was the track's man, who showed up in all the pictures, doing the same damn thing. Behind the horse and sulkey was Jim Benson who had a driving average of 0.089 (run from a formula that awards 1000 points for a win, 555 points for a second, and 333 points for a third, and a zero for all other placements). He still shook his head in disbelief, a horse who had never raced until he was six, a driver with a desperately poor record, and a trainer who was a full-time farmer who in his spare time fooled around with a few pacers. Next to Benson was Clohessey, an older man who looked to be pretty smart. A smile spread across his face as they posed for the winning picture.

He wondered what would be next for this horse. Clohessey could take him up through the ranks of races, non-winners of two, then of three, then of four, then of five, then of six before having to place him in tougher races. He was a horse that would eat up the competition in all of the non-winner races at least until he got to the non-winners of five and six where the competition might catch up with him. On the other hand who could know what this animal was capable of doing? He watched Clohessey talking with Benson as they took the horse back to the paddock where he would be held in a special stall until he urinated and blood was drawn for the purposes of drug testing. Contrary to the popular perception of harness racing, there was in fact a scrupulous testing program whose intent was to keep the playing field as level as possible.

Limmer was in the process of removing from the packet of tickets his personal $2,000 of bets when he felt a heavy hand on his shoulder. He didn't need to turn around; the presence announced itself by the heaviness of the paw.

"Eight thousand, Limmer. That's not going to go down. When you separate those, give me Chicago's. Then tell me what I'm supposed to say down there." He came around from behind Limmer slowly, letting his grip release as he sat down across from him.

"Hey, how could I know? Cobra, Cobra was as good as what Roberts told me. If that Phantom Express wasn't in the race – it was ours. It's one of those things."

"Yeah? Well if you think that'll play in Chicago, it won't. Fact is if you included him in the bets you coulda made us some dough."

"I know, I know," he didn't like the facial expressions that came from across the table.

"I've been on the phone already. You're not giving me anything. I hate to tell you this. You're in trouble."

"What the hell are you talking about?"

There was a long pause before the Italian spoke, "This isn't personal, Limmer. It's business. Here's the deal, straight from Chicago," he looked hard at Limmer, "You've got a week to make it up, all 8,000, or else."

"Or else what?"

He made a few fists, his huge hands bulging with potential malevolence, "Doesn't need to be said, Limmer. Just make it up." He got up and took the tickets that Limmer had pushed across to him.

"I can't believe this. Hey, it's a chance game. Sometimes you take a bath," he stopped talking – the moron was out of voice-range, his huge back ascending upwards to the betting floor.

Kent Limmer began to sweat profusely. His world was shaken. Could he cover $8,000? Sure. But it would damage his finances. Furthermore, he could never again bet for the thugs, and that was a pretty good source of unreported income, that being their various tips, for successful bets. Even if they wanted him to continue on, he wouldn't. The contract was broken as far as he was concerned.

When the advance sheets came out for the following Saturday, sure enough, Phantom Express was in race two, the condition of the race being non-winners of two. He scanned the field; Phantom Express racing out of the three hole would destroy that crew. He estimated in his head that he would be bet down to something like 1:5, in effect returning 40 cents of profit for a two-dollar bet. There was only one way to win in a race of this nature, and that was for Phantom Express to lose, to not show up in the top three. With that kind of knowledge, a bettor would score huge dividends as the odds would be skewed badly. In addition, the second race was the back end of the daily double. If he could exclude Phantom from consideration, he figured that huge profits could be made on the double.

His decision to call Fred Larkin was dictated by necessity. Clohessey, he reasoned, had cost him a small fortune; now Clohessey could return him to a state of balance.

Larkin was an ex-con who had already done two sessions at Fort Madison Prison in Fort Madison, Iowa, which was the heavy-duty Iowa prison on the shore of the Mississippi River in southeastern Iowa. He was a small-time thug, stupid beyond compare, a man without a hint of reserve or reflectiveness. He knew of Larkin because of their mutual relationship with a Michigan guy that Limmer had grown up with, Tom Presley. It was from a call to Presley that he got Larkin's address and telephone number as well as the analysis of his being a dangerous moron.

They met in a bar in downtown Galena, Illinois, a town that aspired to be a suburb of Chicago even though their mutual distance comprised two hours of lousy road conditions.

The agreement was simple enough. "I'll give you $250 to scare the hell out of this guy. The only message is this, hold back that horse; he can't finish in the top three. This is a one-time only thing. I want you to punch the SOB once, then take off. If he does what he's told, I'll give you another $250. It's that simple, but don't leave him 'til he says OK. Tell him this; it's not just him, but his damn horse also. They'll both end up cripples!"

Larkin shook his head and consented. He passed $250 across the table to him as he tried once again to count the number of distinct scars on the face, hands, and head of this head-shaven, tattooed moron. He stopped at 21, positive that a dermatologist with high intensity lighting could easily triple that number. When the moron left, Limmer, in a rare act of self-examination, was alarmed by the events that had unfolded over the last five days. He was worried that things could easily fall apart on him. After all, the use of muscle was not part of his repertoire.

He remembered the picture in the winner's circle. He could have sworn that the damn horse had caught his eye. It gave him the chills. Well, time would tell.

CHAPTER XVII

Roman Garzo was indeed alive. After Burgess had fired him, he had stumbled on numerous paths while trying to recover his esteem. With his savings as an anchor he had bought a half ownership in a Dairy Queen in Ocala, Florida. It bankrupted in six months. His partner sued, contending that Garzo did not fulfill his end of the commitment in attendance and oversight. Furthermore, he argued, that when present Garzo demonstrably alienated the customer base with his rude and intimidating conduct. The outcome of the trial was against Garzo who had declared bankruptcy. A judgment of $75,000 was still out there, however.

Garzo went south into Florida and became a property manager for a large condominium complex in Vero Beach. That job lasted for four months before the vociferous complaints of the residents forced a change. Garzo was told "to read Dale Carnegie and take a charm-school class" by his supervisor who found that his three-month-old Lexus had $10,000 worth of damage to it the next morning. The cops couldn't make a case, "Garzo's firing may only have been coincidental," they said.

His stay with the ground crew for the Florida Marlins baseball team lasted for less than a month. The reason for this dismissal was seen by him as another example of "American Phoniness". Why did he have to pretend to like people?

It was hardly surprising, then, that he found his way back to harness racing by hooking up with a trainer at Pompano Downs in Pompano Beach, Florida. He was one of two assistant trainers for a stable of 47 horses. He had known the head trainer for years, having maintained a passable relationship with him. He had held the job for 18 months and lived modestly in one of the dorms that existed in the backstretch.

The fact was that Roman Garzo was deeply conflicted. The unholy trinity of Jeremy Burgess, Betty Broder, and Fidel Diaz was united by a common theme of hatred and anger. He knew the toll that the events had taken on him. His soul ached from the takedown that he had experienced. He strongly believed that retaliation and compensation were necessary for a balancing of the scales of justice. This was offset by his requirement for opportunity; he concluded that if these entities crossed his path and gave him a clear shot, he would take it. Otherwise, he would wait. He thought back to Phantom Express and wished mightily that he still lived so that he could torment this hard-luck and vicious horse. His passage to the tannery in Pennsylvania was too easy and too unsatisfying.

He had finished his stable duties at Pompano when he went into the horseman's kitchen. He bought some lunch along with copies of the *Daily Racing Form* and *Sportseye*, and he sat down in the cafeteria. He would study the *Form* and probably place a few bets on some thoroughbred races at the off-track betting windows that Pompano Downs supported. He then opened *Sportseye*, devoted to harness racing. In it he was confronted with a brief article on page five of the newspaper. Garzo read in shocked silence.

Something Wrong Here?
- Six-year-old Pacer
- First Pari-mutual Race
- Destroys Field in 1:54 in Madison

Trainer Willis Clohessey bought Phantom Express, an injured and high-spirited pacer for $800, at an obscure auction in the Amish town of Kalona, Iowa. With bloodlines to kill for, he was purchased as a yearling by Jeremy Burgess for $400,000 in Harrisburg, Pennsylvania. When contacted, Burgess had no comment. Records show a spotted past and a mammoth injury had befallen the colt as a two year old. Given up on – he was pulling Amish buggies some months ago. Clohessey bought him on a whim. Now he has on his hands a potential barnburner that in his first race last Saturday came off the pace to obliterate a field of maiden pacers at Madison Downs. Was it a fluke? Clohessey said in response, "Something tells me the fun is just beginning." We'll keep an eye on this story.

Garzo stared at the paper for several minutes. His left hand started to shake. He got up and walked speedily toward his room, blinded by a huge headache. For a few moments he was fearful that he was having a stroke. When he slammed his door shut, he reached for an unopened bottle of Jim Beam. He filled up an eight-ounce plastic cup and gulped it down in two draws. He poured the same amount again, but now he took to sipping. He sat on the cot and tried to sort out the extraordinary range of emotions that he was experiencing.

Jeremy Burgess was in the midst of a meeting at pretty much the same time but a day earlier. His secretary, Mary, passed him a note that read, '*Sportseye* reporter wants to speak with you. Important she says.'

Burgess turned to his chief operating officer and whispered, "Take over for me, Barney, just for a few minutes." He left the room and said to his secretary, "Put me through to the reporter, did he say what he wanted?"

"It's a she, and no," she responded tersely.

Within a minute Burgess was speaking with Lisa Green. "What can I do for you, Ms. Green?"

"Thanks for taking my call, Mister Burgess."

"I have made it a point to assist the racing industry in any way possible."

"A story has come my way. I'd like your comments."

"What's the story?" He was mentally processing hundreds of possibilities.

"You owned a colt once by the name of Phantom Express according to records kept by the USTA." She let the question/comment hang there in the very best of Valley speak.

What she didn't know was the painful look that crossed his face. Quickly guarded, thinking that perhaps the legless driver was advancing some other kind of lawsuit against his deep pockets he stated stonily, "Ms. Green, I'll have no comment until you give me the full story behind your question."

She cleared her throat quickly. "That wasn't a question, sir. That's a matter of public record. Just needing your reaction really," again with the Valley ending.

"I'm waiting," he said abruptly. He rapped his fingers on his desk, aware that he had upped the hostility between them unnecessarily. He urged himself to soften his tone.

"Records indicate that he was sold to a man named David Meacham in Pennsylvania, and then the trail ended," uplifting the sentence ending.

"Go ahead," he said in a softer tone.

"Sir, if you'd like I'll take you off the record. I'm just trying to validate my facts. I won't quote you without your permission."

"OK. Off the record. He was sold to someone in Pennsylvania. He'd never race again; and the name Meacham I just don't know. The whole thing was done way beneath me. But as I recall this man thought that perhaps the maniac colt could make it in the lower claimers in small tracks like Pocono Downs and some of the other tracks in Pennsylvania. I think he bought him for three cents on the dollar or something like that. Is this about the driver? Chicago qualifiers?"

"No, no," finally she dropped the Valley-speak inflection.

"OK, so just where are you going with this? The horse is long dead, bad luck to the end."

"Dead?"

"Yes, indeed. I was told that he was put on the kill truck for food processing. Why did you say dead in the way you did?"

She didn't answer right away. "He's not dead, sir. That's why I'm calling you. In fact, he's alive, well, and racing."

"No, no. You have the wrong horse. Phantom Express," he articulated carefully.

"Exactly," she said.

"He'd be six by now. Can't be the same horse."

"Look, Mister Burgess. I'm not calling to cause you pain. Last Saturday night he raced in Madison, Wisconsin, his first pari-mutual race."

Burgess was stunned into silence and a slowly rising anger. This could be a source of embarrassment. "Go ahead, how did he do?"

"He won. He beat a three-year-old who's a potential stakes horse called Cobra, Cobra. One minute-fifty-four seconds flat," she said with a aggravating touch of glee.

Was she having sport with him? "And why exactly are you calling me about this?"

"My records indicate that you paid $400,000 for him. I was wondering about the whole thing, given that you apparently felt he was dead and all."

"As is true during this whole conversation, I have no comment. That status still controls. If I will ever comment, I'll make sure to call you." He hung up.

He buzzed his secretary.

"Yes, sir?"

"Get Fidel Diaz down in Valdosta. It's important. I want him. NOW!"

In two minutes Diaz was on the phone. "Fidel, Phantom Express! Tell me all that you know."

He was breathing hard. "Sorry, sir. I was in another barn. Well, not much to say ..."

"Fidel, excuse me? There's a lot to say; open up and be frank with me."

Diaz's voice went up a few pitches. "When you looked into the Chicago catastrophe, you let go of Betty Broder but not before she had told you about Garzo. You took Garzo's side for awhile, at least you kept him on until you confirmed that he was not a good trainer. Then you chucked him and gave me the job. Phantom Express was one of many horses that Garzo ruined in my opinion."

"Phantom Express! Tell me what you know. When he was shipped back to Valdosta?"

"They held him in Chicago for about three months. They almost euthanized him. When he got back here we just let him sit for a few more months. Garzo decided to bring him back, and that was when Garzo was almost killed. Not long after, Garzo was let go, but he had already sold the colt in Pennsylvania. Last time I heard, Phantom Express was used as belt leather and Alpo."

"Well, let me tell you how goddamn wrong you are." Burgess went on to relate his interview with Lisa Green. "Whose decision was it to sell him?"

"It wasn't mine. As soon as Garzo barely escaped those kicking back feet, he ordered the sale. The details of the sale had already been worked out when you came down here and fired him. The only thing I had to do with this was to help load Phantom into the van that came for him. I can't believe that he's back. How did that happen?"

"Are you sure that was the extent of your involvement?"

"Yes sir, absolutely."

"Damn that Garzo! If you're called about this, you don't know anything. Understand?"

"Yes, sir."

Burgess hung up. In his heart he knew that Fidel Diaz was hardly responsible for the events that had transpired. It was his own continuing and prolonged bad judgment about Roman Garzo that was the real issue.

As to the metamorphosis of Phantom Express, he was concerned. He would have his lawyers speak with Meacham in Pennsylvania. After all, if the horse was intended to go to the renderers, that's where he should have gone. It wouldn't be the first time that an embarrassing mistake was off-loaded from the butchers. It was not good for his reputation that such a horse would cause him to be made a fool of by other trackmen. And then there was that whole Wall Street buzz around him wasting his energies and money in such a difficult industry.

Betty Broder sat in her office two days after Phantom Express crushed the field in Wisconsin. She murmured to herself that she seemed to spend half her days keeping accounts, processing bills, and speaking with owners about their damn horses. She heard a knock on her door, and as she looked up the huge presence of Nils Johannsen covered her doorway.

"Betty, sit back. I've got a story for you. You haven't forgotten Phantom Express, have you?" He pulled up a seat across from her.

"No, I have not only not forgotten him, but I had two gumshoes in here last week asking about him for some sorry-assed guy in Iowa who's trying to train him. What about it? He kill someone?"

"Well," he said ponderously, "he raced in Madison the other night, you know."

"Yeah? You have a shoe to drop, Nils?" she asked suspiciously, turning away fully from her computer screen and looking at Nils.

"Sure do. The sucker trounced the non-winners of one field in 1:54. Heard it from Johnny Puckett who saw the race. Came off the pace and ripped up the field in the stretch."

"I can't believe this, Nils. This is incredible. That mother shouldn't even be alive!"

He pushed his arms and hands forward in a futile and pleading gesture. "I know, I know. Just wanted to give you a heads up on this. It's the kind of story that some paper or magazine may pick up on, you know. Course, we both knew that he had potential, even though he was awfully crazy."

"That doesn't help me. Eventually – they'll come back if they do a story and talk about me – screwing up. I don't like this one bit. I honestly thought when you brought up his name that he probably had crippled that idiot in Iowa," she paused, "now I'm looking like the idiot." She shook her head in exasperation. "Best thing that could happen to me is if he crashes another gate and kills himself. And think about it, some goofy small-time farmer in Iowa, going to look like a hero!"

Nils got up, "I know, Betty, life's not fair. The jerks always seem to win, don't they?"

She didn't respond to his comment. "Well, when those two privates came around, I warned them about Roman Garzo. If he's still alive and that freak finds out about the colt, be careful. And Burgess, he's not all he seems to be. Let me tell you. He can be mean."

Nils left, making no further comment.

CHAPTER XVIII

It wasn't the same Willis Clohessey who came to McAbee's office on that Thursday afternoon. Pat remembered him from the week before; and when she told Bertrand that he was fazed and visibly demoralized, Bertrand didn't know what to make of it. He had heard that the horse had won after listening to his answering machine on Monday morning, two days after the race. Willis Clohessey was exultant, but he still wanted McAbee to stay active. McAbee had been all of that through his engagement of Barry Fisk's nimble PC fingers.

And truly, Clohessey was all that Pat had indicated that he was. Clohessey's white hair was ruffled, his posture stooped, and peeking through his high-necked shirt were some contusions around his throat and neck. He seemed to have aged ten years.

"Willis, please come into my office."

"Thanks for seeing me on such short notice," he said unsteadily, his voice projecting a raspy edge. He sat where Bertrand had pointed, at a round table with four seats.

"Willis, forgive me, but you don't look good. What's wrong?" Bertrand asked solicitously.

"My voice has been damaged a bit. Do you have water?"

McAbee had Pat bring in a bottle and glass. Nothing was said until Willis took several deep swallows. Clohessey seemed to him to be the prototypical Iowan farmer. Conversation took place slowly and over due course. McAbee forced himself to constrain his impatience. Clohessey would speak when he would speak. It was his meeting, his show.

After a few more short drinks of the water, Clohessey went on, "You heard my message ... about Phantom Express." McAbee nodded. "I'll tell you that I am so proud of him. I have never had this kind of horse," his sad visage, however, belied the content of what he was saying. He took in more water. "He came out of the race unscathed. A marvelous animal." He stopped speaking.

McAbee conjectured that perhaps the horse turned vicious, thinking of what Betty Broder had said about his being a nasty animal. But he steeled himself from commenting, reminding himself that it was a Clohessey meeting.

"I called Madison yesterday morning to see if the non-winners of two races had filled for Saturday night. It had, and Phantom drew the three hole in a field of nine. I see no reason why he can't repeat what he did last Saturday."

"I imagine not," Bertrand said.

"This morning a car came onto my farm. My back is up a bit as it stops; I don't see many stray cars. But I'm neighborly. I waited for the driver to get out. He walked toward me – a large guy, thick shouldered, empty-eyed. He says, 'You Clohessey?' Right there, the way he said that, I should have taken off for the house. But I didn't." He drained his glass and filled it again from the bottle. "I was standing next to the barn door; I just had poured some fresh water, in fact, for the horses. He stretched out his right arm and pressed me against the barn, hands squeezed my throat." He pulled down his shirt collar. McAbee saw the full range of the contusions around his throat and neck area. "He slapped me on the face and told me to listen to him."

Bertrand stood up and came around to Willis, patting him on the shoulder. "Willis, I'm so sorry. Tell me the rest." He sat down next to Clohessey who took a further gulp of water.

"He told me that Phantom was not to finish in the top three on Saturday night. If he did, that he'd kill me and he'd cripple the horse. He threw me down on the ground and kicked me in the kidneys and then he left." He stopped speaking for more than two minutes, while he sipped water and stared off at some spot in McAbee's office. "To be honest with you, I have no stomach for this, Bertrand. I'm thinking of scratching the horse. I'm too old to fight this kind of thuggery. As a young man, I trained in Chicago. That's a tough place, but I never ran into any of this. It's unbelievable."

Bertrand patted his arm. "You're with my agency now, Willis; we can help. Let's just stay on this if you would." Clohessey nodded. "Had you ever seen this man before?"

"No. I'm sure, no."

"Tell me. What was he driving?"

"A Ford Taurus, beige. I have the first three letters, there were three remaining, I couldn't get them." He reached into his right pants' pocket and pulled out a scrap of paper. "KLB blank blank blank."

"That's great, Willis. That will really help. The car, anything else about it?"

"Ah, no."

"Stay with me for a minute. Dents, scratches, tires, windshield?"

"Can't remem ... hold it – yes – he had a sign on the passenger door. I couldn't read it, but it was painted, reddish paint, three or four lines. No hubcaps either, at least not on the passenger-door side."

McAbee let the conversation sit for a bunch of seconds before resuming, "That'll help a lot. Tell me more about the man; close your eyes, Willis. Just relax and think. I know it's unpleasant."

"Stained teeth, uneven. Needed a shave. He was so thick through the middle. A weight lifter? Brown eyes, eyebrows were joined. About five feet ten. That's the best I can do."

"Clothes?"

"T-shirt, blue jeans, and boots."

"T-shirt? Anything on it?"

"Yeah, but I can't remember, I just can't remember."

"Ink color?"

"Sorry, Bertrand. Can't get it."

"You're doing great, don't get down on yourself. About what he said?"

"I think I told you everything."

Bertrand stopped the interrogation momentarily. "Willis, have you seen a doctor?"

"No. I think that it'll go away. There is some blood in my urine, that I'll watch. If it continues tomorrow, I will. That worries me. His kick really got me good."

Again, McAbee placed a long silence between them. "Let me get back to what he said. Did he give you a reason for wanting him to finish out of the money?"

"Uh ... yes. Yes, he did. He said something to the effect that I cleaned them out last week. Now it's time to replace what I had taken, that's it."

McAbee tried for a long time to gather further information but to no avail. Willis Clohessey had given him everything that he could, at least for the moment.

"I'm going to call my computer man, Barry Fisk. He's been working with some of the information that I got from Betty Broder. Let's see what that brings, OK?"

"Sure. But before you call him. You remember telling me that she said that he was a bad-luck horse?"

"Yes."

"Don't you think it's odd? I mean, everything about him seems to bring hard luck like she said."

Bertrand McAbee was not a believer in such Delphic pronouncements. Thus, he said nothing. However, on an occasional day he would concede that some entities in creation weren't in for a good time, in fact, they were consistently in for a bad time. He answered neutrally, "He does seem to draw some bad cards. I'll be back in a minute, Willis."

He went out to Pat and said, "Pat, try to get Barry on the phone, and inform him that he'll be on the speaker phone with Willis Clohessey who has just this morning been beaten up and is quite shaky. Impress on him that I don't need any crap from him."

Two minutes later his phone buzzed. It was Pat. She said, "He's on the line. Your speaker phone isn't on?"

"Not yet."

"When I went through with what you said, he was insulted. Says that he's always nice. I almost dropped the phone. Anyway, he'll be on his best behavior – yuck, yuck, yuck."

McAbee turned on his speakerphone and said, "Hi Barry." Before Barry could say anything he continued, "Willis, why don't you come over here by my desk. I'll introduce you to the best computer man I know. Barry, this is Willis Clohessey. Willis, this is Barry Fisk." There were muted hellos.

"So Barry, have you managed to get anything for us?"

"Yes," he said crankily.

"We're listening."

Fisk gave a detailed account of Jeremy Burgess and his entry into harness racing. He was probably the single most prolific spender in the sport. However, from what Fisk could uncover, the $400,000 payout for Phantom Express was his biggest single mistake in his history, not that costly errors didn't cluster around a number of his choices, as well as a series of shrewd and prescient decisions. As to Roman Garzo, his story was spotty. He was known to have just dropped off the face of the map for a while only to re-appear. He was a man living in the underground economy; but he would, on occasion, come up for air. He had been arrested on four occasions, but never once had he been convicted. Drunken driving, felonious assault, on two occasions, and one charge of theft had all fallen by the wayside. Currently, he was attached to a barn in Pompano Park, Florida, coming back into the mainline economy for another breath of air.

As to Phantom Express, he had extensive surgery done on him after his accident. There was a sale made by Jeremy Burgess Holdings to a Pennsylvania trainer. Somehow, the horse's papers continued on until Willis Clohessey picked up the horse in Kalona. Clohessey had to pay a fine for the privilege of renewing the horse's outdated paper trail, but as Clohessey knew, he had done so.

Bertrand then told Fisk what had happened to Willis Clohessey, relaying to him the information about the license plate. But he drew a sharper bead on what had happened at Madison Downs last Saturday night. "Someone apparently took a huge hit on the race or races last Saturday. It seems that same person is the one who is taking aim at Willis. Can you fish around on their networks?"

"Sure, I'll give it a try, but it may be hard. Not so much to get their records, but to smell out who the losing bettor is. But sometimes they have privileged bettors who use a card that's tied to a name. If that is the case, then maybe I can get something."

"What does that mean?" Bertrand asked.

"If you bet such-and-such an amount, you are registered in their computer system, you get a free sweatshirt and so on. Of course, in the meantime, they've probably taken your shirt and pants in the process, " he laughed and hung up.

Willis Clohessey had left McAbee's office determined to keep Phantom Express in the race and to keep his eyes open when in Madison. But McAbee was uneasy through Thursday night, and by Friday morning he decided to show up on Saturday night at Madison, unannounced. To his joy, he convinced Augusta that a night at the races would be fun. He drove to Augusta's renovated house in the heart of Rock Island's Historic District, which comprised a five-square block of restored houses from the nineteenth and early twentieth centuries. Close to downtown Rock Island it was considered to be one of the nappiest neighborhoods in the Quad Cities. Augusta had performed a miracle on her colonial-styled home. Its powder blue exterior with black trimming, especially effective on the shutters, and white picket fence always transported Bertrand backwards in time. He wondered whether a person from 1910, looking just at that house alone, would feel that time had never passed. It was her pride and joy.

She came out of the house as he pulled up in front. She was wearing a red, short-sleeved, cotton blouse that caught her snug fitting tan Capri pants at the waist. She had on a heavy gold chain that hung a few inches down from her throat and some large looped golden earrings. As usual, she took his breath away. When she entered the Explorer only then did he notice that she carried a black windbreaker that she casually tossed into the back seat. "We're off to the races!" she said.

During the three-and-a-half hour drive to Madison which McAbee figured would find them there at about six p.m., he gave her a thorough review of all that he knew.

After which she said, "Funny thing about this case. It seems to take on an edge the more you get into it. What do you expect from tonight?"

"He won't throw this race. If the horse is as good as he thinks that he is – he'll probably win. It's possible that someone may try to go after him. I can see that you're wearing your fighting clothes, so I guess that I can relax."

"Hey, Bertrand," she said teasingly, "I thought we were on a date. You never told me that I'd be getting into a fight. You're such a romantic guy. You take me to the races and tell me to get ready to mix it up. You sound like some of my old boyfriends."

McAbee laughed at her feigned outburst. "Don't worry, I'll protect you. Just take off that big hunk of gold that you have draped around you and swing it. They'll run for the hills. By the way, is there a gold mine under your house? Looks like it weighs a ton."

"It doesn't and don't try touching it. I know all about you tricky white men who look for excuses to touch auxiliary assets."

"God! Can't get anything over on you."

"You just leave hanging things be – Mistah!" she said in her most exaggerated way.

McAbee loved the banter that he and Augusta tossed around. But deep down he knew that there were serious feelings afoot for both of them. The verbal ping-pong merely served as a classic defense mechanism through which they could handle what was there and correspondingly avoid handling what was there.

They pulled in the parking lot at Madison Downs at 5:50 p.m. The place smelled new, escaping the seediness for now that some older tracks, deferring maintenance, had fallen to. He bought two programs, and they headed out to the track apron where they saw on the finely graveled track a number of horses being warmed up, especially those in the earlier races that would begin at 7:30 p.m.

He found the warmup color for the second race and then looked for it – blue pads with the number three – Phantom's number for that race. At first he didn't see that number on any horse, although he did see several blue-padded horses in that non-winners of two race.

He felt the tug on his arm first, then the comment from Augusta, "Bertrand, there he is, second race, three. Wow, he's beautiful. An athlete."

It was McAbee's first sight of Phantom. He was caught by the horse's watchfulness – as though he was a General picking up all of the conditions on the field of battle. "Yes, he's really something."

They watched him warm up for about five minutes until he was taken off the track. At this point it looked as though he was anxious to race. McAbee saw no sign of Willis Clohessey who was presumably in the paddock watching over his horse. They went into the grandstand. Each of them ordered a bratwurst, which they ate in the bleacher area off to the side of the main apron area of the track.

At seven p.m. *The Star Spangled Banner* was played as people stood around in varying displays of bad posture and inattention. Unlike baseball and football games where there was a semblance of decorum, it was imperceptible here.

The first race ended with a tight finish that had three horses coming across the finish line with barely a yard separating them. "OK, Augusta, are you going to bet on the second race?"

"You better believe it. I'm putting fifty on Phantom to win. I don't fool around, you know."

"Fifty? Where are you getting that kind of money?" he asked lightly.

"From the sky. I find fifties in my lawn every morning."

"I'll do the same, but if he loses it'll be a tough drive for you on the way home."

"And, when he wins?"

"I don't know what I'll do. I guess I'll have to praise you."

"More like it, Mistah!"

After they placed their bets they went to the rail as the horses were announced by Scott Harris. McAbee noticed that Phantom was at even odds, 1:1. Only one other horse was drawing serious money, Thumbnail, who had the one post. As the race was beginning, with the horses on the gate, he noticed that Phantom was still at 1:1 while Thumbnail was at 3:1. All of the others were 10:1 or over. If a bettor knew that Phantom would fail, significant amounts could be made. He wondered just exactly who was going to be set adrift after this race.

The race started, and Thumbnail took the lead easily. Phantom Express patiently got away fifth on the rail. No one was caught on the outside as the horses began their single-line move around the first, long turn of the one-mile track. The first quarter was slow according to Harris at 29.1. Moving now to the long straightaway there still didn't seem to be any attack being made on Thumbnail. McAbee was concerned that if he wasn't pressed Thumbnail could steal the race by setting such a slow time that he would be uncatchable in the last half of the race, his energy being intact. Then he saw Phantom pull out of fifth place and begin to mount an assault. If he was trying to draw out any horse in front of him for giving him cover or drafting possibilities, he wasn't succeeding. They were content to stay on the rail. Almost on top of the half-mile marker now, Phantom's nose had moved up to the outside of the back tire of Thumbnail's bike who had gone across the half mile at 58.2. It was a somewhat slow half and presumably Thumbnail could open up and fly with Phantom on the outside having to take lots of extra steps as they entered the huge second turn of the track.

Phantom was slowly gaining on Thumbnail as they flew through the third quarter of the race in 27.3 for a three-fourths of a mile in 1:26 flat. Harris' voice picked up intensity as the field now straightened out in the stretch. Even to McAbee's relatively naive eye, it was a race between these two horses as Phantom was now even with Thumbnail whose driver was resorting to his whip while Phantom's driver used only his lines to urge him forward. When they hit the sixteenth pole, Phantom seemed to understand that the time had come because he dug down and drew away from Thumbnail who was no quitter, but had just met a superior horse. Phantom tore across the finish line, winning by a solid five lengths. The final quarter was a very fast 27.2 for a winning time of 1:53.2.

As Phantom was slowed and turned at the first quarter pole to be returned to the winner's circle for the picture ceremony, McAbee noticed that Willis Clohessey was being driven to the winner's circle from the paddock on a golf cart. McAbee went up to the fence and looked at Clohessey who had moved off the cart and went toward Phantom. "Bertrand – get up here for this picture. Please."

McAbee made a dismissive gesture.

"No, I insist. And bring your friend."

After the picture Willis said, "Why don't you two get on this cart and come back with me."

"This is Augusta, Willis, my best investigator."

Willis looked at her and smiled. They shook hands as the cart headed back to the paddock. Willis acted like an excited kid.

CHAPTER XIX

Augusta sensed that Bertrand had become anxious. His attention shifted toward Willis even as he kept a seemingly admiring eye on the horse that paced off ahead of the golf cart as they all returned to the racing paddock.

She overheard him say, "Willis, has anything happened since we spoke?"

"No."

"Have you seen the guy around?"

"No," Willis looked at McAbee in a way that suggested, perhaps, that he wasn't safely out of Madison yet.

She estimated that Willis Clohessey was a close-mouthed Iowa farmer. When she had first run into the type she was inclined to think of them as being slow-witted – a reflection of her Chicago Southside upbringing where success was predicated on verbal quickness and a certain audacity of manner. Her undertaking of studies at DePaul University had given her a chance to sit back and study the white man. As she found with her own African-Americans, they range through the spectrum of personality types. Every race, every nationality, every religion, et cetera, had its good ones and nasty ones, its smart ones and dumb ones, and so on. But Iowa farmers? She had never met one while at DePaul. That came when she finished her degree at Augustana College in Rock Island, Illinois, and when she took on work with McAbee's ACJ Agency. Willis Clohessey was no idiot, the look in his eye told her that. Underestimating him could be a rank mistake.

They got off the golf cart. Willis said, "Phantom has to be brought to the spit box for a urine and blood sample. Stick around and meet him. In the meantime, I'll get you a visitor's pass. They don't look kindly on unregistered visitors. Just sit over there under the TV and look like horse owners. The guards shouldn't bother you." He left.

"Interesting place," Bertrand said without looking at her.

She was presently in a circumstance where McAbee did not appeal to her. He had a way of retreating into another world, as though he was now two men in one. In the one world, he would go through the motions with her, making small talk but barely listening to her answers. She reasoned that if she said 'I'm having a heart attack' in a normal tone of voice he'd say 'OK, you do that' or 'Good, I'm glad you're enjoying it'. The other part of him was unreachable. It was as though he was hearing some far off voice or that a part of him was being lifted into a spaceship where he would ascertain needed information.

The bottom line for Augusta was that she felt as though she was reduced to an object, to something that was just there, like a car bumper or some sort of inanimate object. But she caught herself. Even if some of her thoughts were accurate reflections on how she felt, McAbee wasn't this way often, and when he was it was because he was on a case. But she had to admit, she wanted to give him a good elbow in the ribs to bring him out of the trance in which he was thoroughly ensconced.

Willis came up to the two of them. "You'll have to put these stickers on some part of your clothes. They will keep the guards off your case." He handed each of them a two-by-three-inch label that had stamped on it 'Registered Visitor'. They each removed the backing. Bertrand posted his on his short-sleeve golf shirt over his right breast. She placed hers over the left pocket of her Capri pants.

She said, "This OK?"

Willis said, "Sure. Why don't we go back to the spit box and see if any progress has been made on Phantom."

Augusta asked, "Why do they call it a spit box?"

Willis responded, "A long time ago, before blood and urine samples, they took saliva samples. The stall is the box; the saliva is spit."

Bertrand got up slowly. She gathered that something was still gnawing at him. Finally, he asked Willis, "Did you ever hear of a guy named Kent Limmer?"

"Can't say I have."

That name had been brought up during the trip to Madison. Barry Fisk had pierced the betting software. Apparently, he had tracked down the frequent bettor lists, matched the amounts bet by them the last Saturday night and had deduced that Limmer had exposed himself to a $10,000 loss over all the races that Phantom Express had a part in relation to betting. He wasn't positive, but Kent Limmer fit the profile. The dummy who beat up Willis Clohessey had said too much, which made it just enough to finger Limmer.

Mole that he was, Fisk zeroed in on Limmer, eventually pulling down his phone records. He was still on them as Bertrand and Augusta headed up to Madison.

McAbee said after a few seconds, "I think that he's the man who took some heavy betting losses last Saturday. All of his bets floated around your race. He included every horse except for Phantom. He uses a betting-premium card, so we know how he bet. By doing that he saved himself a few hundred dollars, but ended up losing $10,000. We can't be positive about him, but it sure seems likely."

"If he bet against me again, I guess I'm in trouble."

"My computer guy is going to try to hack into the system to see if his frequent bettor number shows up again relative to your race. If it does, it's more and more conclusive as to whom he is."

Willis looked back to McAbee. "You and Augusta are pretty darn good. I wouldn't want to get on the wrong side of you."

They reached the spit box. Within a few seconds a woman came out with about a cup of urine. She said, "He's done. He's yours."

Willis turned around and looked intently at the two of them. "I'm taking him out of here to wash him down and then walk him until he's dry, and then I'm going back to West Branch. You can watch and then you can walk with me. That OK?"

"Sure," Bertrand said. He never checked with Augusta. It was a nicety. But it wouldn't happen while he was in this other world.

Clohessey went into the stall and retrieved Phantom Express. He was a noble giant. Augusta noticed his flawless conformity, a remarkable animal that was now led to the backstretch. Clohessey soaped and then hosed him off. The horse, with ears back, kept an eye on Clohessey. She and McAbee stood away and watched them both carefully.

McAbee's cell phone went off. He said, "Hello Barry. Anything?"

He listened for a few minutes. There was no effort on his part to speak. His eyes took on a vacant look as they fastened on to, what appeared to be, a roof beam. He said, "So, totals."

He listened again. "Sounds like a sure thing, doesn't it?"

After another silence Bertrand asked, "How's his call list?" Another silence, then "OK. Whenever you get it, just call. Thanks for everything." He disconnected.

Clohessey spoke to the horse. "OK big boy, let's take it easy. Augusta and Bertrand, please stay along his flank and never get behind him, never." The clop of the horse's shoes sounded on the backstretch dirt as Willis led him away and onto still another path. The warm air and the quiet of this part of the backstretch were pleasant to Augusta, who noticed that McAbee was walking beside her with a puzzled look. He was in a state of disharmony. She'd just have to wait him out. All of the dots were not yet connected.

McAbee observed the big horse take casual, long steps, his musculature stretching with seeming effortless motion. He had dealt with pacers a few years back when he had stumbled onto a serial killer. He knew that some horses could look ungainly but race with the heart of a lion, and some horses could look high quality and race with a pea-sized heart. This horse appeared to have the two great attributes together, a magnificent visage and a fierce heart.

But apparently there was more to this animal. He seemed to have a dark side. Some of the information that had come through hinted at a potential killer – a horse who would hurt himself in order to bring down an imagined enemy. But there were also suggestions that perhaps his imagined enemies were actually all too real.

As they walked, he asked Willis, "Is he as dangerous as some of them say?"

Willis looked back, slowed his walk, and said, "He is dangerous. No doubt about that. But he's dangerous because he's scared. He's not dangerous because that's the way he was born or something like that."

"Betty Broder seemed to see him that way."

There was a long silence. "She's a track trainer. She sees an animal, and he's a purse. They're almost all like that. Seems by the time she got him he was already a pretty frightened animal. She didn't have the time or the patience to bring this horse back. She's no therapist."

"Can you unteach fear?"

"To a degree. I can lessen it and make sure that he's not exposed to fearful things. But I'll be honest, he'll always be dangerous. A false move, a startled gesture, a mishandling, a whip, any of those things could provoke him. You don't realize how strong these horses are. If I lose my focus for even a second, it could cost me my life."

"You talked about what you avoid doing. But what positive steps do you take?"

"I talk to him. He loves it when you speak to him. Not harsh or strident. More like, quiet, even, believe it or not, complimentary. He likes compliments, and he likes to be stroked along the neck while I speak to him." Willis stopped and said just audibly, "This is right, isn't it Phantom? You're doing such a good job."

McAbee saw the horse's ears twitch and stand up. Maybe he was wrong, maybe he wanted to see it, but the relentlessly hostile stare appeared to be less menacing and more open in response to the ministries of Clohessey.

"Look here, you two. Come up near him, from the front. Don't move your hands suddenly, just stroke his neck, like this." Willis placed his hands near the top of his head and then stroked downward to his shoulder. "Be firm. It's OK."

McAbee noticed Augusta replicating Clohessey's motion. The horse leaned his head her way slightly.

Willis said, "He likes you, Augusta. Don't be afraid to speak to him."

She did so, "I watched you tonight. You were terrific. I even won some money because of you. I'll buy you carrots or apples, whichever you like best. The next time I see you, you'll have them."

McAbee stroked him likewise. It didn't have quite the effect that Augusta had on him. McAbee wasn't surprised, and for a split second caught a querulous look from Phantom. Perhaps he sensed McAbee's uneasiness.

Willis began to walk him again.

McAbee asked, "How much longer will you be here?"

"At least another hour."

"I'm going to go up into the grandstand and see if I can find Limmer. I think that it's time to speak with him. Augusta – would you stay with Willis?"

"Sure. While you're there, could you cash my ticket?"

He took her ticket and proceeded to walk toward the track apron where he could see that there was a pretty good crowd. He pointed to the sticker on his shirt when he reached a gate where a guard stood; the gate divided the patrons from the track people. The guard said, "Just keep that ID on. If you need to get back in here." McAbee nodded as he passed into the track proper.

He went to a betting window and cashed in both his and Augusta's tickets. He asked the cashier, "Where do the big bettors hang around?"

"Usually upstairs in the restaurant or lounge. Just take the escalator over there."

"Thanks."

By the time McAbee reached the lounge, the seventh race was in progress. Scott Harris' voice was full of excitement; it was the featured race of the night.

McAbee had received a description of Limmer from Barry Fisk. He watched the bettors in the lounge, about 75, and the diners in the restaurant, about 200. He noticed one man in a corner who fit the description of Limmer. But there was an immediate problem. He was being addressed, too intently, by a heavyset, menacing man who was whispering into his ear. It had a bad feel to McAbee. He was positive the comments were not sweet nothings as the man he supposed was Limmer was sweating profusely in the air-conditioned lounge. Finally, the heavyset man arose and patted Limmer on the shoulder – heavily, unfriendly, as it lingered just a little too long and a little too insistently.

He turned and headed toward McAbee who averted his gaze elsewhere, feigning to be looking for someone. He passed without comment.

McAbee immediately went toward Limmer. The look on Limmer's face was not that of a mean man, rather it projected fear and high anxiety.

"Mister Limmer?"

"Yeah?" he said looking suspiciously at McAbee.

McAbee wished that all identifications went down that easily. "Do you have a minute?" he asked non-threateningly.

"Look, I don't know who the hell you are. What do you want?"

"My name is McAbee. I'm a PI in Iowa."

Limmer started to stand.

"If you walk away from here, there's going to be a felony warrant on you within a few days. The choice is yours." McAbee sent him a non-committal look.

Limmer stopped. He looked at McAbee as if trying to ascertain McAbee's angle and the ammunition behind his statement.

His pause told McAbee all that he wanted to know. "Why don't you sit down?" He kept his voice as even as he could.

Limmer sat and said with little conviction, "Well – I'm listening."

"You've lost a great deal of money on betting against Phantom Express." He stopped and gazed at him. Limmer ran his hand through his thinning hair. "This is all known, so I'm glad we don't have to argue or drag out evidence."

"I lose money all the time on all sorts of horses."

"$17,538 on two races."

"I still don't see your point."

"A man came to see Willis Clohessey a few days ago. In my opinion, felonious assault occurred on Clohessey."

"I don't even know what this Clohessey looks like. You'd better be careful before throwing around rumors like this. Hey, look. I don't need this crap. I'm leaving." He got up slowly, perhaps to see if McAbee had any more.

"That's your decision. Of course, Clohessey's being watched; if your muscle man does something stupid, is apprehended, and then turns states evidence against you, you're cooked. It's all pretty simple. If you have any assets – and you do – you'll be taken to civil court and sued. That's it for me. Oh, and one other thing, you probably should bet on him next week. He's just getting better, Mister Limmer."

Limmer took a few steps away from the table, and then came back. He sat down. He said, "McAbee, or whatever your name is, here's the deal. Did you see that guy who was with me before you sat down?"

"Yes."

"He's connected. You understand that?"

"Yes."

"I've got to come up with $20,000 in three days. That means I'm probably going to have to rob my mother. Do you know how that makes me feel? So, you come along, more threats. My life goes from pretty good to a joke in a week, all over a stinking, bad-luck horse!" He stared at McAbee, was it for sympathy? "I'll get the 20 thou. As for you, I'll try to find out what happened and get it ended. By next Saturday, I'd like to be up here with a clean slate; no mob and no you."

McAbee mulled over the offer. He conjectured that Clohessey was the kind of man who could look the other way and let it go. "I'll stay here. Do what you have to do, and give me an assurance. I'm prepared to let it go."

"Be back in a minute." Limmer left the table, already pawing for his mobile.

He was still unclear. Was Limmer's goon his own hire, or had he bargained with the mob? If it was the latter, the issue was moved to a more dangerous level; it might not be possible to call them off given their sensitivity to image and revenge.

Limmer came back within two minutes. His face had just a touch of relief. He sat down, "Just for the record, I don't know who this Clohessey is."

McAbee looked at him evenly. He nodded his head once.

"I feel bad for this Clohessey. I called someone who thought he could end any misunderstanding. Enough?"

McAbee was irked by this seedy gambler who had suddenly become a big diplomat. He said sharply, "Limmer! Yes or no, is Clohessey out of this? I don't need BS."

"Yes, he has nothing to fear."

McAbee arose and said, "If there's any going back on this, it will turn into a very sad story. You'll have a leading role."

CHAPTER XX

McAbee was relieved. Clohessey was accepting that the goon had been called off. He felt that he could now train Phantom without looking over his shoulder. Other than Augusta being a little distant on the way back from Madison, McAbee considered his trip to be quite worthwhile.

But one question still bothered him. Augusta had asked, "Does this mean that the file is closed?" His response was non-committal. Clohessey was probably out of danger, even though some people hung out along the edges, namely, Roman Garzo, and maybe on the outside, Betty Broder, and on the very, very fringe, Jeremy Burgess.

He asked Barry Fisk to continue surveillance of these three and to forget Kent Limmer. By the time that this order had come through, Barry had an "all but certain" take on the goon that Limmer had employed, a man named Fred Larkin who not only showed up on Limmer's phone records but who also had gassed up in Tipton, Iowa on the day Clohessey was beaten up. Tipton was about 15 miles east of West Branch on Interstate 80. He noted that there was no credit card record of Larkin having been in Iowa for at least the last two years. Coincidence? Not likely.

When McAbee had hung up from that call to Fisk he wondered just what kind of laws Fisk had traversed in his avid pursuit of Limmer and Larkin. He didn't want to know. His attorney had warned him to keep a distance from Fisk and to always make sure that Fisk was kept on as an independent contractor. In the words of his attorney, "That little SOB can cause more trouble in 15 minutes with his keyboard, than a busload of hard-core felons." McAbee had hinted to him that he had bought some equipment for Fisk as a way of giving him a bonus. The attorney had never known the amount of money that had actually been given – over $60,000 during a period of about four years. When McAbee thought about his deceit, he winced at the thought of his attorney discovering the true amount of McAbee's involvement, which if truth be told, his secretary, Pat, Jack Scholz, and even Augusta didn't know. Only his accountant knew, who just perceived it as a business expense, not aware of the potential perfidy lying behind McAbee's contribution. His summative judgment was that Barry Fisk had done a lot more good than bad.

On Wednesday morning McAbee received a call from Willis Clohessey.

"Willis, how are you?"

"Oh, I'm fine. I just wanted to say two things. Phantom is in again, non-winners of three, seventh race this Saturday in Madison. They tell me he's going to be featured in the program. I've been on the phone with a reporter from the Madison paper. They're going to do a story on him for the

Friday paper. They all think that there's a lot of fan interest in this. I also got a call from *Hoofbeats* magazine, if he wins this Saturday; they're going to feature him on the cover. Seems they've been working on a story about horses that have made unlikely recoveries. They're calling it fallen angels or something like that."

"*Hoofbeats?*" McAbee asked.

"Oh, that's the official pub of the USTA, the United States Trotting Association. It's a big deal. That's the mother agency that lies behind harness racing. So how do you like that?"

"That's great, Willis." McAbee was pleased to hear Clohessey this enthusiastic.

But then came the ominous part of what he had to say. "But there is a bit of concern." There was a lengthy pause. "I've had three calls over the last day. They're anonymous on my caller ID. I've even tried the call back function on the last one, about two hours ago, but no luck. I didn't know if I should bother you. I guess I've used up my retainer, and you probably have closed the file, but I thought I should tell you. What do you think?"

McAbee ran his mind across a number of strings. "First off Willis, I guess I've put your file in a limbo status. I thought your troubles were over. The calls bother me. I haven't reviewed your bill. I don't know how much has been gone through. Pat is probably still putting it together. Let's not worry about that for now. Answer a few questions for me. Give me some exact times on those calls."

"Yesterday, about four p.m., another about nine p.m., and then this morning, two hours ago."

"The person says nothing?"

"No, nothing, but they don't hang up. I can hear them. After I say a bunch of 'hellos', and 'who is this' I hear the click. Do you think that I'm done with those bettors in Madison?"

"I do, Willis, but obviously I'm not positive. Is there anyone out there with you?"

"No. But I do have a shotgun."

"I'm sure you do. Here's what I think, Willis. In the case of the gamblers, both you and the horse were in trouble, but you were primary. In the case of any others, though, it's not that simple. I think that you're in less danger than Phantom because with the others there's embarrassment, revenge, and sheer hatred going for them. It's toward the horse, not so much at you."

"Bertrand, when you talk this way you have me at a loss. How could you possibly want to purposely hurt a horse?"

"The horse is the symbol of their failure. Destroy the horse, destroy the failure. Kill the messenger, kill the message. But you know this could just be a telephone marketing misfire off a faulty computer program. They could be ringing you for the next month, and it may have zero to do with the horse. The one effect has a possible thousand causes." McAbee caught himself, shaking his head back and forth. He had just completed an exercise in befuddlement he told himself. Willis Clohessey wasn't looking for a passage through the canal of sophistry. McAbee was on hire to act, not to think himself into inactivity.

"Well, I have an offer for you." Willis was trying to recover his enthusiasm. "I'd like you and Augusta to come up again with me to Madison as my guests. She's a marvelous woman, Bertrand."

"I know that," he answered, although he was still thinking about the anonymous phone calls. "Let me check my calendar and hers, and I'll call you back, Willis. And ... let me think about all of this. And ... yes, keep that shotgun handy."

He was on the phone with Fisk within a minute of hanging up. He explained the hang-ups to Fisk, especially the anonymous readout on the caller ID.

Fisk was slow to respond, that in itself was unusual. Finally, he said, "That anonymous thing is almost invariably cell phone stuff, and they're becoming a major hazard to hackers like me. If you could spare me another eight thou I can get a program and a piece of equipment made by some Israelis that can lead me to the Promised Land."

McAbee figured that this was going to be the tax for this year. They both knew that Barry's hourly rate was extremely low, given his expertise. The hidden agenda between them involved the equipment, the programs and whatever else enhanced his hacker abilities.

"When can you get it?"

"I can have it by tomorrow. But it has to be in cash. I have a contact in Iowa City who has it in stock. All sorts of legal problems with it."

"The cash will be in your hands by 9:30 tomorrow. In the meantime, do what you can. I feel uneasy about this whole thing for some damn reason."

"He's a bad-luck horse. Don't you believe in that? Classicist!" He said sarcastically.

"You're probably right, Barry." McAbee hung up before he said what he wanted to say to him – which while it would have felt good would have set back his cause.

Betty Broder had been called by the *Hoofbeats* reporter, Thad Apple, who led off his inquiry saying, "We're going to do a story on Phantom Express. In fact, we're holding the magazine at press. If he wins on Saturday night, he'll be the cover story. There's some real interest perking around this story."

"How so?"

"Well, you know, the sport needs something like this, a kind of breakthrough story that could have an impact, could reach people. My editor is pretty keen on this one, and to be truthful so am I."

Betty felt the headache coming on. It seemed to rise out of her spine as it moved savagely into her neck and shoulders, and then as if picking up momentum and force, made a full attack on her head. Her eyes blurred, and she also felt the onrush of a hot flash. She figured that someday, like lava bursting forth from a volcano, her system would not be able to hold against these experiences, and the result would be a stroke. She forced herself to concentrate on Apple and his question. "What do you want from me?"

"Well, I've heard about the accident. Just got off the phone with the driver, Brian Broad."

"Oh, really," she said suspiciously.

"Yup. Said his life's never been the same. Sad story, kind of. Comment?"

"About what?"

"I don't know. How about the way he drove?"

"Hey listen, enough on that. He knows what he did. He was told how to drive him, then he goes out and does just the opposite. Everyone, up and down the line, got hurt because of what he did." The headache felt like a loose log in a raging river taking aim, searching for something to smash.

"Can you give me some background on Jeremy Burgess? I've been trying to reach him, but he's not available."

"Haven't seen him in four years. I don't do business with him anymore."

"You were with him when the accident occurred?"

"What's this got to do with anything?"

"I hear that the two of you almost duked it out. I'm just trying to get the story right."

"Neither of us was happy. But I wasn't going to take the fall for the kind of horses that he sent up from Valdosta. The kind of people he had training yearlings were terrible, vicious. Phantom was already screwed up when I got him." She caught herself. She was getting emotional, and her feelings were augmented by the savagery of her full-blown migraine.

"Anyone in particular?"

"Hey, that's enough on that too. I've got just one more minute, so get to your questions."

"Phantom Express, what do you think about his comeback?"

"Comeback? Comeback from what? He never did a damn thing. It seems to me that a comeback is a come back from something of note. This colt after six years finally has done something. In totals, there's probably been about a half million thrown at him. He's pissed all that away. So, he wins a few races at a third-rate track in Wisconsin, and suddenly he's God incarnate. Please, give me a break." Betty knew that she'd regret these comments, but it was as though this reporter had lanced a wound. The fury flowed hard and steady. "He's a hard-luck animal. When the stress of racing gets into his brain, he'll crack like a walnut shell. You wait and see. Hey, some of those non-winner races? They're nothing. Wait till he knocks heads with some old veteran horses and a full array of skillful drivers. Then we'll see."

"Would you train him again?"

"On no account, no damn way. He's not done hurting people. He's a walking jinx. The minute's up, goodbye." She hung up and immediately put her head between her arms which were folded onto her desk.

"Sir? That reporter, Thad Apple is on the phone again." Mary Potter, Jeremy Burgess' executive secretary, was nervous. She knew she had to persist, but it was a no-win situation. Damned if you do, damned if you don't.

"This is a call I don't need. A reminder of past nonsense, bad people around me." He scowled at her.

She knew that he was suggesting that she could easily be included under this umbrella comment. "Shall I tell him to call back later?" she asked cautiously.

"No, send it through and ... why don't you stay in here. I'm putting him on the speaker, take a transcript." She could see the anger simmering around his mouth. She picked up her pad and sat ready to write.

"Mister Apple, Jeremy Burgess. You're on speaker. I have limited time."

"I'm doing a feature story for *Hoofbeats*. It's about a horse you once owned, Phantom Express. He seems to have made a full recovery from his accident four years ago. I read about your no comment in the *Sportseye*. I was hoping you'd answer a few questions."

"Go ahead."

"Betty Broder – claimed that your training quarters in Valdosta sent her a crazy horse."

"Sure. It's very easy to blame others."

"So, he wasn't crazy?"

"High strung. I feel that she helped ruin him. That's all for her."

"Are you happy for the horse?"

"Horses are risky investments. It's good to know that we had a sense of quality."

Mary looked over at Burgess. He was doodling on his pad, creating a jumble of arrows aimed at a stick man in the middle of the page.

"Do you think he'll keep winning?"

"He's six years old. All of the stake races for which he was bought are done for him, too old. His potential for big money is now highly limited. But I want to say something else about the colt. Everyone who has worked with him has found him to be unstable, quirky, and a bit crazed. Fine wine improves with age, I have not found that to be true with this kind of horse."

"Someone said, that this kind of horse and this kind of success is an embarrassment for you."

Mary saw his hand stop in mid-arrow. He stabbed the pad hard and said through clenched teeth, "Someone," drawing it out slowly, "does not speak for me. That someone is a moron. Your time is almost up."

"I'm trying to locate a former employee of yours. Roman Gar..."

"I don't know anything about him. This interview is over. Good day." He disconnected the phone.

He turned toward Mary and said, "Give a hard copy of that ASAP." He turned away from her and went back to his computer screen. As she was leaving the office, he said over his shoulder, "Don't ever let him through again."

Mary surmised that it would be best to stay out of his way for at least two days. Jeremy Burgess was one angry man. She had seen enough of him over the years to know that that could turn into viciousness.

Thad Apple called the office at Pompano Downs and spoke with the racing secretary. "Roman Garzo. I need a forwarding address. He left Pompano three days ago. The trainer he worked for said that he just disappeared, cleaned out his room, and left a note that said 'I quit'. Do you have any idea where he is?"

"Nope, and quite frankly, off the record, I could give a damn less."

"Oh?"

"Moody, and always out of sorts. And let me add, we've had to warn him about beating horses. Fined him once, public record, beating up a filly on the track in front of a bunch of visiting kids. His kind is not good for racing. But in answer to your question, he's apparently gone. I have no idea where he is."

Thad thanked him. He drew a line through Garzo's name. Whatever the situation was there, it was not worth pursuing given his deadline. This story was about the phenomenal comeback of Phantom Express and not the mood swings of a washed up trainer.

CHAPTER XXI

———◆———

Sam Roemer was scheduled to drive Chai, Chai, Chai in the seventh race in Madison on Saturday night's card. His profession was dairy farming, which he shared with his father on a spread about twenty miles south of Madison. His avocation, however, was to stay involved in the sport of harness racing. He had regularly driven through the summer on the state fair circuit; but when the Madison track opened, he became a regular catch driver. Typically, he was chosen to drive in about half of the races per card. His racing average, some argued very akin to baseball batting averages, was decent, about 250. He was in neither the upper nor lower tier of drivers.

But, Sam Roemer had another connection to harness racing. One barn of his farm was devoted to caring for recuperating horses that needed fresh air and a relaxed, bucolic setting. He tended to these horses that averaged about

10 at any one time. It was a sideline business that enabled the Roemer family to net about $1000 a month in profit, after all the tax considerations, expenses, and the pay they gave to a hired hand who had it as a primary responsibility.

One of the Roemer's primary clients was Betty Broder who had come across him when she had been racing some Wisconsin-eligible two-year-olds at the county fairs in the state. That was about eight years ago. Things had worked between them. Betty guarded her secret place from other trainers, as she found that Roemer's care was quite effective. In several instances, Roemer was given some really nice bonuses for his work.

Forty-year-old Roemer had no illusions. The harness business would always be a sideline. His father was close to retirement, and it was writ large and indelibly that he would succeed him in this 103-year-old family business. The farm, his wife, and two kids were where his heart was located.

The call came through from Betty Broder on Thursday afternoon.

"Sam, Betty here."

"Hey Betty," he said.

"How are my two pacers doing up there?"

"Yeah, fine. But Boxcar Hideaway is still favoring that right front leg. But you expect that from what you told me."

"He'll need a good five weeks up there before he shows any improvement," Betty said.

"Yeah, sounds about right."

Her next statement threw him off. He was expecting her to ask if there was room for another one of her lame horses. "Listen, Sam, I've been on the internet. I see that you're still driving your share of horses at Madison. Specifically, I'm looking at the seventh on Saturday."

He knew the race as he had already run a check of the card. It was a non-winners of three. "What about it, Betty? You looking at one of those horses?" It was not uncommon when a trainer and a driver had a good relationship for a driver to be asked about a horse he had either driven or driven against. A good report on a horse from such a driver could serve as part of the basis for a purchase offer to its owner.

"Not exactly, Sam. What have you heard about Phantom Express?"

"He's a big deal. I don't hang around the track enough, but I do know that there's lots of chatter. You thinking about buying him?"

"No," she said curtly.

"How can I help you?"

"That colt almost cost me my career a few years ago. I was given to understand that he was dead – Alpo. Somehow he escaped that fate, and this dumb Iowan, ah ... Clohessey, ended up with him. Do you know him?"

"Seen him. Don't know him to speak with."

"How bout this Benson guy, his driver?"

"Don't know much about him either. He's an old-timer. Not a bad driver. Patient, waits for an opportunity instead of making an opportunity. He's like me a catch driver, but I don't know what he does for a living."

"What kind of horse are you driving in the seventh?"

"Chai, Chai, Chai. Great early speed makes the front easily, but if he doesn't grab cover by the half, he runs out of steam in the stretch. Pretty good horse. I'd say he'll go off at about four or five to one." Roemer was at a loss for where she was going in this conversation, but he had the clear impression that there was more to this than just curiosity.

"So, you're going to the front, but you'd like someone to make an early move to give you cover?"

"Yeah, yeah, that's pretty much how I see it."

"From what I can see there's a good chance that's going to be Phantom Express."

"Sounds possible." She had done more study on this race than she had initially let on.

"Quite frankly, I don't need this horse to do well. He's an embarrassment. If he wins, *Hoofbeats* is going with a cover article on him, sounds like they're trying to make him the next Secretariat."

"I don't understand, Betty."

"I know something about Phantom that I think will cause him to break stride. Interested?"

Sam Roemer was decidedly uncomfortable at this point of the conversation. "Well ... OK, but let me hear it first."

"Four years ago he snapped and crashed into a metal gate. The snap was due to a whip. He cannot take a hit. The driver, against what he was told, put the whip on him. Thus, the gate and a big accident. This can be an almost repeat performance, again a whip accident."

"Betty, I'm not driving him. You're not telling me to suggest to Benson that he hit him, are you?"

He got back a sour laugh from her. "No. But nothing says that when the SOB comes up alongside of you when he's passing that your whip couldn't find a piece of his ass. How about it? It's not that hard, you know. Just a good wide slash should do the trick. Maybe two or three. I think you'd take him out of the race."

These were not Sam Roemer tactics. Sure, if he saw an advantage he'd take it – that was the nature of driving. But this suggestion was on the dirty side. Plus, if it was true, he would be endangering the colt and his driver. "Oh, Betty, I don't know about this. Let me think about it, OK?"

There was a long pause before she said, "Hey, Sam. We get those races down here in Chicago on the television. I'm going to be watching. This is really important to me. I feel like I'm being set up on this. I'd do the same for you. Don't flunk out on me, I need this." She disconnected.

Sam looked down at the advance sheet which showed the seventh race. He had the two post – the lead would almost certainly be conceded to Chai, Chai, Chai. She was probably right, Phantom would probably come after him at about the half mile, his post was the four, making it a perfect position for pulling out and challenging for the front.

McAbee was scheduled to pick up Augusta at five p.m. at her place. He was in his office on that Saturday from noon on because he was engaged by a medical group to expose their financial manager who appeared to have defrauded the group by over $125,000 over three, all-too-diligent years. Besides meeting with two of the doctors he had engaged the services of Moishe Berenson, an accounting wizard with a decidedly mean-spirited and vicious disgust for frauds. Berenson was used sparingly by McAbee because he could lose his objectivity once he discovered fraud, both for the felons and their victims. He worried about the meeting between Moishe and the two docs. To his surprise, it went well. Apparently, Berenson granted clemency to overworked doctors whom he felt had a pass for trying to oversee a business.

When they were all departed, as he was dialing Barry Fisk, he wondered why it was that he had so many cantankerous contractors around him. He concluded that it was a remnant from his days of managing a college faculty.

"Yes?" Barry answered.

"I'm going to Madison soon, Barry. Do you have anything for me?"

"I have the equipment, I loaded it, it's unreal. I don't know who's better, Indians, Israelis, or the Chinese. But right now I'm leaning toward the Israelis."

"Right, until next month. Then it will be India," Bertrand said mockingly. "Tell me, anything on those three hang-ups, which apparently became four this morning."

"The problem with cell phones is their fluidity. They're stolen, they're gifted, and they're ubiquitous. That's what this Israeli software is all about. I take it from my source that these are really a gift from the Palestinians who were doing so much damage that out of necessity the Israelis put their best minds to the task of creating a tracking system on cell phones."

"OK Barry, now tell me do you have anything?" Barry Fisk was at his worst when he had information that others didn't. He would go on and on talking, knowing the frustration that he would cause. If he was in person, his small legs would start a slow and inexorable set of kicks while he sat, tipping off a sharp listener to his secretly-held knowledge.

"The calls are coming from a cell phone registered to none other than Roman Garzo."

"No?!" McAbee said.

"The software is really good. Now, here's the rest. Garzo has been making his way up from Florida. I know that he called this morning." His smugness came through in his voice. He continued, "He's in St. Louis."

"That was this morning? He could be in Madison tonight."

"No. He checked in at a Fairfield Inn in Collinsville, Illinois. The track there gets the Madison signal for their off-track betting. I'm pretty positive that's where he'll be."

"How do you know about the Fairfield?"

"Credit card – ABC," Fisk said professorially.

McAbee remembered his attorney's advice, a basic 'don't ask, don't tell'. He regretted asking a question for which he knew the answer. But he did want more information. "So, he left Pompano on Monday?"

"Yes. He went to Orlando, stayed at a Motel Eight. Once I got the phone connection, I got to his credit card. I don't know where he stayed on Tuesday, no card used. On Wednesday he was in Dalton, Georgia, at a Howard Johnsons. On Thursday he made it to Chattanooga, a Motel 6, on Friday he got to Metropolis, Illinois, Holiday Inn, and now he's in the St. Louis area. He's in no hurry. I don't know, of course, if he's meeting anyone or whether he has anyone with him. He doesn't charge meals. It's pretty much gas and motels on his MasterCard; the rest is cash. He doesn't use the phone much, but he has been making the calls to Clohessey. I'm going to do a full workup on him, but it'll take me a day."

"You have my cell. Call me right away if you get anything more on him. I especially want to know his whereabouts. I'm worried for both the horse and Clohessey."

Bertrand hung up and headed toward his Explorer. He was now mentally fixed on Roman Garzo and his potential for trouble.

He parked in front of Augusta's house at five p.m. sharp. Tonight she was in snug black pants, a black knit short-sleeved shirt, and silver ornamentation on her wrists, ears, and around her throat. She wore heels that accentuated her height. McAbee sucked in breath when he saw her, statuesque, beautiful, and overwhelmingly present.

"They're on the gate for this seventh race," Scott Harris intoned, "They're a sixteenth of a mile from the start ... they're off and pacing and quickly to the lead is Chai, Chai, Chai – falling in behind is Charleston Chew, then to Bluesman, then to Phantom Express fourth. In the fifth spot is Sluggo, sixth Toothache, and rounding out the field is Breakfast Bargain. Chai, Chai, Chai remains comfortably in the lead as he hits the quarter at 29.2. There is no change in the order as they head down the backstretch approaching the three-eighths pole. Chai, Chai, Chai gets an even bigger breather in this second quarter as he slows the pace. Out of the four hole is Phantom Express who takes up the assault on the leader. This consecutive winner of two races charges by Bluesman, now he's even with Charleston Chew, and he's coming up onto Chai, Chai, Chai and his driver Sam Roemer now urging his horse to stay in the lead. Phantom Express, whoa, Phantom lurches out, away from Chai, Chai, Chai, almost off stride but now back as he pulls ahead of Chai, Chai, Chai, Jim Benson getting control over Phantom. They're now at the half at 58.1 as Phantom Express starts to pull away from the field that remains unchanged in order except for Phantom. They're coming on to the three-quarter pole and Phantom Express has the lead by five lengths and is pulling away from the field with every step. The three-quarters is hit at a blazing 1:25.3. This race is essentially about who is going to place and show as Phantom tears into the stretch led by driver Jim Benson. Oh look at this folks. He's up by 10. He shows no sign of quitting. Chai, Chai, Chai is done as Bluesman looks to be second and Toothache takes third. Unbelievable! Phantom hits the finish line at 1:52.3 under a tight hold. Looks like we're onto non-winners of four for this six-year-old pacer with a history that defies explanation!"

Harris turned off his microphone and yelled back to the camera and monitor director, "Can you believe that? I'm not sure, but I think that Roemer tried to hit Phantom. I want to watch the replay. He veered out; I thought Benson was going to lose control over Phantom Express."

"I'll tell you right now," the director said, "he did take aim at him. I wouldn't be surprised if he gets fined. The judges had to see it, surely they saw it from the starter car."

"Hey, whose that black babe standing next to that balding guy with glasses? God, she's a knockout. Look, he's putting his arm around her waist, and she's smiling. He's a lucky sucker, isn't he?" Scott switched on his microphone and said, "In the winner's circle for the third-straight week – Phantom Express, driven by Jim Benson, owned and trained by Willis Clohessey of West Branch, Iowa, birthplace of President Herbert Hoover. Also celebrating, friends of the aforesaid." He switched off the microphone. "My God that chick is stacked. And she's no twenty-year-old either," he said to no one in particular.

Although he didn't announce it, news had reached Scott two races later from the judge's office that Sam Roemer had been fined $250 and suspended from driving for the next three racing dates. He called the judge's office and asked whether Roemer was going to challenge the ruling. The chief judge, Harvey Lafleur, responded, "He's lucky he wasn't suspended for a month. This horse is a national story. We don't need some damn catch driving dairy farmer pulling some dirty trick on us. If he even looks the wrong way for the rest of this meet, he'll be tossed."

Willis Clohessey's emotions were in turmoil. Jim Benson had cornered him after the winning picture had been taken. He told him about Sam Roemer, and the whip incident. Clohessey had watched the race on a small TV monitor and had seen Phantom lurch out, but he couldn't tell why this had occurred. Now he knew. Benson was surprised by the incident because the word on Sam Roemer was that he was a clean driver. Later, Clohessey had been notified of the corrective action taken by the judges against Roemer. He considered the incident to be closed. However, Clohessey did ask Benson to keep his eyes and ears open as to why Roemer did what he did. Benson would.

McAbee and Augusta came into the backstretch after the tenth race. Willis was walking Phantom, cooling him down before the drive home.

McAbee had a mixed look about him, he appeared to be happy, but there was an issue in his eyes. Augusta must have known what was coming because she also seemed tense.

McAbee said, "Wow, what a victory. We're really impressed, Willis, and happy for you."

Willis told them about the Roemer incident, which in turn drew that distracted look from McAbee. Willis confirmed once again what he had thought about McAbee, that he was prone to float away into some nether world. It was as if things were supposed to converge to a pre-set standard. When they didn't, the look came over him. Augusta, on the other hand, kept herself in focus.

"Willis, I have some news that you should hear. We've been tracking this Roman Garzo. He seems to be heading your way. He also, this is a sure thing, has been the one doing the hang-ups on you. What I don't know is whether he'll end up in West Branch or up here in Madison. I've spoken with Augusta. She's willing to stay at your farm for a few days. Just as extra eyes, you know."

Willis didn't hesitate. "Yeah, that's good. I think that the time has come. Those calls don't have any appearance of good to them. When can you come, Augusta?"

"Well, he's in the St. Louis area tonight. How about tomorrow, about noon?"

"I have a spare bedroom, and I welcome you. And," he looked at McAbee, "I know my bill is advancing. It's OK. Phantom is paying for everything. So, send it on; this isn't charity work, Bertrand."

That same night Jim Benson went to the Pacers Bar and Grill, a few blocks from the track. It was an old building; probably housing a number of different bars over the years. He had heard that it had been bought by a cadre of drivers and trainers and renamed. It clearly was positioning itself to be the place in Madison for the harness people. It was packed with such as Jim made his way toward the bar. He ordered a beer. While he waited he was tapped on the shoulder. He turned to see Sam Roemer. Benson tensed, prepared for trouble.

"Jim, we've never formally met. I'm Sam Roemer," he extended his hand, they shook.

"Yeah?"

"Do you have a minute? I'm sitting by the phone booth over there," he pointed to a place to the right of the bar and adjacent to the entry hallway leading to the bathrooms.

"I'll be there in a minute," he said hesitantly. Roemer turned and left for his table. Benson paid for his beer and as he was heading for Roemer he heard a boisterous yell of his name.

"Hey, Jim Benson, over here, over here." It was Duane Calvert, a regular and leading driver at Madison.

He went over to Calvert who was sitting with some other drivers. "I'll come back. I'm going to have a chat with someone."

"Just want to tell you, great drive on Phantom Express. My horse, Bluesman, left the track sulking."

"Thanks, I'll come back." Benson was pleased by the notice from Calvert. In his estimation, Calvert was the very best driver, bar none, at Madison. He worked his way through the crowd and saw Roemer at his table. He was by himself. Benson sat down. He said, "You wanted to talk?"

Roemer was a bit glassy-eyed and perhaps, just perhaps, his cheeks were tear-stained. He held Benson's eyes, "I'm sorry about tonight. I just don't do things like that. I apologize."

Benson was at a loss for words. Track people were not known for their ability to apologize. "Well, you know, you almost sent him flying on me. Why did you do that?"

"It's a long story. But between us and for your information in the future, your horse had a trainer a few years ago, Betty Broder out of Chicago." He looked at Benson, checking to see if the name meant anything. Benson didn't know the name. He went on, "She's a good client of mine. Sends me horses, you know. Anyway, she kind of forced my hand, told me to take a few long shots at your horse. Said he doesn't handle whips and all that. At any rate, I did as she asked, my mistake. I'm sorry if I caused you harm."

Benson felt for him. "Sam, he doesn't handle whips. She was right. But you were wrong. But I have no more cause with you, let's just forget it."

"I'm grateful." They shook hands.

Benson got up and stepped outside the bar. He called Willis Clohessey's cell.

"Yeah?"

"Willis, Jim Benson. You home yet?"

"Nope, still have about another hour. What's up?"

"Just spoke with Sam Roemer. He was put up to it by a Betty Broder. You know her?"

"Yeah, I talked with her when Phantom was coming along."

"Well, she leaned on him. She does business with him. Anyway, he's sorry and genuinely apologetic. Just thought you'd want to know."

Willis called McAbee who was just dropping off Augusta Satin at her home in Rock Island. He was quite sure that he had sent McAbee into some kind of trance with the information about Betty Broder.

CHAPTER XXII

━━━◆◆━━━

Roman Garzo set out for West Branch, Iowa from Collinsville, Illinois. He figured that a steady drive of six hours would put him into West Branch. The trip was all interstate, beginning at I-55, proceeding through Springfield, picking up I-74 in Peoria, and I-80 into the Quad Cities, which would take him to West Branch.

Garzo had watched Phantom Express at the Collinsville off-track betting parlor on Saturday night. During the post parade while the caller was announcing the horses he noticed that Phantom still had the imperious look, a slight tilt of the head and the wide-eyed glare. Garzo didn't handle well the spasm of hate that tore through him. Everything in his being urged him to place his huge hands on the horse's throat and choke him to death. There was no forgetting, there was no let up in that deepest part of him where hostility was nurtured on a daily basis by perceived injustice. Even when he was given to understand and feel some small joy that Phantom had been sent to the tannery, he hadn't let go, a permanent scar was etched into his soul. And then, out of the blue, the horse had resurrected. It was as if a cancer in remission had returned with an unbelievable vehemence, metastasizing through every piece of him.

He wasn't about to let this rotten animal escape this time. Only the mode of his killing was at issue. He had placed a blanketed hunting rifle behind him in his truck, alongside of a bullwhip he had purchased in little Cuba in Miami, and beside that a 12-inch hunting knife. If he could kill him each time with each of these tools, he would. But if there could be a fourth time, he would choke the animal to death and watch that haunting face come to its end.

If he was caught it didn't matter. Anyway, he imagined that animal cruelty in Iowa was, what did they call it? an oxymoron, anyway. But if he was hindered by Willis Clohessey, he would kill him too. No one or no thing would stand in his way.

He stopped at a McDonalds in Galesburg, Illinois. He took out his cell phone and called Willis Clohessey. When he answered, Garzo hung up. It was important to know that this unknown quantity be there. When he returned to his car, it was 11:30 a.m. He was about 40 miles southeast of the Quad Cities. He wondered what it was like to live along the Mississippi River. Was it nicer in Illinois or in Iowa? He had never been to Iowa. He wondered if it was all farms, all corn, and all animals.

Augusta Satin headed out of Rock Island at 11:05 a.m. She took route 92, the byway in Rock Island, and caught the exchange at I-280, which soon brought her out of Illinois and into West Davenport and soon onto I-80 west. She calculated the whole trip to be about 55 or 60 minutes.

She had a close relationship with Gramma Didion, a transplant from New Orleans who had followed her man to the Quad Cities back in the sixties. He was employed as a skilled machinist at the Rock Island Arsenal, where among other things, howitzers were built for the armed forces. He died in the mid-80s, but she had decided to stay in Rock Island. Its west end was thoroughly African-American and, because of that, thoroughly satisfying. She adored Augusta's kids, and they reciprocated. Gramma Didion was tough, funny, and a terrific role model for Augusta's children. She had told Gramma that she expected to be gone for at least two nights, then she'd reassess. Gramma, with that magnificent smile said, "Gussie," only she could get away with that, "you stay as long as you please, you hear?"

As she drove she reflected on the case. It was her initial opinion that Bertrand was overreacting to the situation until she had found out that Roman Garzo was behind the hang-up calls. She remembered her meeting with Betty Broder who had tagged Garzo as a malevolent and mean-spirited man. Not that Betty herself was above performing dirty tricks such as encouraging Sam Roemer to lash out at Phantom. Bertrand had said that he was going to see her and lay down the law to her. Her recall of McAbee's initial meeting with Broder suggested that visit would be worth observing as Broder had sent some chilly body language toward McAbee. She would only hear Bertrand's rendition, of course, which she knew he would understate terribly. For he had a way of missing nuances sometimes, especially when emotions were at issue. It was just the opposite when some underlying conceptual issue was out there; then his antennae could reach beyond anyone she had ever encountered. Bertrand sensed disarray or the lack of order like a heat-sensing missile pursued a scorching target.

At 12:05 p.m. Willis Clohessey went into his horse barn where he refilled the water pails and put feed into each horse's pail. As he was doing all of these things he heard a car on the gravel in front of his barn. He looked out to see Augusta getting out of her car. He went to the door of the barn and yelled, "Augusta, over here."

When she got there she said, "So this is where the big guy sleeps?"

"Ah, yes. I'm doing a bit of work around here now. Do you want to say hello to Phantom?"

"Sure. I have a big package of carrots in the car."

"Save them for tomorrow. I have some in the barn."

They went to the second stall to the right of the entry door. "Here he is. He likes carrots." Willis reached over to a cellophane bag and took out some of them. "Just put it out there. He'll bite off half of it. When he comes back for the rest, just be careful he doesn't inadvertently get his teeth on one of your fingers. Whatever you do, try to keep your hand flat so he can't get any part of a bite on you."

He watched her go up to Phantom, who eyed her suspiciously. His cocked head, his long gaze downward always seemed to Clohessey to be a product of fear. Nothing else made sense as he didn't buy the premise that horses could be malevolent. Phantom was amazingly gentle with her. She went through four carrots and even managed to stroke the horse's long face. But the cocked head and long look were never far from him.

"I have a nice, airy room for you. Maybe this country air will do you good," he said.

"Does the room have a view of this barn?"

"Yes."

"Sounds great. I've brought along a few books, and I will keep an eye out for Garzo. I don't know what to expect."

"Me neither. After all, what could he do? I can't see him coming onto my land and hurting the horse. Can you?"

"It seems a stretch to me, but he's calling you for some reason."

"Oh, glad you mentioned it. I had another hang-up call this morning, about a half hour ago."

"Is that right?"

As if on cue, Augusta's cell rang. Willis listened to Augusta.

"Hello," she said.

There was about a 30-second silence as she listened intently. She then responded, "Yeah, I have my .38. And I'll inform Willis."

More silence from Augusta, and then an, "OK." She looked intently at Willis before saying, "That call to you? It came from Galesburg, Illinois. That's less than two hours away, Willis. It was from Roman Garzo. This is on the authority of a man you never met and probably never would want to meet, Barry Fisk. He's one of Bertrand's people who has been working the case. He doesn't make mistakes, unfortunately."

Garzo drove into the city of West Branch. There was a presidential museum there devoted to Herbert Hoover. He went into it and walked around, paying scant attention to the exhibits, his mind focused, rather, on the whereabouts of Willis Clohessey. He went to a local restaurant and ordered a grilled cheese sandwich and Coke. He asked the waitress for a phonebook. The address for Clohessey was 18099 Route Three. He inquired of the waitress. She told him to take a right two blocks up and head out about three miles. There'd be a letter box with that name, or at the very least, a numbered box.

Garzo decided to get a fix on the farm's location and layout in advance of the night. However, he would wait until dark before making his move on the horse. He caught sight of the Clohessey name on the mailbox, slowed down and took in the farm. He saw a black Acura parked along the circular drive to the right of the house, and he saw two barns, one very tall, probably for stacking hay and keeping livestock, and the other a low, long building where Clohessey probably kept his horses. He saw the traditional two-story farmhouse where he in all likelihood lived. Garzo did not see any persons.

He drove away from the farm before making a u-turn at a gravel road a few hundred yards up and went back, again slowing down, calculating distances and approaches to the target area. He saw nothing suspicious or unusual. A half hour later he repeated the process and then headed back into town. It was now about 4:30 p.m. He took a room at the Quality Inn, which was about a quarter of a mile south of town. He took a two-hour nap. He had no intention of going to the farm until at least 11 p.m. He watched some television and eventually saw the day disappear into the Iowa sky. He ordered a small sandwich at a Subway in the now virtually empty downtown where the occasional pickup truck or car loaded with high school kids would rumble through the town's main street.

At about 10:50 p.m. he removed the hunting rifle from the blanket and placed it beside him on the front seat along with the bullwhip. He attached the hunting knife to his belt. He could feel the slow rush of adrenalin coming into him. Justice was about to be served.

Augusta wanted that third ear of corn but resisted. The steak had been perfect, along with the baked potato and small salad. "You should open a restaurant, Willis. You're a good cook."

"Yeah, sure," he said humbly.

They had spent their time exchanging pieces of their biographies. There was a sadness to Willis that Augusta couldn't quite decipher. It seemed to lift only as he spoke of Phantom Express, when his face would lighten up and become animated. She helped him with the dishes, in the ending light of the day they walked out to the barn, checked on Phantom and the other nine horses that were boarding there.

At nine p.m. he said that he was going to bed. "I'm usually up about four. Course I don't expect to see you till later. Just make yourself comfortable. If you need anything, just ask." He left her in the living room.

Augusta watched some television before leaving for her room at the southwest of Clohessey's house. Her view of the barn was excellent, and the half moon threw enough light for her to see the barn door clearly. At first, she found the night to be unusually noisy – the hoots, screeches, chirps all causing her to become distracted. Eventually, she found these very same noises to be soothing and calming as she entered into the world of writer Michael Connelly and Hieronymous Bosch, his conflicted detective.

An unusual noise broke her out of her concentration. She looked at her watch; it was 11:20 p.m. She jumped up from her rocker and went to the window. Nothing was untoward. She listened intently. She wasn't hearing anything, but her eyes kept returning to the barn entrance. The door had been left half-open for air-passage by Willis, who had placed two elastic bands across the opening. Willis said that these bands would hold off any horses that might attempt escape on the off chance of their getting loose from their stall. But the door was not ajar the way it had been, she thought.

She went to her bag and removed her .38, which she holstered to her belt. As quietly as she could, she left the house and started to carefully angle away from there toward the barn.

At the door of the barn she heard a low, snarling voice. It wasn't English; the actual language was hard to tell. She drew her .38 and, crouching, peeked into the barn.

She saw a Coleman lantern's low light. It had been placed on the ground outside Phantom's stall. The stall door was open, and before it a thick-figured man stood. She noticed that a rifle was leaning against the stall wall and that the man was fingering a bunch of tassels with his right fingers. Not tassels, she told herself, but a whip with multiple, hurtful fingers. She could not see Phantom, but she heard some low snorts as the man, was this Garzo? – continued to speak in his menacing fashion.

And then with an alacrity that surprised her, she saw him slash forward with the whip. The sound against the flesh was abhorrent to her as was the loud cry of the horse. Before she could react, three more violent lashes of the whip found Phantom's body. As she came through the barn door with her .38 drawn, the man had already disappeared into the stall, unaware of her presence. She heard thrashing and loud movements in the stall before she reached it and saw the man's powerful hold on Phantom's throat.

"Stop! Stop or I'll blow your head off!" she yelled.

He turned and clearly saw the .38 pointed at him, and then he went back to his passion and hardened his grip on Phantom's throat. She came within five feet of him and fired a bullet into his left leg's calf. He screamed and held his leg, buckling to the pain. With his left leg now collapsed to the straw-laden floor of the stall, he reached to his belt and withdrew a hunting knife. He struggled to get up as Augusta fired twice more at his legs, careful to miss the frantic and confused Phantom. The man dropped to the floor of the barn, having taken a bullet into his left knee and his upper right thigh. He fell down onto the straw and tried to get up, knife still in his hands, when Phantom sent his two back feet crashing into the head of his would-be murderer.

Augusta, in all her days, had never heard an uglier and more gruesome sound as the cranium of this man cracked and oozed out brain matter onto the floor of the stall.

Willis Clohessey came tearing into the barn and grabbed Phantom, who was preparing still another death kick. He caught his halter and quickly took him from the barn.

Augusta sat, against her will, across the aisle of the barn. She had seen her share of white people get pale. She was sure that she matched them in virtually every way possible.

CHAPTER XXIII

McAbee sat across from Betty Broder whose sullenness and defensiveness had not changed from their last meeting. She had no intention of giving this guy an inch of respect or hence her attention. It was a Monday, none of her horses had fared well over the weekend, she was furious with Sam Roemer who had done what she asked but who now was turning against her – as if she was the guilty party.

"Listen, what do you want? How much do I have to do to make it clear that I don't want you hanging around here? You don't belong, you're not welcome." He continued to stare at her, as though she were some kind of leper. He said nothing. "Hey mister, what do you want? I'll get my people, and they'll throw you out of here. Don't keep looking at me like that." He looked away from her as his eyes glided around her small, cluttered barn office.

Finally, he said, "I have a few things to tell you. I'm just not sure about where to begin," he said distractedly.

"What if I help you along by throwing you out of here?"

He frowned at her, shook his head, and ignored her for a bit. Then, he said, "None of this comes easy ... I know about you and Sam Roemer ..."

She cut him off. "Sam Roemer? I have no contact with him. Forget it, Macarer. Just forget it." His stare caused her to stop talking. His look made her feel small.

"I'm not here to cause you trouble, understand that, please. You worked against Phantom Express by telling Roemer to use his whip on him. His race driving license could be put into danger as well as your training license." He held up his left hand and his forefinger – a warning to her not to plead her case. "I repeat, I'm not here to cause you harm. But I do intend to leave with an absolute assurance that you will never again interfere with that horse."

His intense look and riveting gray eyes held her fast. The softness she first construed in him fell away as she heard him speak. Somewhere in that soul of his there was something she didn't want to experience. "What you're referring to is a misunderstanding. When I spoke with Roemer I gave him a tip on how to win the race. I didn't tell him what to do with Phantom Express," her shaded lie hung out there causing her to hope that there was enough truth in it to get this man out of her office.

"You said that Phantom was a hard-luck horse. What did you mean by that?"

He sounded like some kind of college professor to her. "Hah! As far as I can see, anyone! Anyone who has ever come into touch with him has been hurt. He's like a bad coin. Just because he's won a few races, it doesn't mean anything. He'll bring some kind of disaster, you wait and see."

He looked away again, his eyes moving rapidly around her office. He came back at attention by turning toward her, "I want you out of the circuit, Ms. Broder. I never want to hear your name again in reference to him. Your bad thinking, your bad wishing, and your attempt to hurt this horse must stop now. If I hear your name again, in any way that shows you were trying to hurt him, it will cause me to act against you. You will feel the kind of damage you don't need," his gray eyes now burned into her.

She took a deep breath. "Hey, screw that horse! He hasn't ever brought good to me. If all you're asking is that I stay to my own stable and ignore that SOB, you have it. Now, are we done?"

"No. In some ways that was the easy part. I have some news for you."

"Oh?"

"Roman Garzo."

"Hey, no news about him is the best news that you can give me. He's a bum. Phantom didn't bring him any luck either. Burgess fired him because of Phantom. See? Everyone loses who comes near that unlucky horse."

"You haven't heard from Garzo in how long?"

"A solid three or four years. If he came here, I'd have my people throw him out with a pitchfork up his ass."

"You'll never get the chance."

"What?"

"Roman Garzo was in West Branch, Iowa last night. Yes, Phantom's home now. He tried to murder Phantom in his stall at Willis Clohessey's barn last night. Augusta, you remember her, shot him. Wounded, he fell down in Phantom's stall, and Phantom caught his head with a full back-leg kick. He was dead instantly."

Betty stared down at her desk in dismay. Whatever doubts she may have had relative to the pacer were now gone. This horse was indeed a curse. She never wanted to hear his name spoken around her. Mildly superstitious, she now became fully engaged with such a thought pattern, even attributing the terrible weekend showing of her horses, to the curse of Phantom. "This is too much," she said feebly.

"It was not a shock that he would try something bad. But what happened is a shock. When I received the news late last night I decided to drive up here right away this morning. All of this is important for you to know."

"Look, I'm sorry about all that happened. Even a guy like Garzo deserved better. But ... OK, I'll stay totally out in the sidelines from here on in. No interviews, no opinions, no nothing. Mister, you may not believe it, in fact, just watching you, you don't seem to believe in much, but this horse is bad luck through and through. Getting close to him is ... toxic. This Clohessey might be next. Oh, by the way, what was a lady like Augusta doing hanging around Phantom?"

"On assignment."

"She OK?"

"Yeah. Shaken. But OK."

"Did Garzo hurt Phantom?"

"Some neck, mouth, and eye cuts, but Clohessey's vet thinks he'll be OK."

"How about Clohessey?"

"He's fine. He doesn't think that the horse is bad luck. Just that Phantom has been around some pretty bad people. Maybe it's a Karma thing. But my purpose here is simple, and you've answered my question. You're one less thing that I have to worry over. Here's my card if you need to get in touch with me." He passed a business card across her desk.

She took it and read it aloud, "Bertrand McAbee – ACJ Investigation Agency. Well, I'll tell you what, McAbee. If I had a choice, but it'd be a bad one, I'd take Phantom over Garzo."

He got up and left the barn. She sat there for a while. She put the card in her desk drawer. She had never quite met anyone like the strange man who just left her barn. She wondered whether his connection to Phantom would break the circle of bad luck that circumscribed the horse.

Malcolm Horosby was a beat reporter for the *Chicago Tribune*. He had been attending to any and all coverage of horse racing for almost 20 years. Although he knew that everyone in the press room thought of him as being cynical and perhaps a bit on the shady side, he self-identified as a rabid sentimentalist, although it was rather a secret that he kept close to his vest.

His first whiff of a story came from the Madison paper which had run a feature on a harness racing horse. Now Malcolm was very partial to thoroughbreds, even though his current debt load of $34,550 was directly traceable to that breed. He would wonder aloud, sometimes, whether the harness industry wasn't the more honest and self-policing of the two horse racing sports in Chicago. At the end of it all, he was conflicted. But horse stories with a twist were a sure way to finesse the sports editor who couldn't see past the Cubs, Bears, Sox, Bulls, and Blackhawks. So, he made a few phone calls and got wind of the big feature that was coming out in *Hoofbeats* by next Friday, a story held pending Saturday night's non-winners of three victory by the pacer called Phantom Express.

He had a list of names that he would use for his 'depthing' of the story: Betty Broder, Jeremy Burgess, Willis Clohessey, Roman Garzo, and Brian Broad. In the great scheme of things, it would be a future story that he would work on as time allowed.

On Tuesday morning Malcolm was leafing through a number of dailies that were spread across the reading room of the *Tribune* offices. It was rare that he would not give a three-minute scan to the *Des Moines Register*; after all he grew up in Mason City, Iowa, and still had extensive family relations there. He sat down abruptly from his leaning stand when he saw below the crease on the first page a story.

Pacer Kills Former Trainer

A bizarre killing took place amidst a shooting incident in West Branch, Iowa on Sunday night. Roman Garzo, 53, a harness horse trainer was allegedly beating a pacing horse called Phantom Express at the Willis Clohessey farm. He was discovered by private investigator, Augusta Satin, who fired three shots at him, each hitting him in various parts of his legs. Falling to the ground the horse kicked Garzo to death.

Garzo had once trained the horse as a yearling in Valdosta, Georgia, for the Burgess Stable. Fidel Diaz, the manager of the Burgess Stable, commented upon hearing the news of Garzo's death, that "There was bad blood between this man and this horse. I am sad about the whole thing."

The horse, Phantom Express, has a checkered past, including a reputation for being high strung and uncontrollable. Willis Clohessey, who currently trains the pacer, has had remarkable success with him at Madison Downs in Madison, Wisconsin. The horse had been bought by Clohessey at an auction in Kalona last fall.

Private Investigator, Augusta Satin, employed by the ACJ Agency in Davenport, had been at Clohessey's farm because of a number of phone calls that had been perceived as hostile. Neither Clohessey nor Satin would comment about the incident. West Branch police and the Iowa Bureau of Criminal Investigation continue to look into the matter.

Horosby said to himself that this was a gold mine waiting for discovery as the story now became high priority. His first call went to Betty Broder, with whom he had tenuous contacts marked by mutual distrust. He calculated that the tough, old dyke saw him as being a nosy and stupid reporter.

"Betty? Malcolm Horosby, *Tribune*. Like to get a comment from you."

"What about?" she said defiantly.

"Well, I'll give you the choice, Roman Garzo or Phantom Express."

There was a long pause before she responded, "I have nothing to do with either one of them. I have no comment, and don't call here again."

"Ah ..." He was glad that she wasn't on a phone that could be slammed because the 'ah' was the last sound he got in.

His call to Jeremy Burgess, 'the Jeremy Burgess!', was shunted to a media relations guy named Timmy Hawkins who read verbatim, Malcolm thought, the following: "Mister Burgess has nothing to say about the incident in Iowa. Both the pacer and the former trainer have not been associated with Burgess Stables for almost four years. He has and will have no further comments about this matter. Good day, Mister Horosby."

At this point, Horosby decided to dig in, there had to be a story here precisely because everyone was zipping up.

Willis Clohessey had Phantom's injuries treated by his veterinarian, Doc Stout, who declared that the horse was fit to race on Saturday night. "Just keep the salve over the eye. If this Garzo had come another half inch closer, he would have taken the eye, and maybe in another 10 or 15 seconds irreparably damaged the windpipe. When you take him out, test his air intake. I think he's OK, though."

When Willis returned to his house, his phone was ringing. He said, "Hello?"

"This Clohessey?"

"Yeah."

"Willis, I'm calling from the race office in Madison, Phil O'Brien. I'm writing two races. One, non-winners of four, purse is $5000. Two, the open, it goes for $13,000. We all think that your horse could probably do it. We'd be obliged if you entered him in the open."

"I don't know about that. When do you need an answer?"

"We draw in two hours. I have your entry for the non-winners of four. But we'd love to see you in the open. This horse is becoming a national story, you know. I'm getting loads of calls on him. This Garzo, did he hurt him?"

"Yes, but he's OK. I just had him out, and he seemed fine. The open race? Those are the best horses on the grounds, aren't they?"

"No doubt. The open is the best race we run all week. It's the feature of features, and it gets shown nationally, and it's bet pretty heavily."

"It might be too much for him," Willis said doubtfully.

"Willis, it could help the track. We need the national exposure, and this would be incredible. I'm asking you, please, on behalf of everyone up here." With the silence came a further plea by the racing office secretary, "You know he wouldn't have any trouble crushing the non-winner of four field. I'm authorized to guarantee you $2500, which is what you'd get from the $5000 purse off of a win, if you don't win that amount in the open. How's that for an incentive?"

Willis shook his head in wonderment. Finally, he said, "OK, enter him into the open."

"Willis, I owe you one. Thanks."

McAbee stood as Augusta walked into his office on Tuesday afternoon. It was the first time that he had seen her since Saturday night, having dropped her off after the race. They had been in contact by phone several times, however.

Her face was taut. Pat followed her into the office and asked if either of them wanted coffee. They declined as Pat left and closed the door. McAbee arose and hugged Augusta who returned it with surprising vigor. They remained clinched for at least five seconds before separating and sitting.

"Augusta, I feel bad for you. You didn't need this."

"It's OK. I just keep seeing Phantom's back feet driving into Garzo's head. I can't get it out of my mind." She shook her head in dismay.

"You warned him off. It's not your doing, you know."

"Yeah, yeah, I know that. Rotten people dig their own graves, and that's what he did ... but still, I just feel lousy."

McAbee said nothing, determined to let Augusta lead the way.

She continued, "I'm glad that you went up to see Betty Broder."

"Oh, yeah. Was she happy to see me," he smiled.

"I'll bet. So, where do we go from here?"

"I'm closing the file again. I know that he seems to be jinxed. But I don't try to get caught up in that stuff. I received a call from Willis about ten minutes ago. He's entering Phantom in the open up there, the best race they have, on Saturday night. We're invited. How about it?"

"You know I'll say yes. But I'll be honest with you, Bertrand. There are clouds around me and harness horses, and this horse? Maybe he is jinxed. But," and now she rang up that huge smile, "you're not, and count me in. Plus, I never cashed in my winning ticket after last Saturday's race. So ... another hot date with a hot guy. After all, who else would take me to the races on a Saturday night?"

"Only me and a few million others if they had the chance," he said earnestly.

CHAPTER XXIV

———◆◆———

Horosby finally got the advance of the *Hoofbeats* story on Thursday. But he needed some kind of insider to give him an edge. He went back to the very beginning of the horse's pedigree, researching the bloodline of Phantom Express. He spoke with Walt Scott and Roger Theroux who would only say that Phantom was a high-strung animal. He traced the details of the sale at Harrisburg, running down the unsuccessful bid of Martin Blum whose only comment was, "I consider myself lucky to have lost the thing."

A datum was given to him about the handler of Phantom at the sale, Jimmy Mason, whom Horosby tracked down. Did he remember the colt? "Sure do. Nothin' wrong with that horse that gentle talkin' couldn't cure." But he only got that from Jimmy after he briefed him about the animal's history. "Seems he's finally in the right hands," was his last comment.

An old friend, a reporter for the *Miami Herald*, got him access to Fidel Diaz on the condition of anonymity. Horosby now began to get the drift of the real story around Garzo and Phantom. He wasn't surprised that Garzo-types were in racing, but he was shocked that a man of Burgess' class and brilliance would ever hire him.

So, by the time he had disconnected from Diaz, he had a sense of the story. Betty Broder was proudly sent a $400,000 raving maniac of a horse by Garzo. Broder was no charmer herself, but he had never heard anywhere that she abused her horses.

He caught up with the record of the qualifier from which Brian Broad had lost his leg. Broad was bitter. He now worked at a hospital assisting in a rehab unit with amputees. He knew nothing of Roman Garzo, but he did speak about a woman who worked for Betty Broder named Alicia. A call to Bogey, the race secretary at Balmoral, gained him a phone number and address for Alicia who was now a groom at the thoroughbred track in Arlington, northeast of Chicago.

She spoke about the time that Phantom had gone berserk after he saw a whip whisk by him and how she was disciplined by Broder. The name of Nils Johannsen was given to Horosby.

Johannsen would only allow that the pacer had to be handled with gentle authority, no whips please. "There must have been a miscommunication with Brian Broad. But Anton La France was supposed to drive. He had been briefed about the qualifier, but he was sick. Poor man's dead now. Could have been a great driver."

He ran down the Pennsylvania trainer, David Meacham, who had bought Phantom from Burgess with the hope of getting him to race. He was full of scorn for the horse. "Piece of wild crap. Tried to kill me twice. Sent him off with a few others for dog food. I don't know how he got back from that. Some Amish must have seen his build and decided to take a chance with him in front of the canner's gates. I find it hard to believe that he's racing and winning. Must be on some wonder drug, or they did a lobotomy on him. Are you sure this is the same horse I had?"

When Malcolm Horosby went to his editor with the story, he drooled as he listened to Horosby. At this point, he said, "You gotta go to Pennsylvania and find that Amish guy. I want this story. This is the best horse piece that I've heard since Seabiscuit. It's got everything! Get on a plane to Pittsburgh today. Don't come back until you put this part of the puzzle together."

It took Horosby two days to track down Josiah Riesling, 20 miles south of Lancaster. Riesling was weeding his garden. A gaunt man, he wore glasses and had a white beard that extended down from his jaw by about four inches. He was in his late fifties or early sixties. His eyes were kindly as he stopped his work and looked up at Horosby.

"Can I help you, sir?" he spoke with a slight accent that Horosby couldn't place.

"You could if you're Josiah Riesling."

"I am he," he wiped his brow with a blue handkerchief.

"I have a story to tell you. Do you have a few minutes?"

"Well, I guess. Come to my porch, and we'll sit. My wife will serve us some lemonade and cake." They went onto the porch of a small, white house. Horosby was directed to sit on a rocker as Riesling went into the house and came back in a minute and sat. "She will bring it to us soon. If you are ready, I shall listen to your story now."

Horosby told him much. He noticed that Riesling would shake his head and sigh on several occasions. The poppyseed cake and lemonade were incredibly delicious. Finally, Horosby concluded, "Phantom was saved by you. I'd like to hear the story. That's why I've come to Lancaster."

"It is a good story. A story of God, indeed, who teaches us in many ways. I am of the belief to allow myself to use vehicles when my work takes me out of the area. There is a slaughterhouse where horses are taken when their day is done. I go there once a month. I had seven horses that I was delivering when I went there. This Phantom was not with me. He was with Hans who is one of us. He also trucked horses, back then. As I was unloading, I noticed that he was taking out the horse you speak of. He handled him with great caution. He had been told that he would kill if he made a mistake in how he cared for him. I was struck by the beauty of this animal – his stature, his bearing. Some animals are noble and proud. He was. For his weight Hans would receive $500 for him. The horse would be dead in less than an hour. I bought him from Hans who wondered about my sanity. I took him home, and he did fine with my personal wagon, and then I gave him to my nephew who eventually went to Iowa. I never had a problem with the horse. He's very smart."

"Did you ever lay a whip on him?"

"No, lines, only lines, and only gently."

"Tell me, what do you think of what has become of him?"

"I don't know what to say except that God is delivering messages. One message seems clear, I think. This mistreatment of God's creatures is not right. Payment will be collected."

"Please tell your wife that the cake and lemonade were great. By the way, your nephew, the one who put him for sale at Kalona, do you know where he is?"

"No. He has left us. He is shunned. He does not exist!"
The kind eyes flashed in anger. Horosby understood, shook
hands, and left.

It was Friday. He wanted to be back by nightfall so that
he could begin his story and head for Madison Downs and
the open on Saturday night.

Scott Harris was in his announcer's booth at six p.m.
There were six horses entered for the open on that Saturday
night. It wasn't the first time he had studied this eighth race;
it fascinated him. He picked up his phone and punched out
the number of Cory Fritzen who was the track handicapper
who posted the track's projection of the odds. He answered
with a terse "Hello?"

"Scott up here. Hey, I'm looking over the eighth race
tonight. I don't understand your morning line of 8-1 on
Phantom Express."

"What's not to understand? It's my calculation on how
the odds will be at race time. He's a rookie. He's racing
against old timers too who have each won over a quarter of
a million dollars apiece. It's one thing to race against non-
winners of two or three, it's another thing entirely to race
against old class horses. People might bet him down because
of all the hype, but I don't see him winning or even getting
that close in fact. Also, it's a short field, only six horses. He's
got the five hole, and there's tremendous inside speed. I don't
see him getting the lead, and short fields favor the front end.
I think that Topsoil will get the lead and keep it all the way
around."

Harris saw that Topsoil had post two, Fritzen rated him
at 2-1, a co-favorite with Citizen Malone who had the three
post. Periodical Room, a nine-year-old gelding who blew hot
and cold during his long career had post one. He had a 5-1

next to his name. Saddleburns occupied the four post, a solid colt that seemed to finish in the money with consistency, even though winning was rare. His odds were 6-1. In the six hole, Scott read Gifting Hours who was also an old-class horse but who was coming off of a month and a half layoff. He was a great closer who could, on occasion, score a last quarter in 26 seconds. Because of the layoff and the short field, Fritzen put him at 8-1.

Fritzen continued, "Young horses, and like it or not Phantom is young by way of experience, the old horses intimidate them. Hey look! For your sake and the track's sake, I hope Phantom can keep winning. But I just don't see it."

"I don't know about your calculations on this one."

"Oh, another thing. Phantom has Benson. Not a top driver by any means. In fact, I think that both of them, the horse and the driver, are out of their class. Anything else?"

"Nope. Thanks."

Scott studied the page for another ten minutes. The qualifier from Balmoral was still on Phantom's line (a history of his last six races), ending with the DNF designation. But as he studied the last three lines, he saw a dominant animal that was tearing up his competitors, race by race.

Scott kept his eye on Benson and Phantom Express when they came out for warm-ups after the second and fifth races. Phantom came onto the track like a proud gladiator, head stretched high, but tilted, giving the impression that he was looking down in scorn at what appeared in front of him.

His gait and stride were even and strong as Benson kept him in second gear, probably warming up Phantom at a two-minute, 40-second clip. The late July and still warm Wisconsin night had a quality to it that made Scott think what it might have been in the 1920s. The timeless sport of harness racing, with that touch of the nineteenth century, the close and humid night that made people move slowly and carefully – it just seemed like he was transported into the past.

After the seventh race he introduced the winning horse, his driver, his trainer, and his owner who dutifully stood for the winning picture pose. And then he heard the rise in murmur, the track apron was suddenly being peopled as never before as the patrons came out from behind the glass doors and the air conditioning to watch the open race and see the curiosity, Phantom Express. The excitement of the fans caught Scott's attention, and he in turn found a voice that articulated the tension of the environment.

"There are 15 minutes to go before the featured open race and arguably the best six horses in Wisconsin. Make sure your bets are placed early. Don't get shut out at the windows."

When there were 10 minutes to post, the loudspeaker blared the trumpet sound so universal at tracks after which Scott said, "And now, ladies and gentlemen – the race you've all been waiting for, the featured eighth – an open race for a purse of $13,000. Number one with red pads is Periodical Room," Scott paused giving the drivers time to line up in numbered sequence. He watched Periodical Room pace slowly in front of the grandstand. "The two horse with a blue pad is Topsoil, the three horse with a white pad – Citizen Malone, the four horse wearing a green pad is Saddleburns, the five horse with a black pad is Phantom Express, and with a yellow pad – the gray horse – Gifting Hours." He then reviewed the horses, again, this time listing their drivers and owners. "Eight minutes remaining, please place your bets."

He took out his binoculars and looked toward the paddock area from where the horses had come. Along the fence near that area he eyed Willis Clohessey, the balding guy, and that statuesque black woman. All three of them looked edgy and, he speculated, why not? If Phantom could do well in this race he would move into a totally new tier of competition. In fact, it might not be long before Phantom would outgrow the Madison Track, by simply being too good and thus destroying betting pools. When that happened, it would be on to Chicago and ultimately New Jersey where the best horses in the country resided. "Two minutes to go."

A minute later the starting car appeared on the track and moved slowly toward the head of the stretch. It spread its wings. "One minute to go, one minute." In the distance, Scott heard the starter say, "Drivers, let's turn 'em." He watched the drivers slowly turn their charges in the direction of the gate and then move them toward the numbered square that matched their pad numbers. "The horses are moving toward the gate, last chance for you to place your bets. In post-position order for this open race: Periodical Room, Topsoil, Citizen Malone, Saddleburns, Phantom Express, and Gifting Hours. They're at the eighth pole, the sixteenth pole, they ... are ... off and pacing and Topsoil, Citizen Malone, and Saddleburns off aggressively as they hunt for early position," Scott said excitedly. "It's a torrid pace as Topsoil and Saddleburns go at it and Citizen Malone drops into third. Fourth is taken by Periodical Room, fifth Phantom Express, and Gifting Hours is viewing them all. Topsoil has the lead, Saddleburns is caught out as Citizen Malone closes the gap. Saddleburns is parked as he continues to go stride for stride with Topsoil. They hit the first quarter pole in 26.4 – a brutal pace by any account! Horses settle in but Saddleburns is parked and in trouble as he searches for some rail but can't get it. He begins to drop back, desperately seeking a hole as Topsoil now slows the pace slightly. Gifting Hours moves out of last place and begins to move up as he goes three wide getting around the fatigued Saddleburns who now finds the end of the pack, falling in behind is Phantom Express who moves off of the rail tracking Gifting Hours. Topsoil in front hitting the half-mile marker in 54.1. He is followed on the rail by a menacing Citizen Malone who is followed by Periodical Room – third on the rail. Gifting Hours is making some headway as he nears Citizen Malone who stays pinned on Topsoil's back. Phantom Express is second over, and Periodical Room is locked third on the rail. Saddleburns has pulled up and is out of the race. Gifting Hours is positioned to show that huge kick in the last quarter as he takes aim at Topsoil. They near the three quarters, they hit it at 1:23 flat – a savage pace cut by Topsoil. This fivepack is now in the stretch for the final quarter. Gifting Hours moves parallel to Topsoil, Citizen Malone is going inside – having drafted for almost the whole race, and Phantom Express is right behind Gifting Hours. Tiring is Periodical Room. Three pacers are now in a ruler line – on the outside Gifting Hours, in the middle Topsoil, and on the rail Citizen Malone. Phantom ... Phantom Express swings out from behind Gifting Hours – he's four-wide – with an eighth of a mile left – what a finish this looks to be, Topsoil is tiring, Citizen Malone puts a nose out front, Gifting Hours still there, and Phantom Express now head to head with Gifting Hours now with Citizen Malone – unbelievable! Phantom Express to the lead, Phantom Express – Phantom Express wins in 1:50.2, second Citizen Malone, third Gifting Hours. Four straight wins, but this one is special. One extraordinary victory for this six-year-old as he ties a track record for his class. Hold all tickets until the race is declared official."

He turned off his microphone and yelled back toward the TV monitor, "This is so huge! I can't believe what I just saw. These horses are a tough crowd, he whipped them."

Scott noticed that the 'official' sign came on. He turned on his microphone and said, "The race is official. In the winner's circle the grand Phantom Express with trainer and owner Willis Clohessey, driver Jim Benson, and friends of the trainer. Payoffs are: 10.80, 5.00, 3.60, for number five, exacta 5-3 pays $29.20. The replay of this race will start in 30 seconds. Look at your monitors on this. This was a great race, a record was tied by Phantom Express." He switched off his mike and yelled back – "Who in God's name is that babe with the balding guy? She is too hot!"

CHAPTER   XXV

Before the race, Jeremy Burgess sat in the quiet of his study and sipped on three fingers of Glenlivet. He switched on his TV monitor, tuning in his satellite as the Racing Network came in clearly on his 72 inch HDTV.

He read the racing program that he downloaded from Madison Downs the previous day. His only interest was the Saturday night open which was to begin in ten minutes. All during the day a variety of phone calls had come his way, seeking comment on Phantom Express, Roman Garzo, or Burgess Stables. He chose to use his spokesperson to deflect the onslaught. The very last call had come from a *Wall Street Journal* reporter. It wasn't the first time that the *Journal* had sought comment about his commitment to harness racing and his apparent losses reaching into the millions. His new corporation was a publicly-traded enterprise; they had hinted and taunted, he had run these expenses through the corporation. He was fair game for this unusual story about a horse that had endured sadistic mistreatment at his state-of-the-art stable in Valdosta.

He watched as the pacers came onto the track. The pacer had killed a man, and yet they let him race. Amazing. He had that same look, a horse peering down on everything about him. A look of disgust and disdain. He should have died in Pennsylvania in a tannery and canning plant. He went back to the program. By any account this horse should not even be in an open race. Being invited to race in such was for extremely good horses that had proven themselves over the years, not this stunt which was being taken advantage of by the track's marketing department.

He would on occasion invite friends in to watch races with him, for example, when his stable was racing at the Meadowlands. But this wasn't the night for this. This wasn't his horse. This was, if anything, a symbol of incompetency and foolishness. He heard Harris, the announcer, who sounded as though he had just smoked some crack to ratchet up his enthusiasm, "Two minutes." The camera isolated on each horse for about 10 seconds. He watched Phantom again as he finished his glass of Scotch.

He observed the horses moving to the extended gate on the starting car and was instantly relieved when Phantom was backed into fifth place. But he wasn't pleased when Topsoil was pressed to a brutal first quarter, making it possible for the horses in back to come on at the end. When he saw Phantom grab cover behind the formidable closer, Gifting Hours, he sat erect, all the while hoping that Phantom would lapse into discouragement as he raced against such old pros as these. He surmised as the stretch came up that Phantom would probably get a fourth, well beyond his real talent. The race had just shaped up for him, it seemed. When he saw

Phantom pull out four-wide from behind Gifting Hours he stood up and shouted at the screen, "No, no, you can't you filthy bastard!"

When the horses crossed the finish he sat down, tried to drink from his empty glass of scotch, and then hurriedly poured a full eight ounces into the same glass. A feeling of depression and hatred hit him as hard as he could ever remember. It wasn't so much the small fortune that he spent on him as it was that the pacer was a symbol of his ineptness. If his life had been snuffed out in that Pennsylvania tannery, it would have been a forgotten story. Now the horse was a national story, and he was in the middle of it, the butt of the joke, for some.

Now, what to do? He could declare adulation for Phantom and pretend to celebrate with Willis Clohessey and his pacer. This very thought turned his stomach. He could attempt to buy the horse back and perhaps ride the positive spin around him. "Yes," he said sourly, and watch him go down the tubes again, even more of an embarrassment.

He could send a professional, not the likes of Roman Garzo, to maim the animal in Clohessey's barn. But this ran against a personal adage, 'Trust no one unless you have to'. He couldn't trust anyone, as it turned out, for such a mission. No one could know. Even these hired killers seemed to always keep some incriminating evidence with them as a way of protecting themselves from a double cross from their patron, and sometimes as a way to double cross their patron.

No, the answer was simple. It would have to be done by him. He had no connections to Willis Clohessey; his absence from any immediate circle around the horse was enormous. The vicissitudes of horse ownership included that some of them died in the most unexpected ways. Jeremy decided at that moment to murder Phantom Express. He had a 60cc syringe of the barbiturate Beuthanasia, from which one simple injection into the neck vein would achieve his goal. Roman Garzo was a fool. He seemed to want to beat or choke the 1200-pound animal to death. An injection would take a few seconds, done in a flash. He drained the glass of scotch as he looked at the winner's circle wondering what those two were up to at the back end of the sulkey, the black woman and the white man. They sure didn't look like horse people.

For Willis Clohessey, Sunday was a day of mayhem. He hadn't gone to bed until four a.m. His phone started to ring at 7:15 a.m., from there it was almost unending. By nine a.m. he asked Josh Swift to come over and give him some assistance with chores. "After all, Josh, You're the one who talked me into bringing him to Madison for those qualifiers." By 11:30 a.m. he had received calls from such notable entities as *60 Minutes*, ESPN, Fox Sports, and National Public Radio. As the producer from NPR said to him, "This story has great potential. It involves a killing, a close encounter with a slaughterhouse, the Amish, a comeback, to say the least. This has a Seabiscuit resonance. Congratulations, Mister Clohessey."

By one p.m. he had called McAbee. "Bertrand, Willis here. I've been called by every sports editor and show producer out there. Serves me right for having a listed number, I guess. I know that you've closed the file, but every time you do that someone else pops up. Is there any way you or Augusta could come out? I think that I need help."

"Is Phantom safe?"

"Oh, yeah. Josh, my neighbor, is over helping in the barn. I guess I just need advice and just maybe an eye around here just in case. Phantom seems to draw out enemies like a leech on blood. More and more people want to come out here to see him and take pictures, interview, you name it."

"Do you have room out there for a white German Shepherd?"

"Does he have manners?"

"He's a fashion consultant on etiquette."

Willis laughed for the first time that day. "Bring him out then. Augusta is always welcome too."

There was a silence on the line. It carried for too long. Was McAbee upset? "I'll run it by her, Willis," he responded neutrally.

Just as he had hung up, the phone rang. "Willis Clohessey here."

"Willis, you might remember me. I'm the racing secretary at Balmoral, Bogey?"

Willis remembered him very well. He was slightly surprised, thinking that Bogey was old enough to be long dead. "I do remember you, Bogey. What can I do for you?"

"We want your horse down here next Saturday. We're starting a series here. Three elimination races and then a final. Each Saturday we eliminate until we end up with the best 10 for the final."

"Appreciate it, Bogey. But I owe allegiance to Madison."

"Thought you'd say that. Talked with the Madison folks. They're OK as long as we give them a huge pitch that Madison is where he got his start and all that. They figured that you'd almost have to say yes to this deal."

"How so?"

"The purses are $30,000, $30,000, $30,000, and the final is $125,000."

Willis shook his head back and forth. This was unbelievable. "That's a lot of money."

"Listen, you've got the hottest horse in the pacing industry. We're going to do a full-page ad in each Chicago paper about this. I know that he's only run four races, but what a huge story he's become."

"When do you need an answer?"

"How about now?"

"No," he said flatly. "I want to think about this and also make some calls. When is the latest you need an answer?"

"Tomorrow at nine a.m."

"Give me your number, and I'll call back."

And the calls kept coming.

At 3:15 p.m. he saw a red Explorer pull into his front yard. He was pleased to see McAbee and Augusta exit the vehicle. McAbee went to the rear of the SUV and opened up the back door as he stood aside for a big, white dog that leaped out of the trunk area. That dog was ready to give a full all-point inspection to the farm when McAbee brought him to heel, placing a leash on him.

Clohessey came out of the house and onto the porch. "Hey you two. I'm so glad that you came. It's been a zoo here. So, who's this big guy?" He walked toward Scorpio whose ears were up and alert. He let Scorpio sniff the back of his hand for a few seconds, and he then crouched in front of the dog and petted him. But like his owner, there was something indefinable lurking. This was not the kind of dog who would show a burglar the way to the family heirlooms. "Plenty of bedrooms out here, and I want you to make yourselves comfortable. Augusta, you could stay in the same room, and Bertrand, I have one upstairs for you. That OK?"

"Sure," he said absent-mindedly.

"The dog can roam around or I can put him in one of the barns. Would he stay on the property?"

McAbee said, "I don't think so. But he could guard Phantom. He'd never bother a horse. He's not an idiot, my Scorpio."

McAbee and Augusta retrieved their overnight bags from the Ford and were shown their rooms. At the behest of Willis, Scorpio came along into the house.

"Willis, you'll find him to be a very good dog who as a menace will be quite an ally for us."

Willis thought that this was quite possibly true.

Clohessey announced at 8:15 p.m. that he had decided to call Bogey in the morning and enter Phantom down at Balmoral. "I'm also going to go to bed. I'm exhausted. You two make yourselves comfortable. There's all sorts of stuff in the fridge and cupboard. Take what you want. If you're going to leave Scorpio in the barn with Phantom, make sure that he's leashed because I'm leaving the doors open. It's too hot otherwise for the horses. Don't pay any attention to me in the morning tomorrow – I'm usually up before dawn."

"We'll sit on the porch here for a while Willis. You have a good night," McAbee said as he was aware that the surroundings demanded muted tones. When Willis left, Bertrand asked Augusta, "Would you like to take a walk?"

"I'd love to."

"Scorpio, come on." Scorpio got up from the porch step where he had been lying down and came alongside of McAbee. There was a truck path that Willis had carved out between the rows of corn stalks. The three of them went along it leisurely, enjoying the light from the moon which was not many days shy of being full. McAbee had memories of unusually magnificent moments over his years, a particular occurrence at a particular time, a smile that brought out the essence of another person, a place that was riveting in its beauty, the sun of a special day, the celebration of a hard-fought victory. Instantly, he knew that this moment would register as being one of those special times as he took Augusta's right hand and he glanced at Scorpio who was three feet ahead – tail wagging, ears up, and the definitive smile that only dogs had.

"Pretty nice out here, Bertrand."

"Augusta, more than nice. Splendid and unforgettable. But it wouldn't be without your being here."

"You say that to all your girls. I know your tricks," she said jokingly.

He laughed gently, but quickly said, "Augusta, I really mean it." As he tightened his hand on hers, Scorpio came back and fell in stride with them.

"I didn't think it was possible, but I'm getting a bit chilly. I don't understand that; it can't be less than 75 degrees."

He took his hand from hers and put his arm around her neck. "Does that help at all?"

"Yeah, but it's not enough, I'm afraid." She turned toward him.

He put his arms around her waist, and they came together. "Wow, I'm not feeling cold. It's damn nice being next to you," he whispered in her ear.

"Likewise." They kissed, long and intense.

He didn't know how long the kiss went on, but he felt Scorpio insinuating himself between their legs. He broke away, saying, "Scorpio!"

She laughed. "So, you have this jealous animal to keep you out of harm's way."

"Harm? Hardly. Maybe we'd better get back though."

"Yeah, we've wandered pretty far," she said with what seemed to be a touch of irony.

He kept his arm around her waist or his hand in her hand as they meandered back to Clohessey's porch. "I'll get some lemonade or a beer or a Coke. Which would you like?"

"The lemonade is great. Scorpio needs something too, don't forget."

He came out with two lemonades, went back into the house and came back with a bowl of water and some Cheese Nips. Eventually, he settled down on the wide porch that stood on the front of the house, balanced between the front steps and door of the house.

"It's so quiet and peaceful here. I can't believe the difference. It's only when I get out here that I can sense all that's missing in my life," she said. "So, Doctor Bertrand McAbee, what am I to infer from your behavior?"

Bertrand knew that eventually this would come. His gigantic procrastination with the relationship was unacceptable and unfair to Augusta and truly to himself also. "Augusta, you know that I think the world of you. There is no woman that I'd rather be with than you. When I'm with you – everything is brighter. That goes without saying, but I'll say it anyway. I feel in harmony with you." He looked over at her. She was gently rocking back and forth, her eyes were closed. Maybe he had pushed too far forward. He said, "Augusta, say something to me before I really make a fool of myself."

"Nothing you just said to me I couldn't return back to you in the same measure. You're kind of a hero to me, Bertrand. You've never treated me in any way other than nobly and respectfully. You may think, 'big deal', but believe me if you had to be around some of the complete asses that I have had to, you'd know how much of a compliment I mean. I know that I used to be pretty good looking. I've had lots of crap tossed my way, like a piece of meat on a scale."

"Wait, wait," he interrupted, "Used to be? Please. You're more smashing now than when I first met you all those years ago."

"Thanks for saying that. Yeah, maybe I need to hear that, but it's not the point. My point is this. I'm willing to go anywhere you want to go in the relationship, Bertrand, A to Z. But I know some things about you that perhaps you don't know that I know."

Bertrand said, "I'm listening."

"I know that you're still part walking wounded from your past marriage. My sources are too good for you to deny this. In fact, they're so good that even if you're sure this wasn't the case, I'd feel that you were in denial."

Bertrand swallowed hard. She had it pegged right. "Well ..."

"No, let me finish. I also know that you're not an apt subject for Oprah. You're not into self-disclosure. What will come from you will come from you. I'm really pleased that I make you feel good and that you see us in harmony. There's also great chemistry in your kisses and hugs. All that's great. But I think that you and I both know that you need time. I'm ready to go anywhere you want to go, Bertrand, emotionally, sexually, intellectually, you name it. But," she turned and looked through to his soul, "It's going to be on your clock. Other than the occasional tease, I'll never try to push you or ask you to go places you're not comfortable. That's also me; that's who I am." She stopped, her hand slapped down on the arm of the rocker.

After a few minutes he said, "That's why you're the only woman for whom I have any interest. I'm a lucky man. Thanks, Augusta." He got up and went toward her. She stood, and they kissed. And again, Scorpio did his thing as he wheedled his way between their legs.

She said, when they separated, "That dog really watches out for you, doesn't he?"

"For me? Hell, I thought he was protecting you."

Later, they took Scorpio into Phantom's barn. McAbee staked him to a 20-foot chain. He would have full access to Phantom's stall, just in case another Roman Garzo was out there. Scorpio stretched out and gave McAbee a big smile. He preferred to stay in the stable.

After two more prolonged good night kisses, he headed for his upstairs room. The noise of the night was extremely quiet. He was sleeping in short order, Augusta heavy on his mind.

CHAPTER XXVI

———◆◆———

Bertrand awoke at 8:15 a.m. A full sun had found his bed along with the distant sound of a tractor. He had slept well through the night. He wondered whether he was the last bum out of bed. By 8:45 he was in the kitchen, having noticed that Augusta's bedroom door was open, her bed made, and she was missing. For an instant, his mood sagged. He went to the refrigerator and withdrew a carton of orange juice, a loaf of uncut wheat bread, and some butter. There was a three-quarters full carafe of coffee in a black Krups urn. He cut two slices of bread and inserted them into the toaster, putting the setting on light. Just as he was about to sit he heard the screen door open. The first thing he heard was the patter of dog feet on the linoleum floor. Scorpio came running into the kitchen. Two seconds later, Augusta appeared.

She placed her hands on her hips, dropped her right hip about three inches, and said, in full taunt, "Well, I'll be. The eastern dude has found his way out of bed. All the chores are done, all the farmhands are in full stride, all the cows are milked, all the horses are run, all the sheep shorn. But here comes Bertrand McAbee – laborer extreme."

While he petted Scorpio he looked up at her, catching the flair of her hips. He looked away so that he could maintain focus on what she said, "There aren't any sheep here you big liar, and anyway I was up at 2:30 and in fact did most of those chores you say are done."

She came over and stood in front of him. She wore blue jeans and a loose celery-green t-shirt. "So? Do I get a hug this morning, or do you love 'em and leave 'em?"

He laughed and got up and gave her a brief hug. "That's all, my toast is getting cold." He said teasingly.

"Well, at least I know where I stand. Do you mind if I sit here to bother you?"

"A rhetorical question. Please."

She poured herself a cup of coffee and sat. "Sleep OK?" she inquired.

"Marvelously. You?"

"Yes, but I heard Willis. Then I took a flood of thoughts, dozed off and on, and got up around 7:30. But guess what?"

"What?"

"When I went out to the barn Willis was just taking out Phantom for his exercise. I sat on the cart with him. It's a lot of fun. I could feel him, straining to go. But Willis kept him tightly reined. The thing about this is that it's mesmerizing. He went around his small track about eight times. It really is another world out here, the horse, the place."

"Tell me about it. But I don't know about this place when Iowa winters pop up. It's idyllic now."

"Willis told me that he'd like us to stay out here – you, me, or both of us for the week. He's worried. By the way, he's in love with Scorpio."

"Who isn't?" At that point, apparently hearing his name and perhaps the affectionate tone used, Scorpio came up to McAbee and nuzzled his leg. He then backed away and eyed the remaining portion of toast. McAbee gave way and handed it to him. He looked at Augusta and said, "I know, I know – I'm weak. He regularly takes advantage of me. I'll call Pat and see what holds down in Davenport. Can you stick around?"

"Partially, at least for the next two days. Then I'll have to go back for a day or two. How's that?"

"Fine. So, we can do two days together if I'm right. This is turning out to be a great mini-vacation."

The house phone rang. It stopped in two rings. McAbee was puzzled, causing Augusta to say, "He has an extension in both barns."

"Ah, I see."

Willis came into the house a few minutes later. "Good morning, Bertrand. Did Augusta tell you that she drove the big guy?"

"She did. She tells me that she wants to get a driver's license and race him in Chicago this Saturday."

"Ha. I was just called, by the way, from Balmoral. I gave them the OK about an hour ago. They drew for Saturday night. Phantom has the three post in the ninth race, and boy are they playing this thing up. You'd think it was the Kentucky Derby."

"Is Jim Benson going to drive?"

"I hope so. I have a call into him. I put down a TBA on the advance sheet."

"TBA?" McAbee asked.

"To be announced. Has Augusta told you? I really want your presence out here, either one of you or both for the week. Is that possible?"

"We were just talking about that. I think that we can work out something."

"Oh, don't forget Scorpio. His presence in that barn at night is really reassuring to me."

"I see. So, you're saying that Augusta and I are luxuries, but Scorpio is a necessity?" Bertrand joked.

Willis thought for a minute and then said, "I didn't say that, but now that you voiced it ... ". He laughed after a few seconds, making sure that he was not misinterpreted.

McAbee smiled. Maybe Scorpio had scored himself a client. "OK, Willis. You've got a deal. We'll just hang around, keep our eyes open, and if we can be of help – let us know. We'll try not to get in the way."

Shortly thereafter he cleared his office calendar with Pat. "I'll be able to get down there in an hour if anything essential is in play. Oh, and please call Gloria, my neighbor, and let her know what's going on. She'll worry. Augusta is here too. Unless something critical comes her way, she'll be here until at least Wednesday."

Pat said, "You two be careful out there."

Bertrand felt his face redden just slightly. Defensively, he said, "It's pretty calm out here. I don't foresee any problems."

"Great." She hung up.

He shook his head back and forth and pursed his lips. It probably was a neutral and unloaded comment. He figured, though, that it had landed on some lingering thoughts of his own, those being not entirely innocent.

Monday and Tuesday passed quickly. Augusta and Bertrand had dined in West Branch that Monday night; they enjoyed a grilled steak meal with Willis and his neighbor, Josh, on Tuesday night. He and Augusta never, however, reached that point of closeness again that they had had on that Sunday night. Both were watchful for each other. They didn't want what they had to be destabilized. Bertrand turned off his bed light at 11:45 p.m. He had been reading Ammonius Marcellinus and especially his treatment of the Emperor Julian AKA Julian the Apostate. He thought that Marcellinus' Latin was crisp and thoughtful as he fell asleep thinking what it was like to live in 363 A.D. (CE) when Julian was dying of battle wounds in Persia and St. Augustine was nine years of age in Northern Africa.

Jeremy Burgess drove out of Highland Hills, north of Chicago, onto the Dan Ryan where he soon hooked up to the East-West Tollway (Interstate 88), which took him into Interstate 80 in the Illinois Quad Cities, which in turn would bring him to West Branch, Iowa. At most it was a four-hour drive. He was using a company car. He hoped to have it back in the parking lot by six a.m.

He had called his secretary and informed her that he was ill and would take Wednesday morning off; she was to cancel all appointments and reschedule. She took pains to remind him that Scott Horosby, the *Tribune* reporter, was becoming more and more persistent for comments about the horse and some incidentals around the story. He told her that he did not want to hear that name Horosby again. No person knew that he was headed for Iowa, and if luck was in his favor, as it often was, no one would ever know.

His call to Willis Clohessey, from a public telephone, on Tuesday afternoon was taken by a neighbor, Josh something or other. With anonymity secured he had gotten directions to the farm as well as where the horse was kept on the farm.

Burgess represented himself as a reporter from the *Louisville Courier*, he was wondering if he could have 15 minutes with Willis and a picture of Phantom Express. The pseudo-reporter was expected to be there at about 10 a.m. on Wednesday morning, long after Jeremy Burgess' work would be done.

He took the first pass by the farm at midnight. The light of the nearly full moon was pervasive, enabling him to quickly ascertain the basic building layout. He came back and pulled the black Maxima off to the side of the road. Black-clad he pulled the black balaclava over his head. He left the keys in the ignition. Walking across the road, he entered the farm property. From his conversation with Josh it was clear where the barn was – he was scheduled to be there next morning for an interview, after all.

Burgess fingered the syringe gingerly. It still had the plastic sheath in place covering the business end of it. He had secured it two years back, from an old veterinarian in Illinois who had become a supplier for a number of horsemen. The beneficial factors in dealing with him was that he was in the initial throes of Alzheimer's and he never asked questions as long as cash was paid. Burgess had told him that he had a 20-year-old horse that was dying, and he wanted to end his life with dignity. "The horse will be dead within five seconds. In fact by the time you empty the syringe you can start the funeral ceremony. Thirty bucks, please," the old coot said. If the rumor was correct, he wouldn't remember to whom he had sold the syringe by the next day.

If his luck held, Phantom Express would be dead and the embarrassment caused by the horse would cease. Questions of who killed the horse and why would never end. Burgess, at least, thought that he was in the clear from it all. Surely, no one would think that the great Jeremy Burgess would take such a risk as actually killing the horse himself.

The stillness of the farm augmented his every step as he stood behind a tree, making an effort to fully capture his bearings. The farmhouse itself was without any inner light. Josh, whatever his name, had said that Phantom was just off the entrance of the barn, that was where Willis would be working at about 10 a.m. tomorrow morning.

He noticed that the door of the stable had been left open, hardly a surprise given the oppressive July heat. He came from behind the tree and proceeded across the circular grass area toward the barn entrance. He noticed that there was a sash of sorts spread across the opening of the barn. The inside of the barn was quite dark in contrast to where he stood outside. He came within five feet of the doorway, standing to the side. His eyes grew more accustomed to picking up some detail in the darkened stable.

From his pocket he removed a small flashlight, which he kept in his left hand while his right hand held the sheathed syringe. He was confident that he would recognize the horse that had such remarkable features. He now found a stillness in himself – in the next minute he could complete the task by killing the horse and being in his car heading for Interstate 80.

He crouched under the rubber line that extended across the entrance. An occasional snort or neigh came from down the aisle. He moved toward the first stall and flashed his light into the stall, a small horse looked back at him curiously. He instantly turned off the light. He went to the next stall and again the light shone on a horse, but it wasn't Phantom, it was a gray horse.

The unmistakable Phantom was in the third stall. His ears were pinned back, his head was cocked, and his left eye caught the flashlight and, it seemed, the malevolent presence behind the light. The horse backed away and paced back and around the stall. Its look was one of audacity. Burgess's hate-filled eyes were now familiarized with the low light of the barn.

He went to open the gate, and as he did he noticed in his peripheral vision a movement of white to his left. He pulled off the plastic sheath of the syringe as he advanced into the stall. A sharp whinny came from Phantom and then he heard a deep growl and bark from behind him. His brain stayed in focus – sink the needle into the horse's neck vein. He came up to Phantom, whose face quickly bolted away from him, but whose full flank rammed him. He stumbled. The needle went into his wrist as he cursed. It had stabbed him deeply. He pulled it out of the back of his hand, and then plunged the needle into the neck of the horse. He realized that the plunger had already been depressed a bit, but now he fully pressed down on the plunger as the frantic horse tried to pull away. At this point the dog had made its way into the stall as the 1200-pound horse collapsed against his shoulder and knocked him down as it fell pinning his own weakening legs. He felt his body going numb and he vaguely sensed a growling dog tearing at his arm. He wondered why he couldn't move. He heard running, yelling; he heard a horrid rattle from the horse and saw and heard, but couldn't feel, a feral dog in full attack. And then there was nothing.

CHAPTER XXVII

———————◆◆◆———————

McAbee had never seen a man cry as much as Willis Clohessey had on that bitter Tuesday night. He thought back to the time he and Augusta had reached the barn and had put on the neon ceiling lights that lit up the entire inside of the building. McAbee sensed the strange silence. Scorpio, whose growls and barks had awakened them, had now gone strangely quiet.

At first, he only saw Phantom whose long and beautiful body was still, then he saw the black-clad man, Scorpio crouched to his side waiting for the slightest move to spur him into an attack. The man's legs were buried under the horse. Augusta had gone to the man and touched his neck for a few seconds. She had turned, saying, "He's dead, there's a syringe in his hand. Don't go near it." She went to Phantom and laid her hands on him for a few seconds, "Oh, Jesus,

Bertrand! This man must have murdered Phantom. He's not breathing either."

McAbee remembered taking Scorpio out of the stall and chaining him deeper down into the barn. He had copious amounts of blood on his muzzle. He petted him and tried to calm down the now shaking Shepherd. It was then that Willis came in, only to very quickly break down into fits of sobbing. Through the night the yard was filled with flashing red lights. The Sheriff declared the barn a crime scene; the Iowa Bureau of Criminal Investigation was called in.

They sat around Willis Clohessey's kitchen table awaiting some kind of release from the IBCI detective who had already questioned each of them twice.

Finally, the burly investigator came into the kitchen at about 11 a.m. "I'll tell you what I think happened to him. First off, the dead man is Jeremy Burgess. He had motive to kill this horse from what you all have said. The needle found in his hand – it's at the lab now, I assume that he must have fallen or the horse moved on him or that dog unsettled him or whatever. It seems he took in part of the contents of that syringe. There was enough to kill both of them obviously." He looked at McAbee, "You're lucky the dog didn't catch any of that needle's contents. He did quite a job on Burgess's arm, by the way. I'm sorry, Mister Clohessey, but I have to take the horse's body to the vet lab in Ames."

By late that afternoon Bertrand and Augusta were taking their leave of the West Branch farm; Willis Clohessey had insisted. He wanted to be alone.

"Willis, we're so sorry."

"Ah, there's nothing you can do if someone is that bent on murdering. If it wasn't for you and Augusta and Scorpio, he probably would have gotten away with it. At least, he got his just desserts. But you know," his sad eyes took them both in, "he was a magnificent horse. God knows what he could have done. But now it's coming to me that he was terribly jinxed. Everyone had said that he was bad luck. Funny ... he really was. He broke a lot of hearts, either directly or indirectly. I don't think that I'll ever see another horse like him no matter how many sales I go to. He was magic, and just like that – he's gone."

There was quiet between them as they drove to Augusta's house in Rock Island. Scorpio was still a bit shaky and was resting near the back door of the SUV.

Augusta said, "Do you think that there's such a thing? A bad-luck horse? A bad-luck person?"

"Yeah. The Greeks and Romans talked about it all the time. Fortuna. Some people or animals in this case are meant to be well served by it, and some not so. Some of it we make ourselves. But many times, it's out of our control. And sometimes, I think," he reached for her hand and took it in his, "we have it right next to us, but we're too dumb or too self-engrossed to realize that Fortuna is with us."

Augusta leaned over and kissed him on the cheek as they drove quietly into the western fringe of the city of Rock Island, Illinois.

AFTERWORD

- Scorpio, fully recovered, has picked up a certain air about himself.

- John Howles is no longer an identity thief. He was a victim of a prison stabbing. He died in surgery.

- Willis Clohessey bought a few promising yearlings at a September sale in Illinois. One of them, in particular, had that Phantom look about him.

- Augusta Satin went out on a date with a detective on the Moline P.D. It was a bust. He could only talk about the Chicago Cubs.

- The banker, John Austin, is tracked periodically by Barry Fisk. Austin can't seem to shake his anti-semitism.

- Betty Broder bought four horses at auction when Burgess Stables in Valdosta was sold off.

- The ACJ Agency is doing well. Its founder, Bertrand McAbee, is in a decided fog of sorts. He still sees in his mind the magnificent image of Phantom Express tearing toward the finish line. But did he fail, ultimately, Willis Clohessey and Phantom?

About the Author

Joseph A. McCaffrey isn't a classics professor. He's not a P.I. either. But he is a professor of philosophy at St. Ambrose University in Davenport, Iowa. Sometime back he was proposed a job not unlike that which his protagonist, Bertrand McAbee, was offered and accepted. The fictional McAbee stories are explorations of roads untaken. Other McAbee adventures include *Cassies Ruler*, *Confessional Matters*, *The Pony Circus Wagon*, and *Scholarly Executions*.

Printed in the United States
33930LVS00002B/115-222

9 781420 854855